I0628240

Sweet Angel

Book V of the Commitment Series

BADGER BLISS BOOKS

DEDICATION

To all the sweet angels who left us too soon.

You will always be remembered…you will always be loved.

ALSO WRITTEN BY KAREN D. BADGER AND
AVAILABLE FROM BADGER BLISS BOOKS:

ON A WING AND A PRAYER

YESTERDAY ONCE MORE

THE BLUE FEATHER

ALL MY TOMORROWS

1140 RUE ROYALE

The Billie/Cat Commitment Series:

IN A FAMILY WAY

UNCHAINED MEMORIES

HAPPY CAMPERS

COLLECTIVE IDENTITY

SWEET ANGEL

RELATIVE-LY SPEAKING

www.badgerblissbooks.com

Sweet Angel

Book V of the Commitment Series

A BADGER BLISS BOOK

By

Karen D. Badger

NOTE: If you purchased this book without a cover, you should be aware that it is stolen property. It was reported as "unsold and destroyed" to the publisher, and neither the author nor the publisher has received any payment for this "stripped book."

This is a work of fiction. All characters, locales and events are either products of the author's imagination or are used fictitiously.

SWEET ANGEL - BOOK V OF THE COMMITMENT SERIES

Copyright © 2015 by Karen D. Badger
www.karendbadger.com

All rights reserved. No part of this book may be reproduced in any manner whatsoever without written permission from the publisher, save for brief quotations used in critical articles or reviews.

Cover art by Andrea Ramsay, romanticfae00@gmail.com
Cover design by Karen D. Badger

A Badger Bliss Book
Published by Badger Bliss Books
Georgia, VT 05468

www.badgerblissbooks.com

ISBN 13: 978-1-945761-09-6
ISBN 10: 1-945-761-09-1

First Edition, June, 2015
Second Edition, August, 2016

Printed in the United States of America and in the United Kingdom

ACKNOWLEDGMENTS

As usual, my beta readers provide an invaluable service. They find my mistakes, express their opinions about my characters and plot, and help me to improve my skills as a writer. They are an essential part of the writing and editing process. I find myself fortunate to have an outstanding and wonderfully diverse group of women who lend their time and talents to my making my books the best they can be. That said, I'd like to express my extreme gratitude to my wife, Bliss, my mom, Ellie Atherton and my very good friends, Donna Brown and Carol Poynor, for their hard work and for being forthright and honest in their opinions and feedback. You guys rock!

Special thanks to Sheri Barnett for validating the medical information in this story…and for being my pseudo-little sister (love ya, Big Guy!).

Finally, I couldn't do this without support from my family…including those related by blood, and those related by love. Thank you all for being a part of my life.

CHAPTER 1

It was an early Saturday afternoon. The sun was bright and high overhead. A slight breeze filled the air, but did little to dispel the heat. The sounds of suburbia were everywhere. Children playing...birds chirping...water splashing in a backyard pool...the sounds of a sprinkler gracing the neighbor's lawn with a much needed blanket of moisture...the steady hum of a lawn mower.

Billie pushed the mower back and forth across the front yard, leaving neat, overlapping stripes of mowed grass behind her. Beads of sweat lined her upper lip while streams of salty sweat rolled down the side of her face from her hairline. The sun beat across tanned arms, shoulders, and long muscular legs, left bare by a scantily cut tank top and cut off denim shorts. On her head sat a baseball cap, lent to her by her son more than a year ago to cover up baldness from brain surgery. Dark hair, having long since grown out beyond her shoulders, was pulled back and neatly entwined in a French braid. White ankle socks and construction boots adorned her feet, while aviator sunglasses protected her piercing blue eyes from the sun's rays. The sun reflected off the sheen of sweat that covered her bronzed skin. Motorists and passersby alike extended greetings as Billie pushed the mower across the yard.

Along the walkway leading from the front porch to the sidewalk, Cat busied herself planting fresh annuals. Kneeling in the grass along the walk, she dug straight, neat trenches with her garden spade, readying the soil to accept the colorful flowers. With a complexion too fair for prolonged exposure to the sun, Cat wore a wide-brimmed straw hat banded in white silk on her red-gold hair, which had also been entwined in a French braid.

A sleeveless button-down shirt with tails tied under her breasts exposed a firmly sculptured abdomen and tiny waist, while cut-off denim shorts adorned her slim hips and thighs. Leather sandals graced slender feet while John Lennon sunglasses perched on her finely chiseled nose. White garden gloves with red polka dots protected delicate hands from the grit and grime of gardening.

Cat sat back on her heels and wiped the sweat from her brow with the back of her gloved hand, spade still hanging loosely from it. She looked around and caught sight of Billie out of the corner of her eye and for the next few moments, watched her push the mower back and forth. She found herself admiring the way the muscles in Billie's legs contracted with each step, while her deltoids bulged with the effort to push the mower along in a straight line.

Now that's what I call eye candy, she thought to herself, grinning smugly at the knowledge that the bronze goddess was all hers.

Cat couldn't believe she and Billie had been together for more than six years already. Seth was only six, and Tara was four when they met. She remembered how tenuous her relationship with Billie had been in the beginning. When they first met in an aerobics class, Cat didn't know Seth even existed. She only found out later that he had spent nearly six months in a coma after being hit by a drunk driver passing his school bus. That certainly explained why Billie was reluctant to spend time with her in the evenings. She discovered later that Billie spent each evening after teaching her aerobics class, sitting by her son's bedside in the hospital.

To be fair, Cat had to admit that at first, she wasn't forthcoming about Tara's existence either. Billie only found out about her when she showed up at her apartment one day and Tara answered the door because Cat was too ill with appendicitis to answer it herself. Cat credited Billie with saving her life that day. By that time, they had fallen in love and although their joint secrets complicated their lives, they worked through them and committed themselves to each other and their children.

So much had happened to them since that first day at the gym. Not long after they blended their families and moved in together. Billie's ex-husband, Brian, broke into their home with intent to rob them in punishment of Billie for not giving him money for drugs. Unfortunately, Cat and the children were home, and in an attempt to protect the children from him, she succumbed to Brian's advances. The only good thing that came from that encounter was their baby girl, Skylar, who had just turned six years old.

Life changed significantly from that point on. As a lawyer, Billie successfully lobbied to change the marriage laws in their home state of New York, allowing them to legally marry, followed by the adoption of each other's children. Then the unthinkable happened—Brian once again invaded their lives and their home, holding Cat and the kids hostage, and shooting Billie in the head during an attempted rescue.

Cat felt tears fill her eyes as she recalled the painful memories. They would have lost Billie that day had it not been for the medical training Cat received years earlier while studying to become an anesthesiologist. She managed to tend to Billie's wounds while waiting for the ambulance and after a time, Billie made a full recovery…at least they thought she had.

One morning, nearly a year after the shooting, Billie was unresponsive and landed back in the hospital. Scar tissue from the gunshot wound was blocking vital functions in her brain. Cat found herself in the unfortunate position of having to make a potentially catastrophic decision about Billie's treatment, one that could put her in a wheelchair for the rest of her life. As it was, Billie recovered full mobility, but not her memory. Worst of all, Billie didn't remember her, nor their life together, insisting she wasn't gay and becoming fearful and angry with Cat's outward displays of affection.

Cat was devastated at the thought of losing the one person who made her complete. With the help of her family and their best friends, Jen and Fred Swenson, Billie's memory slowly returned. Cat truly didn't know how she would have coped without Jen's help. Jen kept her encouraged at times when

Billie's lack of memory seemed hopeless, and she was always there for them when they needed someone to watch the kids at a moment's notice. She truly felt blessed to have such dedicated and loving friends in Jen and Fred.

Billie stopped and made eye contact with Cat. The lawn mower continued to purr beside her as she stood with one hand on her hip, the other holding the safety shutoff bar on the mower, her weight shifted to one hip, and her eyebrows perched high on her forehead.

"You look like you're a thousand miles away. Is everything okay?" Billie asked.

Cat rose to her feet and approached Billie, stopping only when a hair's breadth separated their bodies. She looked into Billie's face and smiled seductively, then reached behind her neck to pull her down into a kiss.

The mower suddenly died as Billie released the emergency shutoff bar to wrap her arms around Cat. The kiss deepened until Cat's knees were too weak to support her. Little did they care that they were in full view of passersby and neighbors alike. Moments later, they broke apart and looked once more into each other's eyes.

"Not that I'm complaining, mind you, but what was that for?" Billie asked.

"That was for being the most beautiful creature on Earth," Cat replied, grinning ear to ear.

"Not true," Billie replied. "And I know this because *I* am looking at the most beautiful creature on Earth right now," she added as she smiled and lowered her head for another kiss.

Suddenly, the sound of a man clearing his voice echoed in her ear. The ladies' heads turned quickly in the direction of the sound.

Cat smiled as she lowered her arms from around Billie's neck and turned around in her wife's embrace. Billie maintained her current position, with her arms circling Cat's waist from behind.

"Hi Bert," Cat said cheerfully. "What have you got for us today?" she asked.

"Good afternoon, ladies," he said. "Well, let's see, a few bills, a sales flyer, and, oh yes, a letter, from...ah, let me see...yes, from Michigan," the elderly mailman said, shuffling through the envelopes before handing them to Cat.

Bert smiled at the ladies as he watched Cat flip through the envelopes. These two ladies held a special place in the old mailman's heart. Not only were they sociable, kind and very beautiful, but they treated him with respect, even going so far as to insist he come in from the cold and share hot chocolate with them one very frigid winter day as he delivered mail. And as far as their lifestyle was concerned, it didn't concern him one bit. He had seen some pretty unique people in his many years of delivering the mail, but all that mattered to him was that they were good, decent people, and treated him considerately...just like these two ladies did. Bert wished all of his deliveries were this pleasant.

Cat thanked Bert as he walked away then handed the letter from Michigan over her shoulder to Billie. "This one's addressed to you, love. It's from your mom."

Billie released Cat from the circle of her arms as she took the letter. She looked at the handwriting, nervously recalling the first time she and Cat met with her mother just three months earlier.

The meeting had been uneasy and tense. Billie had learned that her mother, Laurel, sold her as a baby for drug money nearly thirty-four years earlier. She also learned that she had a half brother, Dylan, and a homophobic stepfather named Jim, whom she had yet to meet. That was one introduction she was not looking forward to.

The search for her mother had started quite by accident. While attempting to construct genealogies for themselves, she and Cat discovered that the two people Billie had spent her entire life believing were her parents were in fact, not. They had purchased her on the black market and had raised her as their own. It wasn't until ten years after their deaths that she learned the truth.

While searching for their roots, Billie and Cat interviewed Cat's grandparents, Josephine Wycliffe and Alexandria Spirakis, a wealthy elderly couple from Charleston, South Carolina. The physical resemblance between Billie and Alexandria was stunning, so much so, that further investigation lead to the revelation that Alex had given birth to what she was told at the time, was a stillborn baby girl fifty-five years earlier. Even though Alex was told otherwise, she was convinced in her heart that the child was still alive. The connection she felt to Billie, combined with the physical resemblance between them, was too strong not to wonder if the child she had lost so many years earlier could be Billie's mother. So started the search that led to Laurel…Alex's daughter and Billie's biological mother.

Billie's first encounter with Laurel was unpleasant to say the least, mostly due the intense feelings of anger and betrayal she felt for the woman. She just could not understand how a mother could sell her child for drugs. Admitting that her life probably would not have turned out as wonderful as it had if Laurel had kept her was not enough to erase the feelings of desertion and betrayal.

Several painful confrontations ensued before the women struggled to come to terms with each other in an attempt to build a mother-daughter relationship. Since that time, they exchanged letters, e-mails and phone calls, managing to build a friendly camaraderie, but lacking that deep emotional bond shared by a parent and child. Three months later, the relationship was still distant and admittedly, Billie was having a hard time completely letting go of the hurt.

"Billie?" Cat placed a hand on Billie's arm and drew her out of her trance as she stared at the envelope.

Billie snapped back to awareness at the sound of Cat's voice. She smiled nervously.

"Billie, are you all right?" Cat asked.

Billie just nodded and sat down on the porch steps. For several moments, she looked at the front of the envelope. The slope of the penmanship prompted a thought that her mother's handwriting was similar to her own. She slid her little finger under the flap and tore it along the top of the envelope. She retrieved the letter and placed the empty envelope on the step beside her and looked nervously at Cat.

"Do you want me to read it to you?" Cat asked.

Billie seriously considered Cat's offer for a few moments before she declined. "No, I'll do it."

Cat lowered herself to the step beside Billie and picked up the empty envelope. She inspected it absent-mindedly as Billie read the letter to herself. When Billie was finished, she took a deep breath and sighed.

"Is everything okay?" Cat asked.

Billie pulled Cat in for a hug. "Everything is fine, Cat. At least it is now," she replied.

"What do you mean?" Cat asked, concern edging her voice.

Billie held the letter in front of her. "Laurel says here that she and Jim went through some rough times after she returned from South Carolina. Apparently, Jim feels threatened by my presence...and Alex's," Billie explained.

"Threatened?" Cat asked. "How so?"

"She thinks he's afraid of losing her to us, I guess," Billie surmised.

"Billie, I hope he doesn't force her to choose between him and her child. If that happens, he will surely lose. Laurel made it very clear that she won't allow him to come between the two of you," Cat reminded her.

Billie nodded as she scanned the letter once more.

"Apparently, she let him have it with both barrels, accusing him of being insecure and close minded," Billie said, paraphrasing the letter.

"Wow," Cat exclaimed. "But didn't you just say that everything's fine? I guess they worked it out."

"It appears so," Billie replied. "Maybe he realized that an open heart has limitless capacity."

Cat smiled at her wife's eloquence. "I sincerely hope so, love. In any case, I'm glad they're okay now. I'd hate to see a good marriage ruined because of ignorance and bigotry."

"Amen to that."

"So what else does the letter say?" Cat asked.

"Well, it says here that she wants to come for a visit next month."

"That's great," Cat exclaimed, sitting up straight, a smile beaming from her face. "I've been anxious for her to visit. I mean, she has yet to meet her grandchildren, and besides, the more time you spend with your mother, the stronger the bond will be between you. I think it's wonderful that she wants to visit."

"Yeah, wonderful," Billie said, almost sarcastically as she pulled Cat back into her embrace and rested her chin on top of Cat's head.

"Billie, I thought you wanted to work things out with her. Are you having second thoughts?"

Billie released Cat and stood up. She moved a short distance away and turned around to face her.

"Cat, while we were still in Michigan, I told you the anger is gone…and it is, but I am having a hard time letting go of the hurt. I'm having a hard time forgiving her. I really want to, but I don't know. It's just hard. I can't get over the fact that she sold me, Cat. How could she do that? I would die before I did anything so heinous to any of our children."

Cat stood on the step and opened her arms, motioning Billie into them. From her vantage point on the steps, she was face to face, nose to nose with her.

"Well, we finally see eye to eye on something," Cat said, grinning. "Ouch!" she yelled as Billie slapped her behind. "I was only joking," she said rubbing her backside. "Look, honey, I totally understand how you feel. I could never do such a thing to a child either, and to be honest, I'm pretty disappointed in Laurel myself, but she *is* your mother. Besides Alex and Seth, Laurel and Dylan are the only blood relatives you have," Cat explained. "Blood is thicker than water, you know."

Billie stubbornly held her gaze, not wanting to agree with Cat.

"Billie, you *know* I can see into your soul. You know I can see the struggle going on right now between your heart and your head. I can see it because your heart belongs to me. Sweetie, listen to your heart. It will never lead you astray as long as I possess it," Cat pleaded.

Billie leaned her head back and looked up at the sky as Cat's arms remained locked around her neck. She knew Cat was right, but her stubborn nature would not allow her to totally forgive and forget. Laurel had hurt her deeply, and it was a hurt that would take time to heal. She closed her eyes and released a long frustrated sigh.

"Billie, look at me," Cat urged as she placed one palm on the side of Billie's face and pulled her head back into an upright position. "Open your eyes, my love."

Billie never could resist Cat's requests. She opened her eyes and smiled at the mischievous grin on Cat's face.

"That's, better," Cat teased before continuing. "Honey, I think it's a good idea for Laurel to visit. I really think the two of you need time together...you know, to get acquainted," Cat explained.

"I'm not sure I *want* to get too acquainted with her, Cat."

"Billie, I know you are worried about being hurt again, but anything worth having is worth taking a risk for. I would love to see you have the kind of relationship with Laurel that you have with your own children...that I have with *my* own mother," Cat explained. "Now wouldn't that be rewarding?"

"Yeah, maybe you're right," Billie said as she lowered her head for a kiss, not quite reaching Cat's lips before a small body pressed itself between them.

Looking down, both ladies saw their youngest daughter wedged between them, her arms wrapped around Billie's thighs and her head resting on Billie's abdomen. Billie took a step back and picked the child up. Skylar immediately put her head on Billie's shoulder and closed her eyes. A frown creased Cat's forehead at her daughter's odd behavior.

"Where are brother and sister, love bug?" Billie asked.

"They're still at 'Rissa's and Stevie's," the little girl answered softly.

Cat brushed the red-gold hair off Skylar's forehead, noting the pale, ashen look to the child's skin. "Sky, honey, do you feel all right?" she asked.

She placed her hand on the Skylar's forehead then looked at Billie. "She has a low-grade fever."

Skylar nodded but continued to rest her head on Billie's shoulder.

Billie also reached up to feel the child's forehead. "Sky, are you sure you feel okay?" Billie asked. She glanced uneasily at Cat.

Again, Skylar just nodded and snuggled deeper into Billie's neck.

"Billie, why don't you bring her inside and put her to bed? I'll get a couple of children's pain relievers from the medicine cabinet and bring them up to her, right after I call her pediatrician," Cat said.

Billie carried Skylar to her room and stripped the little girl of her shoes and jeans, leaving her socks and T-shirt on. She tucked her into bed and pulled the covers up under her arms. Billie kissed her on the forehead and once again, frowned at the heat radiating from her daughter's skin.

"Baby girl," Billie said, running the back of her hand across Skylar's forehead. "You feel hot, honey. Does it hurt anywhere?" she asked.

As before, Skylar just shook her head then yawned broadly while fighting to keep her eyes open.

Moments later, Cat entered the room with two chewable pain relievers and a glass of water. She approached the opposite side of the bed from Billie and sat down. "Here, sweetie," she said to the child, placing a hand on the Skylar's back to help her sit, while her clinical mind, tempered by years of medical training, registered the intensity of heat she could feel through her T-shirt.

Skylar took the tablets from her mother and chewed them, then drank the glass of water. Both mothers tucked her in and then sat with her while she drifted off to sleep.

Billie looked at Cat. "What did the doctor say?" she asked.

"He said just what I expected him to, that children will run fevers for no reason at all. If she's still sick tomorrow, we need to bring her in," Cat replied.

"You're a doctor, Cat. What do *you* think is wrong with her?" Billie asked worriedly while she stroked the hair from Skylar's forehead.

Cat hated to be put in this position. She completely understood why most doctors preferred not to treat family members. She was so afraid of making a bad diagnosis and having her loved one harmed or to suffer because of it.

"It's hard to tell, Billie. The doctor is right. It could be anything from an ear infection, to cutting her molars. If the fever is still there tomorrow, we'll have her looked at," Cat explained again.

"Okay," Billie replied.

"Come on, she's asleep," Cat said.

She kissed Skylar's cheek then rose from the bed and followed Billie out of the room.

CHAPTER 2

"Where's Sky?" Tara asked as the family sat around the kitchen table, preparing to eat dinner.

"She's in bed, sweet pea. She was running a fever this afternoon," Cat said, turning around to look at her middle child from her position at the stove.

Billie placed the final plate on the table. "Knowing Sky, she'll be hungry after sleeping all afternoon. Maybe I should go wake her," she suggested.

"Good idea. If she sleeps much longer, she'll be wide awake and wanting to play all night," replied Cat.

"We'll be right back," Billie said as she headed for the living room.

"Is Sky gonna be all right?" Seth asked, a worried expression on his face.

Cat placed a plate of rolls on the table and approached her son.

"She's fine, honey. She's just running a fever. I'm sure it's nothing." Cat brushed Seth's bangs off his face. "You need a haircut, young man. Thank you for being concerned about your sister," she added.

Just then, Billie entered the kitchen carrying a groggy Skylar in her arms.

"Here she is, Mama," Billie said, a silent message of concern passing between them as their eyes locked.

Cat instantly read the look on Billie's face as she opened her arms for the child, who went into them eagerly. Skylar wrapped her legs around Cat's waist and arms round her neck, then laid her head on her mother's shoulder and snuggled in close. Cat carried her over to one of the kitchen chairs and sat down with the child straddling her lap.

Cat placed her lips against Skylar's forehead and noted that she was still running a fever.

"Billie, would you get the digital thermometer for me, please?" she asked, watching as Billie immediately went to fetch the requested object. "Sky, honey, do you hurt anywhere?" Cat asked.

Sky shook her head. "I'm just tired, Mama," she said in a faint voice.

Billie returned with the thermometer and handed it to Cat, who placed it under the child's tongue. Skylar immediately rested her cheek against Cat's chest while they waited for her temperature to register on the thermometer. Billie paced back and forth nervously glancing at her wife and child.

Sparing a glance at Seth, Cat noted that he too, was worried about his baby sister, and that Billie's pacing was doing nothing to alleviate his fears.

"Billie, honey, could you please finish setting the table?" Cat asked, noticing that Seth and Tara had yet to be fed. Besides, Billie's pacing was making *her* nervous too.

Billie stopped pacing and knelt on one knee next to Cat and Skylar. "Cat?" she asked, stroking the child's head.

"Billie, please. Worrying about it won't make the fever go away. Please, take care of Seth and Tara. We'll be finished here in a minute," Cat said.

Billie rose to her feet and carried the rest of the dinner to the table.

"Mom, I'm worried about Sky," Seth said as he pushed his food around his plate with his fork.

"She's probably faking' it," accused Tara, as she dove into her food.

Billie leaned over to address both children. "No, I don't think so," she said, rubbing Tara's back. "She feels pretty hot to me. Mama will give her some medicine for the fever then I'm sure she'll be fine. We'll take her to the doctor's tomorrow if she's still sick in the morning," Billie explained to the children.

A beep from the digital thermometer immediate drew Billie's attention to her youngest child. "Cat?" she asked.

"Ninety-nine point six," Cat said, looking at the thermometer in her hand. "That's only one degree above normal.

It's not unusual for kids to run a low grade fever like this," she said, glancing at Billie encouragingly.

A look of relief crossed Billie's features as she approached Cat and took their daughter out of her arms. Hefting her high into her own arms, she looked at the child and asked, "Are you hungry, pooh bear?"

"A little," Skylar replied. "I'm thirsty too," she added.

"How about a glass of milk?" Billie asked.

"Milk might not be a good idea, Billie. Even a low grade temp might cause it to curdle," Cat interrupted.

"Okay, no milk. So, what do you say to Kool-Aid?" Billie offered.

Skylar's face brightened considerably. Kool-Aid wasn't usually allowed at the dinner table, so this was an offer she couldn't refuse as she nodded her head vigorously.

"Hey, no fair!" Tara whined as her sister received the special treat.

Billie turned to Tara as she lowered Skylar into her chair. Grinning, she addressed Tara. "I'll tell you what, rugrat," she began. "We'll let your sister drink milk if you volunteer to clean up the cottage cheese that will surely result from the curdled milk in her stomach."

"Ewwwwww!" Tara and Seth screamed together. "That's gross, Mom."

Billie looked around the table and caught a look of reprimand from Cat. She leaned close to Skylar and said, "Uh, oh, it looks like Mommy's in trouble again."

Skylar just giggled and happily sipped her Kool-Aid.

Cat watched her wife and daughter settle in at the table. *Anyone would think you actually gave birth to her, love.* Cat thought as she marveled at the bond between the two.

* * *

Dinner at the Charland house was normally a time of controlled chaos, as was the case this night. Stories of the day's events passed back and forth across the table as everyone vied for their turn to speak. Billie and Cat loved this time of day. It was a time when the whole family was together and interacting on a personal level.

After dinner, the kids disappeared into the family room to watch TV while Cat and Billie cleaned up the dinner dishes.

"She didn't eat very much," Billie said as she scraped Skylar's plate off into the garbage disposal.

"Well, I'm sure the fever is affecting her appetite," Cat said. She took the plate from Billie and loaded it into the dishwasher then placed a comforting hand on Billie's arm. "Sweetheart, you're going to make yourself sick worrying about this. Look, I'm worried too, but there's not much we can do until morning, short of a trip to the emergency room, or an after-hours visit with her doctor. I don't think a one degree fever warrants an action that dramatic," she explained.

Billie took a deep breath and nodded as she handed the remaining dishes to Cat. "You're right. I know I'm over-reacting, but I can't help it. She's our baby," Billie said.

"I'm beginning to think she's more *your* baby than mine. You spoil that kid rotten, you know," Cat said with a knowing smile.

"I can't help it. She looks so much like you that I can't resist loving her to death," Billie said, leaning in to steal a kiss.

"You, my dear, are nothing but a big softie," Cat teased. "All three of the kids know exactly where your buttons are, and they don't hesitate to push them."

Billie pulled Cat close for a passionate kiss. "I'll show you who the big softie is when I turn you to mush later my love."

"Is that a threat or a promise?" Cat asked breathlessly.

"Oh, that is definitely a promise," Billie responded.

Minutes later, Cat and Billie joined the kids in the family room, armed with a big bowl of popcorn, ready to settle in for an evening of family time together. Five minutes into the movie, Skylar climbed into Billie's lap and snuggled. Billie's arms automatically wrapped around the small body, as she subconsciously placed a tender kiss on the child's head.

Cat looked over at them and smiled, silently saying *I told you so* with her eyes. Billie responded by sticking her tongue out at the redhead.

Cat's eyes widened at the gesture. "Is that how you plan to keep your promise later, my love?" she whispered into Billie's ear. She grinned ear to ear at the blush that rapidly colored Billie's face.

Sometime later, after the children were tucked into bed, Billie kept her promise, and made several more in the process.

* * *

Cat and Billie were awakened the next morning by a small body pouncing on them. "Mama, get up. I'm hungry."

Billie lifted her head to see Skylar straddling Cat, shaking her awake. Cat had been sleeping on her stomach with her arms tucked under her pillow, so she had no defenses to use against the child.

"No. Go away," Cat said sleepily.

"Mama, come on," Skylar whined.

"Tell Mommy to cook breakfast for you," Cat suggested.

"No way! Mommy cooks yucky," Sky replied loudly, not seeming to care that Billie was right there to hear her insult.

Billie decided to take advantage of the child's protest by adding a little of her own. "Yeah, Mama. Mommy cooks yucky. Sky wants *good* food…just like *you* cook."

Cat shot a look at Billie that guaranteed revenge was forthcoming in the very near future, before turning her attention back to the child.

"Pumpkin, can't you wait a little longer? It's way too early for Mama to get up," she whined.

Billie looked at the clock on the bedside table and was surprised to see how early it really was. Grinning, she reached over and pulled Skylar off Cat, and threw the giggling bundle down between them on the bed. She proceeded to tickle her unmercifully.

"You little rugrat," Billie exclaimed. "Do you know what time it is?" she scolded through peals of laughter.

"Time to eat," Skylar replied.

"No, it's time to sleep," Billie returned.

Skylar sat up and placed her hands on her hips, much like Cat did when she was disgusted. "Mommy, it's six-thirty o'clock!" the child exclaimed.

Billie slapped her own forehead. *God I hate mornings*, she thought to herself before suddenly remembering Skylar's illness from the day before. She brushed an errant lock of red-gold hair from the child's face. "How are you feeling this morning, love bug?" she asked.

"I'm hungry," replied Skylar as she threw herself back down between her mothers.

Cat had rolled over onto her side to face Billie and Skylar. She propped herself up on one elbow and felt Skylar's forehead with her free hand. It felt cool. "No fever this morning," she said. "That's good."

Skylar lay there between her mothers, beaming up at both of them. "Can we eat now?" she asked.

Billie looked at Cat. "Well, you can tell she's *your* daughter all right," she observed, grinning ear to ear.

Cat swatted Billie on the arm then addressed Skylar. "Honey, go wake up brother and sissy, then I'll come down and make breakfast for all of us. Okay?" she asked.

"Okay, Mama. Hurry up, I'm starving," Skylar said.

After Skylar scooted off the bed and ran to wake her siblings, Billie looked at her wife with a grin on her face.

"What's that grin for?" Cat asked.

"I was just wondering when Skylar turned into 'Mini-Cat'," Billie commented.

"Mini-Cat?" Cat asked.

Billie sat up and placed her hands on her hips. Shaking her head side to side, she put as much attitude as possible into her reply. "*Mommy, it's six-thirty o'clock!* Does that look familiar, Cat?" she teased.

Cat narrowed her eyes at Billie, an indignant look on her face. "She's just hungry. She's a growing girl," she said, defending her daughter's behavior.

"She's just like you, Cat. When it comes to food, she has a one-track mind," Billie pointed out, trying not to laugh.

Cat pounced on Billie and straddled her waist. She pinned Billie's hands to the bed above her head. "One-track mind?" she said evilly. "I'll show you a one-track mind, tough guy," she said, lowering her lips to Billie's. The kiss deepened, their tongues fighting for space in each other's mouths as Cat stretched her length out on top of Billie.

With little effort, Billie freed her hands and immediately caressed Cat's back, moving down to cup her bottom, effectively pulling their bodies closer together. Cat responded by grinding her hips into Billie. With a muffled cry, Billie flipped them over and propped herself up on her elbows, placed on either side of Cat's head. She placed feathery kisses across Cat's jaw and neck, while pressing herself firmly against the smaller woman below her.

"God, Cat, do you have any idea what you do to me? One look, one touch, and I'm mush in your hands," Billie declared, kissing the hollow between Cat's collarbones.

Cat arched her body toward Billie, eyes closed, head pushed back into the pillow as she entwined her hands in her Billie's dark hair. She pulled Billie's mouth closer to her neck. "I need more, Billie. Please love me," she responded.

"Mama, Seth and Tara are awake. Can you make us pancakes?" Skylar said from the doorway.

Billie dropped her forehead to Cat's chest and groaned.

"Damn," Cat said under her breath. "Okay, sweetheart, I'm coming...I wish." The last part of that comment was meant for Billie's ears only.

Billie chuckled and rolled off Cat to lie on her back, hands clasped behind her head.

Cat stood beside the bed and looked down at her lazing wife. She reached for a pillow and smacked Billie in the face with it. "Out of bed, big guy. You've got sausage duty. On your feet, soldier."

Billie grabbed Cat, and pulled her back down onto the bed beside her. She rolled over on top of her. "And what will you do to me if I go AWOL, Sarge?"

"I'll have to confine you to quarters, Private...mine, to be exact," Cat answered wickedly.

"And if I cooperate?" she asked.

"Confinement to quarters, followed by...let's see...lots of pushups and laps," Cat threatened.

"Laps?" Billie asked, raising her eyebrows into her hairline.

"Laps," Cat said.

"Laps as in running, or laps as in *laps*?" Billie asked suggestively, flitting her tongue over her lips.

"Well, there's not a lot of room for running in my quarters, Private," Cat replied.

Billie was off the bed in two seconds flat. Standing at attention, right hand saluting, football jersey falling to mid-thigh, she said in a clipped military voice, "Private Charland reporting for KP duty, sir."

CHAPTER 3

"Billie, you need to give your Mom a call," Cat said.

"I'll do it later when I'm not so busy," Billie replied.

"Busy? You call what you're doing, busy?" Cat asked as she watched Billie swing back and forth while stretched out on the hammock.

Cat and Billie relaxed in the back yard of their home while the children, along with their friends Karissa and Stevie, played kick ball nearby.

"Hey, keeping this thing swinging is hard work," Billie teased.

"No, really, love. You need to call her. She wants to visit next month, right? Well, next month is only a week away. We'll need to plan activities, time off from work, meals...," Cat rambled on.

"All right. All right. I'll call," Billie said as she attempted to roll out of the hammock.

The next thing they knew, Billie was flat on her back on the ground under the hammock. Cat tried her best to suppress a grin, but it was a losing battle.

The kids were not so subtle. Within seconds, they were upon her, all five of them, burying the fallen woman under a football huddle.

"Five against one—no fair," Billie yelled as she struggled to make her way from beneath the pile of juvenile bodies. After a few moments of futile struggling, she resorted to her secret weapon. "All right, I guess I've got to play dirty," she said as she proceeded to tickle each one of them away until she was on her feet and surrounded on five sides by vultures circling in for the kill.

Suddenly, they were wet. Cat had retrieved the garden hose and sprayed each of the children, and Billie. Standing there totally shocked and totally soaked, all five pair of eyes looked toward Billie for their next move. Billie looked at the kids, then at Cat, an expression of shocked betrayal on her face. Finally, she pointed to Cat and yelled, "Get her!"

Cat suddenly found herself fleeing from a crowd of six as they chased her around the yard. Soon, she was soaked from head to foot as well.

"I surrender! I surrender!" Cat screamed as they finally backed off.

"Serves you right, Mom," Seth laughed as he looked down at his wet mother lying on the ground.

"Mom, since we're already wet, can we go to Stevie and Karissa's to swim in the pool?" Tara asked.

"Me too! Me too!" Skylar said, jumping up and down.

"Is Jen or Fred home?" Billie asked before giving permission in the event there would be no adult around to supervise.

"Mom is gone to the hairdresser's, but Dad is home," Stevie replied.

"All right then. Grab your suits and towels…and behave," Billie called out to the retreating children as they ran toward the house.

Billie looked down on one very wet Cat sitting on the ground in front of her. She pulled her to her feet then took Cat's face between her hands and kissed her soundly. Releasing her suddenly, she grinned then went to make her phone call.

Cat watched Billie walk away. *Damn, she looks sexy with wet hair*, she thought.

* * *

Billie stood in the living room shivering, cell phone in one hand, while dialing with the other.

Cat placed a large warm, bath towel around Billie's shoulders. "Cold, my love?"

"Freezing," Billie said.

Cat had followed Billie into the house, intent on changing into dry clothes after the water fight in the yard, when she noticed Billie shivering. *Well, I got her wet... the least I can do it warm her up.*

Cat wrapped her arms around Billie's waist from behind and laid her head between her shoulder blades. Her fingers made lazy circles on Billie's stomach as she dialed the phone. By the time Billie dialed the whole number, Cat's hands had made their way up to her breasts. Cat felt Billie press herself back into her in reaction to the caress.

"Hello, Jim? Jim, this is...ah!" Billie said, throwing her head back as Cat pinched her nipple. "Ah...Jim, this is Billie, is Laurel home?"

Cat's hands roamed under Billie's T-shirt as they waited for Laurel to pick up the phone.

"Cat...," Billie warned as the hands moved higher.

"Hmmm," Cat murmured into Billie's back.

"Hello? Hello, Laurel, this is...oh God, Cat," Billie said involuntarily as both of Cat's hands slipped under her bra, each one capturing an erect nipple and squeezing hard. Billie was nearly exploding with desire. Reaching around with her free hand, she placed it on the small of Cat's back and pulled her in tighter, grinding her bottom into Cat's abdomen.

"Cat? Is that you?" asked the voice on the other end of the line.

The voice pulled Billie back to reality.

"Laurel," she said a little too hurriedly. "Laurel, no, this is Billie. Cat...well, Cat...," Billie stammered.

"Cat is right there, teasing the hell out of you while you're trying to talk to me," Laurel finished for her daughter, a trace of laughter in her voice.

"As a matter of fact, that's exactly what she's doing," Billie admitted. "She's on to you," Billie added to Cat after covering the receiver with her hand.

"Oh God," Cat said, embarrassed that her mother-in-law had caught her in the act of foreplay with her wife.

Billie turned her head sharply to look back at Cat, and stuck out her tongue in a *serves you right* kind of gesture.

"Don't wear that tongue out. I have plans for it later," Cat said over Billie's shoulder, loud enough for Laurel to hear. Now it was Billie's turn to blush.

"You know, Billie, this is all very entertaining, but somehow I don't think you called me to discuss foreplay. I take it you received my letter?" Laurel asked.

Cat's hands were on the move again.

Billie reached back and slapped her butt.

The hands continued to move.

"Ah, the letter...yes, I did receive it. Yesterday, in fact," Billie replied.

Snap. Zzzzzzip. Cat's hands inched their way inside the waistband of Billie's cut-offs.

Billie turned around sharply to confront Cat.

Major mistake. Cat immediately went for the delicious orbs that were now at mouth level.

Billie once again forgot that she had her mother on the phone, as she reached out and pulled Cat's head in closer. "Oh God, Cat, that feels so good," she moaned loudly as Cat inhaled first one, then other sensitive nipple into her mouth, sucking hard and biting gently.

"Billie. Billie!" the voice from the phone shouted, once more snapping Billie back to reality.

Billie raised the receiver to her ear. "Laurel," she said, "Look, I'm sorry, but I'm gonna have to call you back."

"That's a good idea, Billie. Tell Cat for me that she's a wicked woman, all right?" Laurel asked. "I'll talk to you shortly. Bye."

Billie placed the receiver on the cradle as she looked down at Cat, barely disguised passion in her impossibly blue eyes.

"Uh-oh. I'm in trouble, aren't I?" Cat said as she looked up at Billie.

Billie nodded and said, "And I'm gonna *love* dishing out the punishment."

Grinning ear to ear, Cat turned on her heel and high-tailed it out of the living room and up the stairs to their room, Billie right behind her.

Billie caught Cat by the arm just as she made it into their room and struggled to control her as Cat fought to get away.

"Hold still," Billie commanded, almost losing her grip on Cat's arm. Billie was surprised at how squirmy Cat was. Finally, she maneuvered herself behind Cat and wrapped an arm around her waist, lifting her off the floor and planting her on one hip.

Cat's feet were completely off the floor as she found herself helplessly trapped. "Let go of me, you brute," she shouted.

"Brute? I'll show you who's a brute," Billie threatened as she walked over to the bed, sat down, and threw Cat over her lap, face down.

Bracing herself against Billie's legs, Cat lifted her upper body off Billie's lap. "You wouldn't dare!" Cat challenged as she realized what Billie was about to do.

"Wouldn't I?" Billie replied, landing a sharp blow on Cat's wet denim-clad bottom.

"Aaahhh!" Cat screamed.

Whack!

"Billie, you stop that, this minute," she demanded, trying to cover her bottom with her hands in anticipation of the next blow.

Whack!

"Damn it, Billie," she screamed again.

Whack!

"Okay, okay. I'm sorry," Cat pleaded, her pride hurting far more than her backside, and her libido curiously aroused.

Billie stopped her hand in mid-swing and brought it down lightly across Cat's backside to rub away the sting from the previous contact. Of their own volition, Cat's hips began to rotate, pressing her bottom into Billie's hand.

Billie reached under Cat and unfastened Cat's shorts. She worked them off her hips, taking the lace panties with them and exposing her bottom, warm and slightly pink. Billie ran her hand over the warm skin, gently caressing and soothing, before placing tender kisses on each cheek.

Cat moaned loudly as her hips moved in time with Billie's caresses.

"God, Billie," Cat said as she rolled onto her back across Billie's legs.

Billie slipped her arm under Cat's back and raised her into a semi-sitting position. "Are you all right?"

Cat smiled. "I'm fine, love," she answered.

"I didn't hurt you, did I?" Billie asked, genuine concern in her eyes.

Cat's smile broadened. "You can punish me like that any time you want."

Billie helped Cat to her feet and led her to stand between her legs, while she remained seated on the bed. She wrapped her arms around Cat's waist then slid her hands under Cat's T-shirt. Soon, Cat's shirt and bra joined the shorts and panties on the floor.

Cat stood naked in front of Billie. She could feel the warmth radiating from her backside, each pulse of heat sending pangs of desire to her core in remembrance of how the heat came to be there.

God, I can't believe how turned on I am, Cat thought to herself as she pressed her body forward into Billie's embrace.

Billie placed butterfly kisses on Cat's abdomen, each one causing Cat to catch her breath and clench her stomach muscles.

Billie cupped one of Cat's generous breasts, bringing it to her mouth. Cat's knees weakened as Billie took the swollen nub into her mouth and suckled it gently before moving to the other.

Cat had her hands resting on the small of her own back, arching her upper body toward Billie's mouth, but quickly moved them to Billie's shoulders for support when her knees gave out.

Billie supported Cat with both hands around her waist as she closed her legs and invited Cat to sit on her lap, facing her. After Cat was seated, straddling Billie's knees, toes pressed into the floor, Billie spread her own legs open again, forcing Cat's legs apart, exposing her most vulnerable parts.

"You are so beautiful, my love," Billie said as she pulled Cat down into a kiss while her right hand caressed Cat intimately.

"Is this for me?" Billie asked, noting how ready Cat was.

"Only for you," Cat replied as she pressed herself down onto Billie's hand. Cat's forehead fell onto Billie's shoulder at the intensity of the invasion. "Oh, God, Billie. More. I need more."

Billie added a second finger and thrust deeply into Cat. Cat screamed out her desire, begging for more as she rose up and down frantically. A third finger pushed Cat very near the edge. Finally sensing that Cat was about to explode, Billie drove herself deep and hard over and over into the smaller woman on her lap.

For the next several moments, Cat repeatedly screamed out Billie's name as she rode the wave to fulfillment. Finally, she crashed into the sea of love that was her wife.

Cat lay like a rag doll in Billie's arms, totally overcome by the intensity of passion she had just experienced at the hands of her lover.

Billie pulled Cat in closer and took firm hold of her waist as she rose to her feet. Cat instinctively wrapped her legs around Billie's waist and locked her ankles; her arms still draped around her tall lover's neck. Billie reached down and supported Cat by her still-warm bottom as they stood there for long moments, mouths locked in a passionate, soul-sharing kiss.

"Let me love you," Cat said between kisses.

"Oh I intend to do just that," Billie replied as she moved toward the bed.

Suddenly, their passion-filled moment was interrupted.

"Mom! Mom, Skylar hurt herself!" the two women heard Seth shout from the hallway.

All thoughts of unfulfilled passion fled. Billie quickly put Cat down and headed toward the door while Cat threw on a robe and followed her. Seth was in the hall waiting for them.

"Where is she, honey?" Billie asked her son urgently.

"She's downstairs, Mom. She hurt her leg," he explained just as Cat emerged from the bedroom, having quickly donned dry shorts and a T-shirt.

"Seth, sweetie, is she bleeding?" Cat asked.

"No, but it hurts her real bad. She's got a really big bump on her shin," he explained as he led his mothers to the stairs.

Down in the living room, Tara and Skylar were sitting on the couch side by side, Tara with her arm around her little sister, while Skylar whimpered.

Billie was immediately by her side, soothing her tears while Cat knelt on the floor to examine the bruise. Billie looked at Tara, reaching behind Skylar to rub her older daughter's back. "Thanks for taking care of your sister, love," Billie said, drawing a huge smile from the little tomboy.

"It doesn't look like anything is broken," Cat said. "How did this happen?" she asked, looking back and forth between the three children.

"We were playing baseball in Stevie's yard. I was pitching and Tara, Sky and Karissa were playin' the field," Seth said. "Stevie hit the ball and it got Sky in the shin."

Billie cringed at the description of the speeding ball smacking her daughter in the leg. She was sure the ball was going well over a hundred miles per hour on impact.

"Ba...baseball is stupid," Skylar stammered between tears.

"I told you to get your glove down, Sky," Seth said. "Coach says the ball won't hurt you if you don't let it go under your glove."

"Stevie is stupid," Skylar said. "He hit me with the ball."

"Sky, honey, you know that's not a nice word. Stevie didn't hit you on purpose. The ball just happened to go in your direction," Cat tried to explain to her daughter as she poked around the bruise.

Satisfied that nothing was broken, she asked Billie to get the cold compress from the freezer. "Well, little Missy, looks like you're going to be confined to the couch for a while with an ice pack on your leg," Cat explained just as the phone rang.

"I'll get it," Billie said as she rose to her feet. "Hello?" she said into the receiver.

"Hi, Billie, this is Jen. Is Sky all right? Stevie told me what happened. He feels horrible. Is she okay?" Jen asked nervously.

"She seems to be fine, Jen. Cat doesn't think anything is broken. She's sitting on the couch right now with an ice pack on it. Tell Stevie it wasn't his fault, okay? Things like this happen.

She shouldn't have been playing baseball with the older kids to begin with," Billie said to their best friend and neighbor.

"Well, you know how she is, Billie...determined and stubborn, just like her mother," Jen remarked.

"I'll tell her you said that, Jen," Billie joked.

"You insufferable, two-toed, knock-kneed rat," Jen exclaimed. "You're going to get me in trouble, you know," Jen responded.

"I love you too, Jen. We'll keep you posted, okay? Talk to you later," Billie chuckled before hanging the phone up.

Billie turned to her family. "That was Jen. She said Stevie is feeling really bad about this," she said.

"Stevie is mean," Skylar insisted.

Billie knelt down beside her daughter as Cat adjusted the ice pack on her leg. She turned Skylar's face toward her. "Now, Sky, do you *really* think Stevie made the ball hit you on purpose? Do you?" she asked again.

Skylar looked at her mother and reluctantly shook her head. "I guess not," she admitted.

"Well then, I think you need to tell him that you're okay and not angry with him," Billie explained.

Cat was listening to the conversation between her wife and daughter and admired the way Billie was handling the situation.

"Seth, honey," Cat said, "why don't you run over and invite Fred, Jen and the kids to a cookout this afternoon. That will give Stevie and Skylar a chance to make up, okay?"

"Cool," Seth responded as he ran out the door.

Billie looked over at her wife and smiled. "Good idea," she said.

Cat rose to her feet. "Well, I guess I'd better get to work. I've got salads to make." Then, turning to Skylar, she asked, "Are you feeling better, rugrat?"

Skylar nodded her head vigorously.

"Don't worry, Mama, I'll keep her company," Tara said. Then to her little sister, she added, "want to color with me, Sky?"

Secretly worshipping the ground her big sister walked on, Skylar beamed under Tara's attention. "Really?" she asked. "Sure, let's color," she said excitedly, her bruised leg all but forgotten.

CHAPTER 4

The next week, all was relatively quiet at the Charland house. Monday was the first day of summer vacation, and that meant the mornings were more relaxed, with no mad rush to organize the children in time to catch the school bus. Billie and Cat had a standing arrangement with their respective employers about shifting their work hours to accommodate the children's school schedules. Cat started work at an earlier hour so that she was out in time to pick the children up at daycare shortly after the school bus dropped them off. Billie, on the other hand, went to work later so that she was able to put Seth and Tara on the bus before leaving home, and then drop Skylar off at daycare prior to going to work…usually arriving home again just before dinner. It was an arrangement that had worked out well for them.

During school vacations, their schedules remained the same—just less rushed. The only difference was that Billie dropped the two girls off at the daycare center on her way to work.

This morning, Cat was reluctant to go to work, lingering in bed longer than usual and dragging her feet when she finally did get up.

Billie had the girls sitting around the kitchen table eating a breakfast of cereal and juice when Cat finally meandered down the stairs, a total lack of enthusiasm on her face. She stopped in the doorway between the living room and kitchen and leaned against the casing.

Billie put the juice back in the refrigerator and approached Cat with open arms. Cat went into them eagerly, resting her head between Billie's breasts and wrapping her arms around her waist.

"Are you all right, Cat?" Billie asked, placing a kiss on top of the red-gold locks beneath her chin.

"Cramps," Cat said.

Billie smiled knowingly. "Maybe you should stay home today," she suggested, rubbing her hands up and down Cat's back.

"I would love nothing better than to stay home, curled up in bed with a hot water bottle pressed into my abdomen, but I'm scheduled for an early surgery. I doubt the hospital will be able to find an anesthesiologist to replace me with such short notice."

She squeezed Billie a little harder. "I need some drugs," she added, referring to the menstrual medication they kept on hand.

Billie released Cat and pulled a chair out at the kitchen table. "Here, you sit down with the girls, and I'll get it for you." Billie filled a coffee cup for her before heading to the bathroom medicine cabinet.

While Billie was gone to retrieve the medicine, Cat looked at her daughters then rose to give them each a good morning kiss.

She wrapped her arms around Tara from behind and hugged her tight, then planted a firm kiss on her cheek. "Good morning, dumpling," she said as she moved on to her younger daughter. "You too, rugrat," she added before sitting back down. Still half asleep, it took a moment for her senses to acknowledge that something wasn't quite right.

Having noted from the kiss on Skylar's forehead that the little girl seemed to be running a low-grade fever once more, she called into the other room. "Billie, bring the thermometer back with you, okay?" Looking at Skylar once more, she said, "Sky, are you feeling all right, honey?"

Billie came charging into the room. "Thermometer? Who's sick?" she asked.

"Sky feels warm again. It's pretty low grade, but I can feel it," Cat said, taking the thermometer from Billie and placing it under Skylar's tongue. She took her own pain relievers with her coffee as she waited for the digital thermometer to beep.

Billie felt Skylar's forehead. "Sky, do you feel all right, honey?" Billie asked.

Skylar nodded her head vigorously just as the thermometer beeped.

Cat took the temperature gauge out of her daughter's mouth. "98.9," she said. "That's not too bad. Sky, do you hurt anywhere? Are you tired?" she asked.

"No, I feel good. Can I have some more juice?" Skylar asked, handing her glass out to Billie.

"*May* I have some more juice," Billie said, correcting the five-year-old's verbiage. "And what's the magic word?" Billie added.

"Please?" Skylar said, grinning ear to ear at her mother.

Billie took the glass and kissed her daughter on the head before retrieving the juice. Bringing it back to the table, she handed it to Skylar who immediately began drinking. "Do you want more, Tare?" Billie asked her older daughter.

"Sure, thanks," Tara replied as Billie filled her glass.

"So, what do you think, Cat?" asked Billie.

"She seems fine. Her temperature is pretty much within an acceptable range of normal. Ask them to keep an eye on her today at daycare and to call one of us if she seems to be ill or sluggish at any point during the day," Cat suggested.

"All right," Billie said as she watched Skylar finish her juice.

"Wanna play dolls with me, Tare?" Skylar asked her sister, a hopeful look and puppy dog eyes displayed blatantly on her face.

Tara rolled her eyes at Cat and Billie, but agreed to play anyway. "Let us know when it's time to go, Mom, okay?" Tara called over her shoulder as she led her little sister down the stairs to the family room.

"All right, sweetie," Billie replied as she watched her daughters go.

Cat smiled. "Tara seems to be taking quite an interest in her little sister these days," she observed.

"Yeah," I noticed that too," Billie said, reaching out to rub Cat's back as she sat doubled over in her chair. She sat down in a chair next to Cat and reached for her hand. "C'mere," she said.

Cat climbed into Billie's lap and snuggled into her wife's shoulder as Billie wrapped her long arms around her.

"Are you sure you can't take the day off?" Billie asked. "I hate to see you go to work in such pain."

"I'm sure. The meds will kick in soon. I'll be all right," Cat added, placing a tender kiss on Billie's neck.

Billie held Cat tight, neither woman saying anything for long moments, as their hearts spoke volumes.

Finally, Cat broke the silence. "Billie?" she asked.

"Yes?"

"When does Laurel arrive for her visit?"

"Her plane lands at two-fifteen on Friday," she replied.

Cat nodded and closed her eyes against the pain in her abdomen. Billie placed a kiss on her cheek.

"Billie?" she asked again.

"Yes?"

"I'm nervous about Seth staying home."

"Cat, he's twelve years old. I think he's a little too old to be going to daycare, and besides, Jen is home all day and she offered to keep an eye on him," Billie explained.

"I know, but, well, I'm worried about him being alone," Cat confessed.

"Sweetheart, he'll be fine. In fact, I'd be willing to bet that he'll either be at Jen's for most of the day, or Stevie will be here. He has strict instructions to go nowhere but here and there. He'll be fine, Cat. Don't worry about him," Billie said, trying to soothe her wife's fears.

"I can't help it. I still remember how fragile he was the first time I laid eyes on him, so vulnerable laying there in that hospital bed. It was love at first sight. It broke my heart to see him like that. I can't believe that was six years ago," she said. "I guess I'm just being overprotective."

"Yes you are," Billie replied, kissing her on the head again. She chuckled as a thought came to her.

"What's so funny?" Cat asked, lifting her head to look at her wife.

"Knowing Seth, the day will be half over before he even gets out of bed."

Cat smiled. "You might be right. Are you sure he isn't *my* son?" she asked, referring to the standing joke about getting her out of bed in the morning.

"Oh, he's your son all right. He's definitely your son," Billie exclaimed.

* * *

"Billie Charland," Billie said when she picked up the phone. She cradled the receiver between her chin and shoulder while she organized the brief she was working on.

"Hi, hon," Cat replied.

"Cat! What a surprise. How are you feeling?" Billie said, stopping what she was doing to savor the discussion with her wife.

"Much better, thanks. Cramps are gone for the most part."

"Good. Is everything okay? The daycare hasn't called you about Sky, have they?" Billie asked, worriedly.

"No, they haven't. Actually, I'm calling to see if you can leave early to pick the girls up. The anesthesiologist who was supposed to assist on a three o'clock operation has taken ill and I was asked to cover," Cat explained.

"Yeah, sure, I can do that. Do you want me to start supper?" Billie asked.

Cat groaned involuntarily into the phone.

"Oh, come on. My cooking isn't that bad," Billie complained.

"Honey, I'm sorry, you weren't supposed to hear that," Cat said apologetically. "Sure, go ahead and start supper if you want. There's some leftover potato salad in the fridge. Just throw a few burgers on the grill and some corn on the cob on to boil and that should do it. Okay? Oh, and remember to turn the grill to medium—not high," Cat said.

"How long does the corn need to boil?" Billie asked.

"Fifteen minutes ought to do it," Cat replied.

"All right. I can handle that. Do you have any idea what time you'll be home?" Billie asked.

"Hopefully by the time dinner's ready. I've got to go prep. I'll see you tonight, love. Bye," Cat said hanging up the phone.

Billie hung up the receiver and checked her watch, noting that it was already nearly three. She finished collecting and organizing the briefs she was working on then neatly piled them into her briefcase. *I'll finish these at home*, she thought as she snapped the case closed.

She stopped by Art's office on the way out and stuck her head in to let him know that she was leaving early.

"Is everything okay, Billie?" Art asked. "You seem a little distracted today," he observed.

"No, everything's fine. Cat had to cover a three o'clock surgery, so she's asked me to pick up the kids," she explained.

"All right then, I'll see you tomorrow," Art said.

Art sat back in his chair. *Huh*, he thought to himself, *there's something she's not telling me.*

* * *

Billie arrived at the day care at exactly three-thirty. When she walked into the reception area, she noticed Skylar and Tara waiting for her. Expecting to see Cat, they were surprised and excited to see that Billie had come to collect them.

"Mommy!" Skylar said as she ran into Billie's arms and snuggled in to her neck.

"Hi, love bug. Have you been a good girl today?" she asked.

Skylar nodded her head vigorously.

Settling Skylar on her right hip, Billie opened her other arm to accept Tara into a hug. "Hi, sweetness. How was your day?"

"Pretty good," Tara replied. "Where's Mama?" she asked.

"She had a late surgery, so she called and asked me to pick my girls up," she explained.

Tara looked up at her mother and beamed. "Does this mean we get to eat out?" she asked hopefully.

"Actually, no. I have strict orders from Mama to go home and start supper," Billie replied.

"Ah, Mom, I remember the last time you cooked," Tara whined.

"Hey, what is this problem everyone has with my cooking anyway?" she asked indignantly.

Tara looked at her with an expression that said *Duh, Mom, buy a clue!* causing Billie to laugh out loud.

"Well, I hate to break it to you rugrat, but I am cooking tonight. I won't poison you, I promise," she said, chuckling as she carried Skylar out to the car with a pouting Tara following close behind.

Fifteen minutes later, they pulled into the driveway of their home. Tara climbed quickly out of the car and ran into the house to claim the family room TV before anyone else did. Skylar was a little slower. She was pushing the rear passenger door closed just as Billie came around to her side of the car. Billie knelt down in front of her, bringing her to face level with the little girl.

"How are you feeling, sweetling?" she asked, feeling the child's forehead, and noting that it was warm once again. A frown etched itself deeply into Billie's brow.

"I'm tired, Mommy," Skylar complained.

"C'mere, love," Billie said, opening her arms to the child.

Billie carried Skylar directly to her room, and sat her on the bed. She removed first one of Skylar's shoes, and then the other, noticing that even her feet felt warm. Urging the child to lie down, Billie next stripped off her jeans.

After tossing Skylar's jeans into the laundry basket clear across the room, she turned to the child to brag about the basket she had just made when she suddenly noticed something that made her heart stop in her chest. The bruise on Skylar's shin as a result of being hit with a baseball more than a week ago still looked as fresh as the day it happened.

Shouldn't this have healed by now? she asked herself as she watched the child yawn, her little hands balled into fists on the pillow on both sides of her head.

Skylar closed her eyes, mouth stretched open wide to accommodate another escaping yawn. The little girl's eyes were heavily lidded and closing rapidly while Billie tucked her into bed for a nap before supper. She lay next to the child and hummed an old lullaby her adoptive mother used to sing to her until she was fast asleep.

Billie touched the sleeping child's red-gold hair. *Sky baby, I hope you're all right*, she whispered in her mind, before rising to go start dinner.

CHAPTER 5

The operation Cat had anesthetized ran into complications and lasted much longer than expected. It was nearly seven before she finally made it home. Billie spent the entire time between feeding the kids their dinner and Cat's arrival home, pacing nervously around the kitchen.

Cat walked into the kitchen and wearily threw her car keys on the table. "I'm beat," she declared, rolling her head around on her shoulders to loosen the tension in her neck. Finally after a few moments of silence, she noticed that Billie was pacing, a worried expression on her face. She stopped her in mid-pace.

"Billie, honey, what's wrong? Where are the kids?" she asked, looking around for the children.

"Seth is at Stevie's, the girls are in the family room. Cat, there's something wrong with Sky," Billie stated.

"What do you mean?" Cat asked, narrowing her eyes.

"Do you remember when Sky was hit on the shin with the baseball?"

Cat nodded.

"Do you remember how bruised her leg was, and how much it hurt her to walk on it?"

Cat nodded. "Billie, what's that got to do with anything?" she asked.

"Cat, Sky was very tired when I picked her and Tara up this afternoon. I put her down for a nap when we got home and noticed when I helped her out of her jeans, that the bruise on her leg hasn't even started to heal yet," Billie explained.

Cat frowned. "You said the girls are downstairs?" Cat asked, heading for the basement steps.

"Yes," Billie replied, right behind her wife.

When they reached the bottom of the stairs, they found Skylar and Tara sitting on the couch facing each other and playing dolls. Skylar was still in her underpants and T-shirt. Cat studied her daughter carefully without speaking; not wanting to alarm the little girl.

"Hi, love bugs," she said to both children. "Did you have a nice day?"

The girls immediately jumped into an animated conversation about their day at the daycare center. Cat noticed that Skylar did look a little pale. After listening to both children talk about their day, she reached up to feel Skylar's forehead. As expected, she was feverish.

"How are you feeling tonight, sweetie?" Cat asked as she nonchalantly examined Skylar's leg for the bruise she received more than a week ago. As Billie described, the bruise was still there, and very fresh looking.

"Sky, honey, did you bump your leg at daycare today?" Cat asked.

Skylar shook her head no.

Billie and Cat exchanged worried looks.

Cat kissed her youngest daughter on the forehead. "Sweetheart, you're running a fever again. I'm going to call the doctor, okay? We'll take you in and let Dr. Sorensen look at you," Cat explained.

"I don't wanna go to the doctor's," Skylar whined.

"I know, sweetie, but if you're sick, you'll need to go to the doctor's to get better," Cat reasoned.

Skylar looked scared. "Mama, is he gonna to pick me with a needle?" she asked.

Cat smiled. "No, love. I just want him to look at you, that's all," she assured her younger daughter.

Skylar crossed her arms in front of her and pouted, knowing she had no choice.

"Come on, bugger," Billie said, holding her arms out to her daughter. "Let's get you dressed, okay?"

Skylar went into Billie's arms and rested her head on her shoulder.

A frown deepened on Billie's face as she felt the heat radiating from Skylar. Leaning in close to Cat's ear, she whispered, "Cat, she's burning up. I can feel the fever through her clothes."

Cat placed her hand on Skylar's back to verify Billie's observation. "Billie, go ahead and get her dressed. I'll call the doctor," Cat said.

Ten minutes later, Cat was tying Skylar's shoes as Billie phoned Jen.

"Hi, Jen. This is Billie. Look, Cat and I are taking Skylar to the doctor."

"Sky is ill?" Jen asked.

"Yeah, she's feverish again. It's the third time in a week. We need to get her looked at. Seth is still there with Stevie, isn't he?" Billie asked. "We need him to come home to stay with Tara while we're gone."

"Why don't you send Tara over here. In fact, she and Seth can spend the night and the day tomorrow if they'd like. That will give Stevie and Karissa something to do too. I really hate vacations. All they do is whine about being bored," Jen said.

"Jen, are you sure you don't mind?" Billie asked.

"If I minded, I wouldn't have offered. Now pack a bag for both of them and send it over with Tara," Jen instructed. "Don't worry about them. Take care of Sky. Besides, I think she'll like an evening being the center of attention for a change."

"All right, Jen. I don't know how to thank you. We'll drop Tara off on the way. Expect her in about ten minutes," Billie said.

"No thanks necessary, big guy. You'd do the same for me, and you know it. Now drag your tail, or you'll be late," Jen warned.

Billie thanked Jen once more then hung up after promising to call her with the results. Giving Tara instructions to pack a small bag for herself, she went to collect a few things for Seth. Five minutes later, they pulled into Jen's driveway and dropped Tara off.

* * *

"Damn it, Cat. What is taking them so long? We've been waiting here for nearly a half-hour," Billie complained.

"Billie, please be patient. There seems to be a lot of sick kids tonight. We just need to wait our turn," Cat explained.

Skylar shifted restlessly in Billie's arms where she had crawled the minute they arrived. Billie reached over and brushed the bangs off Skylar's forehead and replaced them with a kiss.

"Cat, she's even more feverish than when we left the house," Billie observed.

Cat felt her daughter's forehead. She looked at Billie a little worriedly. "You're right, she is. Look, I'm going to see the receptionist. Maybe she can tell me how much longer we'll have to wait."

No sooner had Cat rose to her feet, than the nurse called out Skylar's name.

"It's about time," Billie murmured under her breath. She followed Cat and the nurse to the examination room, carrying a very warm and clingy Skylar in her arms.

The nurse measured Skylar's weight and height then took her temperature, recording the information on the chart attached to her folder.

"The doctor will be right with you," she said, leaving the three of them alone in the room.

As soon as the nurse left, Skylar held her arms out for Cat. Skylar wrapped her legs around her mother and laid her head on Cat's shoulder. The heat coming from her face was radiating into Cat's skin. Cat looked at Billie nervously as she rubbed the child's back. Billie paced back and forth across the room. Neither said a word.

Finally, Dr. Sorensen entered the room. "Now, who do we have here? Let's see, Skylar Charland, age six," he said, reading the chart. He put the chart down on the examination table and folded his arms in front of him. "Well, Skylar, what seems to be the problem?"

Billie took a step toward the man like she was about to read him the riot act.

Cat held her hand up, effectively stopping her. "She's running a fever, Dr. Sorensen. This is her third fever this week.

The other two were less severe—less than 100 degrees—and both gone by the next morning. As you can see by her chart, this fever is much worse. She has also been listless, and she has a week-old hematoma on her shin that is not healing," Cat explained.

Dr. Sorensen looked at Cat curiously. "Am I to assume that you are a doctor, Ms...,"

"Charland. Cat Charland," Cat answered, "and yes, you assumed correctly, Dr. Sorensen, I am an anesthesiologist, now I would appreciate it if you would examine my daughter and give me your opinion of what the problem is," Cat said.

"All right. Bring her over to the table, if you would," Dr. Sorensen instructed.

Cat laid Skylar on the table and took a step away to allow the doctor access to her daughter. Skylar immediately started to cry as the strange man started poking and prodding her.

Billie stepped in and took Skylar's hand. Bending over the child, she talked soothingly to her. "Sky, baby, it will be all right, Mom and Mama are right here with you."

The doctor looked oddly at Billie.

Billie stared right back at him, daring him to say something.

He quickly looked away and finished his examination.

"Well, Ms. Charland," he said, addressing Cat. "She seems to have an ear infection. I'll prescribe some antibiotics for her. She'll be as good as new in a few days," he said, pulling out his prescription pad and beginning to scribble on it.

Cat frowned. "What about the bruise on her shin...and her paleness? She's terribly pale," Cat said.

"Well, her weight and height are normal for a child her age, and beside, summer is just starting. A lot of kids are pale from the winter, so I wouldn't worry about it. As far as the bruise is concerned," he said, examining the purplish skin on Skylar's leg, "shin bruises always take a long time to fade. I'm sure it's nothing," he concluded. "Let's give the antibiotics a few days and see what happens, okay?"

* * *

"I don't like him, Cat. We need to find a new doctor for the kids," Billie insisted as she maneuvered the car through the city streets.

"You may be right, Billie. He was a little impersonal with her," Cat said, looking into the backseat at Skylar. Moments after pulling out of the parking lot of the doctor's office, she was fast asleep.

"I'm glad the pharmacy was still open. At least we were able to get her prescription filled before tomorrow. We'll wake her and give her the first dose when we get home," Cat commented.

Moments later, Billie pulled the car into the driveway. Coming around to the passenger side, she lifted Skylar and carried her into the house, directly to their bedroom.

"Billie, where are you going with her?" Cat asked when she saw Billie carry Skylar right past her bedroom.

"To our room, Cat. I want her near us tonight so we can monitor how she's doing," Billie explained.

Cat just threw up her hands. "All right," she said as she stopped at Skylar's room to collect her pajamas.

By the time Cat joined her in their room, Billie had managed to get Skylar out of her play clothes and ready for her pajamas. Between the two of them, they dressed the groggy child and gave her the first dose of antibiotic, finally tucking her into bed between them.

Billie lay on her side, looking at the child, then over at Cat, catching Cat's eye.

"What are you thinking Billie?" Cat asked.

"I'm thinking that this sweet little angel looks so much like you, and not at all like Brian," Billie replied.

A chill ran through Cat at the mention of her rapist's name. A chill so intense, it was visible to Billie.

Realizing what she had done, Billie apologized profusely.

"Cat, I'm sorry," she said, reaching over Skylar to cup the side of Cat's face with her palm. "I'm so insensitive some times. Forgive me?" she asked, genuine sorrow in her eyes.

Cat smiled. "Yes, I forgive you, love. But say it again, and I'll have to kill you, okay?" she said grinning.

Billie grinned. "It's a deal," she said, lifting herself up onto one elbow to kiss Cat tenderly. "Good night, my love," Billie said.

"Good night, Billie."

Each of them in turn kissed their sleeping daughter.

"Sleep well, kitten," Cat whispered the nickname her father always used for her.

Soon, all three girls were sleeping peacefully.

* * *

The next morning, Billie woke before the alarm. She rolled onto her side and looked at her wife and child sleeping beside her. Skylar was wrapped in Cat's arms, her hair strewn across her tiny features, her arms and legs in a state of disarray around her. Billie smiled as her heart lurched at the sight. She brushed the hair away from the little girl's face and kissed her cheek, noting that it was still warm with fever.

Cat's eyes opened in response to the movement beside her. Billie's gaze locked with hers as she lifted her face away from Skylar's cheek.

"Good morning, love," Cat whispered, accepting a kiss from her wife.

"She's still warm, Cat," Billie remarked.

Cat felt the child's forehead. Raising her eyebrows, she said, "You're right. Maybe one of us should stay home with her today."

"Maybe both of us should," Billie suggested. "I'm between cases right now, so I can arrange to take the time off."

"And I'm not scheduled for any surgeries today, so it shouldn't be a problem for me either," Cat said.

"Good," Billie said, smiling. "Go back to sleep, then. I'm going for my run. I'll be back soon."

After kissing Cat and Skylar once more, Billie rolled over and shut off the alarm, then climbed out of bed and donned her running clothes.

As was the case every morning, Jen was at the end of the driveway, waiting for her.

"Good morning," Billie said as she stopped to stretch her hamstrings, calves and quadriceps.

"'Morning, big guy. How's Sky this morning?" Jen asked as she too stretched out before starting their run.

"Still warm, I'm afraid," Billie answered. "I'm really worried about her, Jen," Billie admitted.

"What did the doctor say?" Jen asked.

Billie scowled. "He said she had an ear infection. She had her first dose of antibiotics last night. He wants to wait a few days to see if it helps," Billie explained.

Jen looked at the irritated expression on her friend's face. "Do I sense something else going on here, Billie? Sounds like you don't have a lot of faith in Sky's doctor," Jen observed.

"I don't know, Jen. There's something about him that I don't like. I can't put my finger on it though," she said.

"Well, it's helpful that Cat is a doctor too. I'm sure she'll step in if she thinks the guy isn't doing his job," Jen assured her friend.

"Yeah, you're right," Billie said, shaking her legs out. "Are you ready to sweat?" she asked Jen, a teasing smile on her face.

Seconds later, the friends began their run.

* * *

The sound of the shower woke Cat from a light sleep. Rolling over, she encountered a foreign body next to her and realized that Skylar was still with her...and still sleeping. That concerned her a little, considering the little girl usually rose nearly as early as Billie every morning.

She kissed Skylar on the forehead, checking the child's temperature at the same time. Acknowledging that Skylar was still slightly feverish, but not nearly as bad as the night before, Cat released a sign of relief and climbed out of bed to go in search of Billie.

Billie was standing under the shower spray, allowing the warm water to cascade over her face and down the length of her dark hair. The needle-like darts of water provided a therapeutic massaging action on her forehead, helping to alleviate the slight headache she could feel building in her skull. A smile graced her face as the rustling shower curtain alerted her to Cat's presence behind her...long before she felt Cat's hands circle her waist and her lips make contact with the skin between her shoulder blades. She instinctively pressed herself back into Cat, who tightened her arms around Billie's mid-section.

"Good morning," Cat said, pressing her length against Billie's back in a full-body hug.

Billie's right hand came down to cover the arms circling her waist, while her left arm reached back to pull Cat closer. "Good morning yourself, my love," Billie returned.

She turned around in Cat's embrace, shielding Cat from the direct spray of the shower as she lowered her face for a tender kiss. "I love you," Billie said, kissing her again.

"Hmmmm," Cat replied, reaching her hand around Billie's neck to pull her down for more.

Finally, the kiss ended, and the women stood there in each other's arms, eyes locked in a loving gaze. "Is Sky still asleep?" Billie asked.

Cat nodded and kissed the hollow in Billie's neck at the spot where her collarbones met.

Billie tilted her head back and closed her eyes. "That feels good," she said, pulling Cat's head closer with a hand behind her neck. "Is she still feverish?" Billie asked.

Once again Cat nodded. "Hmmm, but not as hot as last night," she replied as she began to suck on the sensitive skin on Billie's neck, sending shivers of desire directly to Billie's groin.

"Good," Billie managed to rasp out before her body shuddered with the intensity of emotion she was feeling. "Cat," she rasped out, "Do you know what you're doing to me?" she asked.

"As a matter of fact, I do," Cat said, reaching down between Billie's legs and finding the evidence of her labors.

Billie's knees buckled as Cat caressed the swollen nub she found there. Her right hand immediately went to the shower wall, bracing against an instant meltdown onto the floor of the tub, as her left hand circled Cat's back, pulling her closer. Her stance instinctively widened to give Cat better access.

Cat increased the pace of her caress as Billie's body became more and more heightened by desire. The constant bombardment of the jet spray on her back was increasing the intensity level of the bolts shooting to her groin.

Cat flicked her tongue over Billie's nipples, taking each one into her mouth and biting them gently as her hands made their way behind her tall wife, gripping the firm cheeks of her bottom and pulling her in closer.

"Harder," Billie panted as each nip nearly pushed her over the edge.

Cat obliged and increased the pressure of her teeth on the hardened nipples, biting firmly until Billie moaned in pain. Her entire body was weakened, quivering with pent up desire, waiting to be released. Cat's right hand made its way back between Billie's legs stimulating her as her left hand continued to knead the supple flesh of her buttocks.

"Cat, I can't take much more of this," Billie managed to say between pants.

In one swift movement, Cat released Billie's nipple, dropped to one knee and drove three fingers deep into Billie.

Billie nearly folded in on top of Cat…the only thing holding her up was her grip on the support bar in the shower.

"Oh my God, Cat," Billie shouted as a powerful orgasm ripped through her body, sending it into spasms of desire.

Over and over, a tidal wave of heat crashed into her, her abdomen contracting with each wave. Her legs were totally useless as she sank to her knees beside Cat, spasms racking her body for long moments, her upper body leaning heavily on Cat.

Cat held her close, whispering terms of endearment in her ear as the after effects of their lovemaking began to subside. Finally Cat removed her hand, causing one more momentary spasm to escape Billie's body.

Billie reached down and cupped Cat's face between her hands, the spray of the shower coming down heavily around them. She kissed her deeply. Moving along Cat's jaw line to her ear, Billie spoke her heart.

"Cat, I love you more than life itself. What have I done to deserve you?" she asked. "I am so blessed to have you in my life," she finished, claiming Cat's lips once more in a breathtaking kiss.

Billie gently lowered their two bodies to the floor, with Cat reclining against the back of the oversized tub. Kneeling between Cat's legs, she kissed her thoroughly, starting at her mouth and ending in the hollow at the base of her neck between her collarbones...at the same spot that Cat had started on her. Cat's head was thrown back, her wet hair splayed all around her, eyes closed.

Billie looked at her and thought that she was the most beautiful creature on the face of the earth. Reaching outside the shower, Billie grabbed the clean towel that was hanging on the rack, and pulled it into the shower with them. Folding it carefully, she tucked it under Cat's neck and head to cushion them against the hard surface.

The exploration of Cat's body began in earnest. Every inch of Cat's skin was caressed with kisses as Billie moved over her, nipping, biting, and licking. Each point of contact was met by a moan from Cat's lips.

Several times, Billie had to push Cat's hands away as Cat attempted to guide Billie to that special destination that would provide relief from the building tension and desire. Each time, Billie would gently remove Cat's hands then continue her exploration of Cat's body, teasingly avoiding her final destination.

Cat's desires were rapidly escalating out of control. As Billie suckled her breasts, she felt the impending wave of an orgasm begin, only to be quelled as Billie retreated to another spot on her anatomy.

"Billie, please. I need you," she panted in desperation.

Sensing that Cat would go over the edge with very little assistance, Billie suddenly moved south, gently biting the Cat's passion point. That movement, combined with the sudden needle-like spray hitting her face and chest from the shower that Billie was no longer shielding her from, caused her to quickly fall over the edge.

Arching herself upward as she braced her arms against the tub wall, Cat called out Billie's name over and over as her body convulsed uncontrollably. For long moments, Billie continued the oral massage until Cat was lying limply and quietly beneath her.

Billie looked up and saw Cat staring at her with love-filled eyes. Releasing her prize, Billie kissed the inside of Cat's thigh, then made her way up the smaller woman's body, gathering her into her arms and holding her close.

"Billie, I love you more than I could possibly describe," Cat said into Billie's shoulder. "Please promise to love me forever," she added.

Billie looked into her wife's eyes. "Forever, my love. Forever. I promise."

"Mama?" a small voice said from the other room.

Cat grinned up at Billie. "Good timing," she exclaimed before climbing to her feet.

"I'll be right there, love bug," Cat yelled into the other room as Billie helped her to wash the evidence of lovemaking from her skin.

CHAPTER 6

Cat and Billie watched Skylar's health closely over the next few days. Shortly after taking the medication her temperature would fall, but only temporarily. Within three hours of taking the meds, it would rise again.

Skylar's behavior during this roller coaster ride varied with the fever. As was to be expected, when the fever was high she was listless and irritable, unable and unwilling to eat much of anything. When it was low she was full of energy and wanting to play.

By the third day, Cat was convinced the antibiotics were not working. Instead of seeing the expected improvement, Skylar's fever remained high, regardless of her dose schedule. Billie and Cat had a difficult time getting the child to eat anything, and just barely convinced her to take in enough juice and water to keep her hydrated. She spent most of the third day lying around, alternately sleeping and whimpering.

Cat pulled the thermometer out of Skylar's mouth and read the display. "Her temp is still high—100.6 degrees," she said.

"Cat, I'm not a doctor, but shouldn't her meds be working by now?" Billie asked.

"Normally, yes. I'm beginning to think something is wrong with either the diagnosis or the treatment. The antibiotics are simply not taking care of the problem," Cat said. "I'm calling her doctor to see if they can get her in right away. If not, we'll take her to the emergency room."

An hour later, Cat, Billie and Skylar sat in one of the examination rooms at the pediatrician's office. Skylar was wrapped tightly around Cat and whimpered periodically, resisting even Billie's attempt to cheer her up. After what felt like an interminable amount of time, Billie voiced her extreme displeasure with the situation.

"Cat, what the hell is taking so long? No wonder people hesitate to go to the doctor. Are all doctors like this or is this one in particular more incompetent than the rest?" she asked with intense frustration tingeing her voice.

"Billie," Cat replied, exasperation clearly showing through her voice and mannerisms. "Not all doctors are incompetent... in fact, most are pretty damned good at what they do."

Billie rubbed her hands over her face then dropped them into her lap. "Cat, I'm sorry. I don't mean to insult your profession, it just that every time we come here, we wait for what seems like an eternity. Doesn't Sorensen realize Skylar is sick?" she asked.

Cat had no answer for Billie's frustration, and was saved from having to come up with one by Dr. Sorensen himself, who chose that moment to rush into the room.

"Okay. Who do we have here and what seems to be the problem?" he asked while scanning Skylar's chart.

Billie shook her head in disbelief. *It was only three days ago that he saw Skylar. The least he could do is remember her name.*

Cat glanced nervously at Billie, then prompted the doctor's memory. "Skylar Charland. You saw her three days ago and diagnosed an ear infection," Cat said.

Dr. Sorensen looked blank for a moment then glanced at Skylar's chart. "Of course—Skylar Charland—age five."

"Age six. Maybe you should take a closer look at her chart," Billie said sarcastically.

"Yes...age six. Fever, bruise on her leg," he read from her chart. He looked at Cat over the top of the chart. "How are the antibiotics working?"

"They aren't," Billie replied sharply.

Dr. Sorensen scowled at Billie then looked pointedly at Cat. "How so?" he asked.

"She's still feverish...she's not eating...she isn't sleeping well...the medicine is *not* working," Billie reiterated.

Dr. Sorensen closed Skylar's chart. "I'm sorry. I understand your concern for Skylar's health, but my question was for Dr. Charland."

"Billie's assessment is correct," Cat said quickly.

Billie could feel the heat rise into her face as she struggled not to take the man's head off and hand it to him. She shot a meaningful look at Cat then bit her tongue so as to not cause a scene in front of Skylar.

Dr. Sorensen turned his attention back to Skylar's chart. He made a few short entries then placed it aside. "Well, let's take a look." He took Skylar from Cat's arms and placed her on the examination table.

Skylar immediately began to whimper.

"There, there. Big girls don't cry," Dr. Sorensen said firmly.

Cat reached out and placed a warning hand on Billie's arm.

Billie sat there and gritted her teeth in an effort to control herself.

Dr. Sorensen examined Skylar's ears and listened to her heart and lungs, then picked up her chart once more to enter a few notes. "I think we should give the antibiotics a few more days," he said.

"No." Billie said vehemently.

"No?" replied the doctor.

"What part of that didn't you understand?" Billie said sarcastically. "Look, my daughter has been ill now for nearly a week. She's feverish, weak, listless, and irritable. She isn't eating. She's stumbles around when she walks…she sleeps all the time. Three days of antibiotics has not helped."

Dr. Sorensen thumbed through Skylar's file. "It says here that Caitlain is her mother, not you. I'd like to hear *her* opinion on Skylar's treatment options."

"What did you say?" Billie asked incredulously.

"I said, she's not your biological daughter—she's Caitlain's. What part of that did *you* not understand?" he replied sarcastically.

Billie was on her feet in an instant, her hand reaching for the doctor's throat.

"Billie!" Cat shouted while Skylar started to whimper again.

Billie immediately regained control of herself at the sound of Cat's voice. She leaned close to the doctor and talked in a low, even voice to prevent Skylar from hearing what she had to say.

"You son of a bitch. I've dealt with bastards like you before. We're talking about the life of a child here, not who her biological mother is. Don't you have any compassion in your heart at all?"

She picked Skylar up from the examination table and cradled her gently in her arms. "Let's go, Cat."

Before leaving, Billie turned to the doctor. "You will never get the chance to see one of *my* children again. I may not be a doctor like Cat, but I *am* a lawyer. I hope your malpractice insurance is up to date, because if your incompetence has caused Skylar any harm, I will become your worst nightmare."

* * *

"Billie, slow down, you'll get us all killed," Cat demanded.

Billie glanced into the rearview mirror at Cat who was sitting in the back seat next to a sleeping Skylar. She suddenly realized just whose lives she held in her hands and immediately slowed the car down and stopped by the side of the road. She sat there, staring straight ahead…her hands on the steering wheel.

"Cat, I'm sorry. He just made me so angry. I'm afraid I'm not dealing well with it."

"There's nothing to be sorry about, love. If it wasn't for Sky being there with us, I would have loved to see you deck the son of a bitch. I should have gone with your instincts to begin with, and found another doctor right away," Cat admitted.

"What do we do now?" Billie asked.

"Let's go home. I'll call some of my colleagues and compile a list of good pediatricians that we can choose from," Cat said.

"All right," Billie said, reaching for the gearshift. "Damn!" she said suddenly.

"What is it, Billie?" Cat asked, startled by the outburst.

"My mother is due to arrive tomorrow, Cat. Maybe I should call and tell her to cancel her plans," Billie suggested.

"No, Billie. It's too late for that. No, let her come. I'm sure Sky will be all right in a day or two. There's no reason to cancel her visit," Cat reasoned.

"Are you sure?" Billie asked.

"Yeah, I'm sure. Let's go home. I've got a few calls to make," Cat replied.

* * *

Cat spent the rest of the afternoon contacting physicians until she found one that had a small enough caseload to accept new patients. She set up an appointment for the following day. Hanging up the phone, Cat joined Billie and the kids in the family room where they were watching a *Teenage Mutant Ninja Turtles* movie. Seth and Tara were lying on their stomachs on the floor, eyes glued to the TV, a bowl of popcorn between them, while Skylar was once again curled up in Billie's arms, sound asleep.

Cat snuggled into Billie's side on the couch and kissed her daughter on the head. "I found a doctor, Billie. We have an appointment at ten tomorrow morning. That will give us enough time to see her, and still be at the airport by two to pick up your mom," Cat explained.

"Her?" Billie asked.

"Yes, her. Dr. Alexis Berry. She has a couple of young children of her own, so I'm sure she'll be more sympathetic than Sorensen was," Cat explained.

"Good. Maybe she can get to the bottom of what's ailing Sky," Billie said.

Cat reached over to brush an errant red-gold lock from Skylar's face. "I hope so, love. I certainly hope so. It breaks my heart to see her so listless," Cat said.

* * *

At nine-forty-five the next morning, Cat, Billie and Skylar entered the offices of Dr. Alexis Berry. They were immediately aware of the differences between this office and that of Dr. Sorensen. Where Sorensen's office was drab, sparse and clinical, Dr. Berry's office was bright and cheery. The waiting room was painted bright yellow with blue, pink and green toys painted all over the walls. One corner of the waiting room featured a sunken play area with carpeted steps surrounding it in a Coliseum type layout with stadium seating. A large array of toys and gadgets for children from toddler to pre-teen were positioned strategically around the play area. Skylar was so impressed with the allure of this room that she insisted on being allowed to play, despite her illness.

Cat and Billie sat comfortably nearby while Skylar sorted through the treasure chest toy box. At exactly ten, Skylar's name was called and the threesome was led to an equally appealing examination room, where a very pleasant nurse took all of the standard vital sign readings, even allowing Skylar to wear her stethoscope and making her giggle by calling her *Dr. Charland*.

After the nurse left, Skylar spotted a collection of children's books in a box on the floor and hurriedly scurried off the examination table to sort through her new find. It wasn't long before the door opened once more.

"Hi Sky," Dr. Berry said to the little girl as she entered the room, acknowledging the child before addressing her parents. Squatting down so that she was face level with the child sitting on the floor, she reached out and touched Skylar's forehead. "Not feeling so good today, are you sweetie?" the doctor asked, moving her hand from the child's forehead to her cheek.

Billie liked this woman immediately. She had a totally different manner than Dr. Sorensen. To begin with, she was smaller than Sorensen, who was a very large and imposing man, well over six feet...and she had a soft, gentle, soothing voice. Most importantly, she directed a great deal of the dialogue directly at Skylar, talking *to* her instead of *about* her during the examination.

"I'd like to take your temperature and listen to your heart. Is that all right?" Dr. Berry asked.

Skylar nodded her head shyly.

"Good," said the doctor, smiling as she extended her arms to Skylar.

Without hesitation, Skylar allowed the doctor to pick her up and carry her to the examination table. She set her down on the table and explained each procedure to the child before carrying it out. Soon, she had taken her temperature, blood pressure, pulse, and reflexes and had listened to her heart and examined her ears, all without a trace of fear in the child's face. Cat and Billie grinned at each other, very pleased with the mannerisms of this warm, kind-hearted doctor.

"So how does her ear infection look?" Cat asked.

Dr. Berry frowned and looked at Skylar's ears once more. She clicked off her light and crossed her arms, looking directly at Cat and Billie. "I see no trace of ear infection. What makes you think she has one?" she asked.

Billie's eyes nearly popped out of her face. "She doesn't have an ear infection?" she asked incredulously.

"Dr. Berry, could she have had one recently—like three days ago?" Cat asked.

Dr. Berry shook her head. "No. Ear infections generally take at least ten days before they are gone. If she had one as recently as three days ago, she'd still have it," Dr. Berry explained.

"That son-of-a...," Billie began before remembering they were in mixed company. She bit her tongue to stop herself.

Dr. Berry picked up Skylar's chart and read the name of her previous physician. She sighed deeply. "Okay, it's probably safe to say that we'll be starting from square one here," she said.

Turning back to Skylar, Dr. Berry tweaked Skylar's nose. "You, my girl, are an excellent patient, and for that, you get a lollipop."

Dr. Berry retrieved a lollipop from a drawer beneath the examination table then chose a couple of children's books from the box on the floor. She gave them to Skylar. "Here you go, sweetie. I have some boring big-people stuff to talk about with your moms. Why don't you look at these books while I do that?"

"Have a seat, ladies," Dr. Berry said to Cat and Billie. She sat on the examination stool in front of them. Addressing Cat, she said, "Considering she looks so much like you, I am assuming you are the birth mother, right?" she said with a smile.

"I am her biological mother, yes, but Sky considers Billie her mother as well," Cat explained, a bit defensively.

"Fair enough. I'll address both of you equally," Dr. Berry said. "Tell me about her symptoms and behavior since she's been ill."

For the next few minutes, Cat and Billie both explained to the doctor how Skylar had been tired, cranky and listless all the time. After pointing out how pale she was, they stressed the fact that she had virtually no appetite, and basically spent most of her day sleeping. They also explained to her, the origin and age of the bruise on her shin.

Dr. Berry frowned. "The bruise happened when?" she asked.

"Almost two weeks ago," Cat answered. "Look, I know it should be faded by now, but her last doctor didn't seem disturbed by the fact that it still looks new."

"Caitlain, it says here on Skylar's new patient form that you are a doctor. May I ask what type?" Dr. Berry asked.

"Please, call me Cat. I'm an anesthesiologist," Cat said a little defensively. "Why do you ask?"

Dr. Berry smiled. "Relax, Cat. You're not on trial here. It's just that when I treat the children of other doctors, I need to make sure that they are open to suggestions and ideas beyond what they themselves have already diagnosed, that's all," she explained.

"Dr. Berry, we are open to anything that will help our daughter feel better. I am not a specialist in pediatric medicine. Sky's symptoms are typical of so many childhood diseases, I'm not about to make a misdiagnosis where my own child is concerned. That's why we are here to see you," Cat explained.

Dr. Berry stood and extended her hand to Cat and then to Billie. "Good. I'm glad you feel that way. Maybe we can work together to help this little girl feel better again. As a precaution, I'm going to order some blood work, as it appears her former doctor did not do that," Dr. Berry said. "Like you said, Cat, her symptoms are indicative of a lot of different things. The results of the blood work should help us make a more accurate diagnosis. I'll send the nurse in to draw some blood."

Dr. Berry approached Skylar and sat down cross-legged on the floor in front of the child. "C'mere, munchkin," she said, opening her arms to Skylar.

Skylar went to Dr. Berry without hesitation and sat on her lap.

"We're going to do everything we can to help you feel better soon, little one," she said. "I am going to ask the nurse to come in and draw some blood. You'll have to be brave, because it might hurt a little, okay?"

A look of trepidation crossed Skylar's face. "I'll try not to cry," she said.

"Sweetheart, it's okay to cry if something hurts you. I just want to make sure that you let the nurse do it. We need some of your blood so we can figure out how to make you feel better, that's all," she explained.

Skylar nodded her head in agreement and promised to cooperate.

"Good girl," Dr. Berry said. She hugged Skylar before rising to her feet. Facing Cat and Billie again, she promised them the test results by the following day then left them alone with their child while they waited for the nurse to draw blood.

* * *

Laurel's plane was due to land just after two in the afternoon. Having left the doctor's office by eleven, they had plenty of time to go home, have lunch, and collect Seth and

Tara before heading to the airport. All the way home from the doctor's Skylar raved about the selection of stickers Dr. Berry had given her for being such a good girl.

"What do you think about her, Billie?" Cat asked.

"I really like her. She seems to have a way with children. I like the way she actually talked *to* Sky, rather than over her head to us. I've never seen a doctor actually get down on the floor with a patient. I really do like her, Cat. You done good picking her out, woman," Billie said in her best redneck voice.

"Ya think so, ma?" Cat joked back.

"Yes, Ma'am, yer darn tootin' I do," Billie quipped.

"Mommy, you sound funny," Skylar giggled.

Billie looked at her daughter in the back seat. "You, my sweet angel, were a very good girl at the doctor's, even when they came to take blood," Billie remarked.

Skylar beamed with pride as she held out her arm to show them, for the hundredth time, the bright pink bandage the nurse had wrapped around her arm after drawing blood.

"Yes, you were, kitten. We were very proud of you," added Cat.

Billie maneuvered the car into the driveway and shut off the ignition. "Okay, rugrat, we're home," Billie announced as she climbed out of the car.

"Mommy, can I have a horsey ride to the house?" Skylar asked.

"Sure, sweetness, climb on," Billie said as Cat lifted Skylar onto Billie's back.

Billie made a big show of galloping around the driveway before climbing the stairs to the kitchen door, while Cat stood there and shook her head, wondering for the thousandth time, which of the two was the bigger kid.

Entering the house, Billie galloped through the kitchen and into the living room, depositing Skylar on the couch, then tickling her until she begged for mercy.

By this time, Seth and Tara had heard the ruckus and had come down from their rooms, followed by Stevie and Karissa. Without hesitation, the girls jumped into the tickle war, while Seth and Stevie just stood by the sidelines silently communicating that they thought girls were pretty dumb to be playing such games.

Finally, the fun was over as Cat broke it up, dragging Billie away to help her make lunch for the kids.

* * *

While they were all sitting around the lunch table, Billie took the opportunity to discuss Laurel's visit with the children.

"So, who's excited about meeting your grandmother today?" Billie asked.

Skylar raised her hand and waved it excited. "I am," she said.

Tara shrugged. "It's kinda weird," she said.

"What do you mean, love?" Cat said as she placed a sandwich in front of Tara.

"Thanks, Mama. I mean, she just appeared out of nowhere all of the sudden," Tara explained.

"No she didn't," Seth said. "Remember? Mom and Mama went looking for her. They were helping Grams find her."

"Why would Grams want to find *your* mom?" Tara asked Billie. "Isn't she Mama's grandmother?"

Billie glanced at Cat who was still standing behind Tara.

"Well, it's kind of complicated. You see, by blood, Grams is really *my* grandmother and Grandma Jo is Mama's grandmother," Billie explained.

"Wait a minute here," Seth said. "How did that happen? Grams has been Mama's grandmother for a long time. How can she suddenly be your grandmother too?"

"Maybe it's best to start at the beginning," Cat said.

"You're right, Cat. Okay, it's like this...Laurel is my mother. She had me when she was in her twenties, but she couldn't take care of me, so she gave me to another couple to raise," Billie explained.

"The other couple was your mom and dad—who were killed in a car accident when I was still little, right?" Seth said.

"Yes. Anyway, when Mama and I were doing our family tree, we discovered that my parents were not really my parents," Billie continued.

"So, I still don't get how your mother is related to Grams," Tara said.

"I'm getting to that, dumpling. Now, where was I...oh, yes, Mama has told me for a long time that I look just like her grandmother, Alexandra Spirakis," Billie said.

"You *do* look a lot like Grams," Seth chimed in.

"Yes, and when I finally met Grams and Grandma Jo in person, Grams wondered if maybe there was a reason for that. She told us that when she was a young woman, she had a baby girl and when she was born, the doctor and her uncle told her the baby didn't make it...which was a lie. Instead, they stole the baby from her and put it up for adoption. That baby girl was my mother, Laurel," Billie explained.

"Why did they take her away from Grandma Alex?" Tara asked. "Was she a bad mother?"

"No sweetling, she wasn't. Her uncle told her the baby had died because she wasn't married and he was embarrassed about that. He gave the baby to an adoption agency," Cat explained.

"But Mom, you and Mama weren't married yet when Sky was born. Were you embarrassed about that?" Seth asked.

Billie reached over and touched the side of Seth's face. "Sweetheart, there has never been a time when Mama or I have been embarrassed or ashamed of any of you. We love all three of you very much and are proud to be your parents. Don't ever think differently, okay?" she said.

Seth just nodded and smiled.

"So, if Grams is Laurel's mom and Grandma Jo is Grandma Ida's mom, then Laurel and Grandma Ida are stepsisters, just like me and Sky—right?" Tara asked.

"Not exactly, love," Cat replied. "You and Sky are *half* sisters. That means you have one parent in common. Laurel and Grandma Ida are *step*sisters because they have different parents, but their parents are partners. Does that make sense?"

"Tara is my stepsister and Sky is my half sister," Seth said, "because me and Sky have the same dad."

Cat and Billie shared an uncomfortable look at the mention of Brian.

"You're right, Seth," Billie said to her son.

Cat looked at her youngest child and noticed that she was chasing the food around her plate, but not really eating any of it.

"Sky, honey, you have to eat something. Dr. Berry said that you need to keep up your strength if you want to feel better," Cat said.

Skylar grimaced and made an effort to eat while the discussion turned back to Laurel.

"So, you said Laurel couldn't take care of you. Why not?" Seth asked Billie.

"She had some problems to deal with that were unsafe for a baby to be exposed to," Billie answered.

"Why didn't she look for you when her problems were fixed?" Seth continued with the questioning.

"That's a very good question, love...one that I need to ask her myself. I don't know the answer to that right now," Billie explained.

"Mom, what do we call her when she gets here?" Tara asked.

Billie took a deep breath. "Well, I guess we need to ask her about that. She doesn't have any other grandchildren yet, so maybe you three can help her pick out a grandma name. How does that sound?" Billie asked.

"Cool," said Tara.

"Is Uncle Dylan coming with her?" Seth asked hopefully.

"Not this time, honey. Uncle Dylan is trying to set up a veterinary clinic and he can't take any time off right now. Hopefully, you'll get a chance to meet him soon," Billie said.

"What does he look like?" the young boy asked.

"He's tall, like I am, and he has the same blue eyes I do, but his hair is blonde and curly. It's kind of the same color as yours, Seth," Billie said, describing her brother.

"Wow!" Seth said. "I never had an uncle. I can't wait to meet him."

"All right you three, enough with the twenty questions," Cat exclaimed. We need to be at the airport in about a half-hour, and you all need to wash up first. Now off with you...clean hands and face...clean clothes...scoot," Cat said, shooing them off while she rose to clean the lunch dishes away.

"I'll get these, Cat. Why don't you give Sky a hand, she looked pretty beat at lunch," Billie suggested.

"All right." Cat stood on tiptoe and kissed her, before disappearing after the children.

* * *

In the waiting area near the gate, the three children stood in front of a large window overlooking the tarmac, watching the planes land and take off, knowing that their grandmother would be on one of them. Billie nervously paced back and forth while Cat patiently sat nearby, reading a magazine.

Finally flight 4129 from Flint, Michigan was announced with an expected ETA of five minutes.

Billie stopped dead in her tracks and looked at Cat.

Cat smiled back at her with a look that said, *Relax, it's only your mother.*

When the flight was announced, Seth corralled his sisters and directed them toward Cat and Billie. Skylar immediately raised her arms and asked to be picked up. Billie naturally obliged, placing Skylar on her left hip while the child laid her head on Billie's shoulder.

"My poor sweet angel," Billie said as she placed a kiss on Skylar's head. "I know you don't feel well. You can take a nap as soon as we get home, okay?"

Skylar just nodded her head.

Suddenly, Tara spoke up. "Mom, is that her? That lady over there looks just like you,"

Billie followed the direction Tara was pointing, and sure enough, there before them in the distance, was Laurel.

"Laurel," Billie called, waving her hand in the air.

Laurel spotted them and broke into a huge grin as she made her way toward her family. She stopped within a few feet of

Billie, a tentative look on her face as she waited to see how well received she would be.

Billie smiled and opened her one free arm to her mother, who quickly moved in for an affectionate hug.

"Billie, I've missed you so," Laurel said in a shaky voice as she hugged her daughter close.

"It's good to see you again, Laurel," Billie said a bit clinically before releasing the woman.

Laurel moved on to embrace Cat before allowing Billie to introduce her to the children.

"Laurel, thank you for coming," Cat said as she embraced the older woman. "We've been looking forward to spending time with you."

Laurel placed her hand on the side of Cat's face and smiled. "We have a lot of catching up to do, starting with my grandchildren," Laurel replied as she released Cat and turned back to Billie who was patiently waiting to introduce Laurel to the kids.

"Laurel," Billie said. "This is Seth, he's twelve, Tara, age ten, and Skylar, age six. I'm afraid the little one is sick right now and more than a little shy. We need to get her home to bed," Billie explained.

"What are we s'posed to call you?" Tara asked bluntly.

Laurel raised her eyebrows to the child in a gesture that was so like Billie, Cat had to chuckle.

Laurel knelt on one knee in front of Tara, she cupped the side of the Tara's face. "You know, I've been thinking about that all day, and I think I like Nana. How does that sound?" Laurel said to Tara before looking at Seth and Skylar.

"I like that," said Tara.

"Works for me," Seth said with all eyes turned to him.

"What about you, baby doll?" Laurel said to Skylar as she reached over to touch the child's face. Feeling the warmth, she shot a look of concern toward Cat and Billie.

"I like Nana too," Skylar said shyly.

"Then Nana it is," Laurel said. Turning to Seth, she asked, "Do you know where there's a strong young man that might be able to help me with my bags?"

"I'll help you, Nana," Seth said.

"Can I help too? I'm pretty strong," asked Tara.

Laurel smiled at the little girl and reached out her hand. Tara quickly took it as the trio headed to the luggage carousel.

While they were gone to retrieve the luggage, Billie looked at Cat. "Well, what do you think?" she asked.

"I think things will be fine, Billie. It will take some adjustment, but things will be fine. Here they come," Cat commented as she watched them approach, a nearly five foot-six Seth carrying the larger of the bags, while Tara toted an overnight case. "She's managed to charm our son into doing some work. She can't be *all* bad," Cat exclaimed chuckling.

* * *

The ride home was uneventful, with Seth and Tara talking Laurel's ears off in the back seat. When they arrived home, Seth and Tara promptly headed to Jen's house to go to a ballgame with Fred, Karissa and Stevie. Billie helped Laurel settle into the downstairs guestroom while Cat gave Skylar fever medication and tucked her into bed for a nap.

Cat was in the kitchen making coffee when Billie joined her, leaving Laurel in the guestroom to finish settling in.

Billie walked up behind Cat and wrapped her arms around her. She nuzzled her face into Cat's neck.

Cat wrapped her hand behind Billie's neck, holding her in place as a shudder passed through her body.

Billie turned Cat around and leaned her back against the counter. Lifting her chin with her hand, she noted a lone tear that had escaped Cat's eye.

"Sweetheart, what's wrong?" Billie asked, wiping the tear away with her thumb.

"Billie, I'm worried about Sky. She's so weak and feverish. It's breaking my heart. I don't know what to do to help her. All this medical training and I can't even help my own child. I feel so damned helpless," Cat explained, tears freely flowing at this point.

Billie placed delicate kisses on her forehead. "Shhh, it will be all right, love. We're doing all we can to help her right now. Dr. Berry will know what to do after the blood work comes back," she explained, trying to calm Cat's fears.

Seeing the pain and uncertainty in Cat's eyes, she opened her arms once more. "C'mere," she said, enveloping Cat in her warmest hug.

Cat pressed herself into Billie, wrapping her arms around her waist and resting her cheek on Billie's breastbone.

It was in this position that Laurel found them. Walking in on the tender scene, she was again surprised at the warm feeling that permeated her chest every time she saw them together like this. An aura of love surrounded the two women...an aura so great that it could be felt by anyone who was open-minded enough to see it. Laurel walked up to the pair and placed a comforting hand on Billie's back.

"Is everything okay?" she asked the women.

Billie kissed the top of Cat's head before resting her cheek on it and addressing her mother.

"Sky has been ill now for over a week. I guess it's starting to get to us," she explained.

Laurel turned to Cat. "Is there anything I can do to help?"

Cat, forced a smile and said, "You're doing it right now. Thank you for caring, Laurel."

"Of course, I care. She *is* my granddaughter," Laurel said, smiling.

Billie looked at her mother's profile stoically. *Why am I having such a difficult time accepting your sincerity, Laurel? Is it too little, too late for me?* Billie thought as she closed her heart to the woman's apparent compassion.

Cat, on the other hand, was willing to accept love from any direction as she reached out her hand to Laurel.

"Yes, she is," she said, forcing a smile through her tears.

Laurel glanced at the counter behind Cat. "I see a fresh pot of coffee there. How about I pour us all a cup and we can sit and get acquainted, okay?"

Cat pulled out of Billie's embrace and wiped her eyes. "Sure," she said. "The cups are in the cabinet above the pot. I'll get the cheesecake from the refrigerator and we'll sit and have a nice talk."

* * *

As the three ladies sat around the table, a heavy silence fell over the room, none of them really sure how to initiate the conversation. After trading several uncomfortable glances, Cat finally spoke.

"We're really sorry Dylan and Jim couldn't make the trip, Laurel. Seth is especially anxious to meet his uncle. He's kind of outnumbered in this household," she said.

"He really wanted to come, but his veterinary practice is just starting to get off the ground and he really couldn't leave. Jim, on the other hand…well, Jim has some issues he needs to work out. He's still struggling with the fact that I kept Billie a secret from him for so many years, not to mention—" Laurel explained.

"Not to mention the gay thing, right?" Billie said a little too sarcastically.

Laurel looked at her daughter with regret evident on her face. "That certainly is one way to put it—yes," she replied. "Having a gay daughter is one thing. Having a gay daughter *and* a gay mother is another thing all together. I personally think he's wondering just how straight *I* am," she added.

"Well, I guess I can understand how he might wonder," Cat commented. "After all, there is scientific and medical evidence indicating sexual orientation to be a matter of genetics rather than a personal choice. With two family members overtly displaying homosexual orientation, I guess I can see why he might wonder what your biological makeup is, Laurel," Cat said.

"But Cat, he has no reason to believe *I* am gay. We've been married for twenty-five years. We have a son. How could he even wonder?" Laurel asked.

Cat and Billie exchanged glances.

"I was married too, Laurel, and I have a son," Billie said.

"But Billie, you were unhappy in your marriage, and you knew why. You knew you were in a relationship that wasn't right for you. I *am* happy in my marriage, and Jim *is* right for me. That is something I have no doubt of," Laurel replied.

"Why is Jim so homophobic anyway?" Billie asked. "Was he raised that way?"

"Heavens, no. His parents and siblings are very open-minded. I have never heard a derogatory comment from any of them. I don't know where Jim's intolerance comes from. I wish I knew. I wish I could help him get over it," Laurel explained.

Cat reached out and touched Laurel's hand. "What if he doesn't get over it? Do you think he'll try to interfere in your relationship with Billie?" she asked.

Laurel looked down at her hands and paused a moment before answering. Finally, lifting her eyes to meet Cat's...and then Billie's, she replied. "I have been pondering that very question, and I have decided that I will not allow him to interfere," she said firmly.

Billie sat back and released a disgruntled sigh, shaking her head side to side.

Leaning forward, Laurel placed her elbows on the table and addressed her daughter. "You find that hard to believe?" she asked.

"Actions speak louder than words, Laurel," Billie replied.

"Billie...," Cat warned.

"No, Cat. Let her speak," Laurel interrupted.

"Laurel, I am having a really hard time believing your sincerity. Why the change of heart? Why the sudden devotion to the biological child you discarded thirty-three years ago?" Billie asked.

"Billie, that's uncalled for," Cat scolded.

"Why the sudden change of heart?" Laurel repeated. "It's not so sudden. I have regretted the decision to give you up for thirty-three long years. It was a mistake that I knew I could not correct. It has been hell to live with," she explained.

"So tell me, Laurel, why? Why did you give me up? Or rather, why did you sell me? Couldn't you find any way at all to keep me?" Billie asked pointedly.

"At the time, I didn't think I could," Laurel answered. "Keep in mind, Billie, that I was raped by my own father. Part of me wanted to hate you. Heaven knows giving you up would have been easier if I had," she began.

"Rape is no reason to throw your child away, Laurel," she interjected, reaching out to grasp Cat's hand in a show of support for the memories this discussion was sure to invoke in Cat.

Laurel frowned at the gesture.

"I was a mess, Billie. I had nowhere to go and no one to turn to. My mother was a spineless jellyfish when it came to my father. I couldn't take care of you. Had I kept you, you might have turned out just like me. I couldn't let that happen, don't you see? You were better off with the Watermans," Laurel tried desperately to explain.

Before Billie could say another word, the phone rang.

"I'll get it," Billie said as she rose from the table. Lifting the receiver from the wall phone, she brought it to her ear. "Hello?"

Cat watched Billie as she spoke, noticing as her brow furrowed deeply on her forehead.

"No, I'd like you to tell me now," Billie said.

Billie waited patiently, obviously disagreeing with what the caller was saying.

"Look, I don't want to wait until tomorrow," a pause. "I know you don't usually give this type of information over the phone, but I need to know now...please," Billie finished.

Another long pause.

"Yes?" Billie said.

Cat watched as Billie's eye grew wide.

"Are you sure?" Billie asked, a mask of intense fear falling over her face.

"Billie, what is it?" Cat asked.

"Oh, my God, no," Billie cried as tears rolled down her face.

* * *

Cat and Laurel were on their feet immediately as Billie stumbled backward, releasing the phone and blindly walking around the kitchen, her hand covering her mouth, tears blinding her vision. "Oh, my God, I'm going to be sick," she said, racing to the bathroom with Laurel right behind her.

Cat picked up the phone.

"Hello? This is Cat," she said into the receiver.

"Cat? Cat, this is Dr. Berry," said the voice on the other end of the line.

Cat's heart immediately sank into her feet. *She wasn't supposed to call until tomorrow.* Cat instinctively knew the news wasn't good.

"Cat, I need you to bring Skylar in first thing tomorrow morning. We need to do more tests," the doctor said.

"More tests?" was all Cat could manage through the heavy haze clouding her mind.

"Cat, the blood work came back early. The results are preliminary, so we need to do follow-up work, but indications are that Skylar has leukemia."

CHAPTER 7

"What do you mean, Skylar has leukemia?" Cat asked.

"Cat, you're a doctor. You know what leukemia is. She has all the symptoms and her red and white cell and platelet counts support it. There are several more tests that have to be done to confirm it and to determine treatment. Now, I need you to bring her in first thing in the morning. Can you do that?" Dr. Berry asked.

Cat was in a daze. "Tomorrow? Tomorrow is Saturday."

"I know tomorrow is Saturday, but unfortunately, diseases can't tell time, nor what day of the week it is. Now, I need you to bring her in by nine, all right?" Dr. Berry instructed.

"All right," Cat said before falling silent once more.

"Cat, are you all right?" Dr. Berry asked.

"Uhmm...I...yes, I'm fine," Cat responded somewhat disjointedly as she looked around the kitchen as though she was seeing it for the first time.

"Okay then. I'll see Skylar at nine, oh, and Cat, remember the results are preliminary. If we've caught it early, she has a good chance of survival. Okay? Think positively. We'll do everything we can for her. I'll see you in the morning. Goodbye," Dr. Berry said before hanging up.

In a daze, Cat hung up the phone and leaned against the wall. Within seconds, she had sunk to the floor in a heap, staring straight ahead, but not seeing anything.

Suddenly the backdoor swung open. "Hey neighbor," Jen said, making her usual grand entrance into the room. Seeing Cat on the floor, she went immediately to her side.

"Cat! Cat, honey, what is it?" Jen said in a panic.

Cat looked at Jen blinking her eyes several times before finally recognizing her friend. Taking several gulps of air, Cat fell into Jen's arms and began to cry.

Jen wrapped her arms tightly around her friend, trying desperately to calm the crying woman. "Cat, sweetheart, please tell me what's wrong. Where's Billie?" she asked.

"Sick," Cat said.

"Billie's sick?" Jen asked for clarification.

Cat just nodded.

"I'll be right back," Jen said as she rose to her feet and went to look for Billie, finding her and Laurel in the bathroom.

Standing in the doorway of the bathroom, she saw an older version of Billie, whom she assumed to be her friend's mother, holding Billie's hair and rubbing her back as she emptied the contents of her stomach into the toilet. Laurel looked up at Jen.

"Is she all right?" asked Jen?

"She will be in a few minutes. And you are...?" Laurel said.

"Jen. I'm Jen. I live a couple of doors down. Look, Cat's pretty much a wreck in the kitchen. I'm going to see to her. Do you have any idea what happened here?" Jen asked.

"All I know is that they received a phone call that seemed to devastate Billie...and Cat, by the sounds of it," Laurel explained.

Just then, Billie sat back on her heels, holding her stomach as she looked at Jen, her eyes red rimmed from crying and from being sick. "Jen," she said, reaching out her hand to her friend. Jen immediately stepped forward and took it.

"Billie, honey, what is it? Why are you and Cat is such a state?" Jen asked.

"Jen, Sky is very sick. My baby has cancer, Jen. Sky has cancer," Billie cried.

Laurel gasped audibly.

Jen felt like someone had punched her in the stomach. "Oh, my God, Billie, no," Jen said, feeling the tears spilling onto her cheeks. Then, suddenly remembering Cat sitting crumpled on the kitchen floor, she reached out to touch Billie's face and said, "Billie, Cat needs help right now. I need to go to her, okay? Do you want to come with me?" she asked.

Billie nodded as Jen and Laurel helped her off the bathroom floor. Together, they made their way to the kitchen where Cat was still sitting against the wall. Billie fell to her knees and gathered Cat into her arms, where they clung to each other and cried agonizing tears of pending loss, while Jen paced back and forth across the kitchen, her gut in knots.

Laurel sat at the table, trying very hard to keep her emotions in check.

Jen stopped pacing and reached for the phone. "I'm calling Doc and Ida," she said. "Cat and Billie need their support right now."

Moments later Jen hung up the phone and knelt down to wrap her arms around her friends, rocking back and forth with them as she shared their pain and tears.

Laurel looked at the tableau wrapped around each other on the floor and allowed thirty-three years of loss and regret to come crashing down on her. With every ounce of strength she had, she prayed desperately that Billie and Cat would not experience the same sense of loss through the death of their child.

* * *

By the time Doc and Ida arrived, Billie and Cat had managed to regain some control over their emotions. They'd moved from the kitchen floor to the couch in the living room, where Cat sat tucked under Billie's arm, both women clinging to each other for support. When Jen called Doc and Ida, she had no details other than the fact that Skylar had cancer, so when they arrived, Ida was in quite an emotional state, and Doc had pulled his professional mask over his features.

Laurel greeted them at the door when they arrived. Doc and Ida knew that Laurel was visiting this week, but they were unprepared for just how much Billie looked like her mother, and how much Laurel looked like Alexandria. Ida walked into the kitchen and locked eyes with her sister as Doc went to seek out his daughter.

"How are they?" Ida asked awkwardly, not knowing what to say to the sister she was meeting for the first time. She found herself wishing their first meeting was under more pleasant circumstances.

"Not very good, I'm afraid. They're devastated by what this could mean," Laurel replied.

Ida reached up to wipe an errant tear from her eye. "That poor baby," she said. "Do they know what kind of cancer it is?" she asked.

"Leukemia," replied Laurel. "They have a nine o'clock appointment tomorrow to take her in for more testing."

Ida reached out to touch her sister's arm. "You look so much like Nona, Laurel," Ida commented before hastily adding, "I'm so glad you're here. I'm sure Billie will appreciate your support."

"I'm not so sure about that, Ida. I'm afraid Billie is still having a difficult time forgiving me, although I can't say that I blame her," Laurel replied.

"Do you plan to stay long?" Ida asked.

"I had originally planned to stay for a week, but considering what has happened here, I'll stay for as long as they need me... that is, if they want me to stay," Laurel explained.

"Laurel, Billie and Cat need us right now, but please, we need to take the time to get to know each other before you leave," Ida said. "We missed an entire childhood together, let's not waste the time we have now."

Laurel nodded her head. "Yes, we do. Ida, I have so many questions. There's so much I don't know about my mother, but you are right. Now is not the time. Our daughters need us," she observed.

Ida nodded as she locked arms with her sister and led her into the living room.

* * *

"Okay, explain the symptoms to me again," Doc said to Cat.

Doc and Cat were sitting on the couch together, Doc holding his daughter's hand. Billie and Jen were standing near the fireplace, Billie's arm resting on the mantel, her head resting on her forearm. Jen was standing next to her, rubbing her back and talking to her in low, soothing tones.

"Daddy, I've told you already. Sky has been listless and tired. She sleeps constantly. She isn't eating. She's pale and cranky. All she wants is to be held. She's been running a low-grade fever for over a week. Thank goodness she isn't fighting the liquids. They're the only thing we can get her to take without a fight," Cat explained.

Billie turned from her position at the mantle. "Tell him about the bruise, Cat," she said.

"Oh yeah, two weeks ago, she was playing baseball with the kids and was hit in the leg with the ball. The bruise refuses to heal," Cat explained as she looked back over at Billie. *My God, Billie, you look like hell. I just want all these people to go home so we can hold each other and work this out,* Cat thought.

Seeing the look on Cat's face, Jen leaned in to Billie's ear. "She needs you, Billie," Jen said.

Billie looked back and forth between her wife and friend and nodded, then went to sit by Cat, opening her arms and accepting Cat into them.

Doc stood up and started to pace. "So Alexis has the blood tests back already, huh? Do you mind if I call her to discuss the results?" Doc asked.

"You know Dr. Berry?" Cat asked.

"Yes. She was one of my residents several years ago. A fine doctor if I say so myself," he said.

"No, go ahead. We're willing to do anything if it will help Sky," Cat said.

"Mama?" a small voice was heard from the stairs.

Six pair of adult eyes turned toward the voice.

Cat forced a smile onto her face. "Sky, sweetie. C'mere love," she said.

Skylar stumbled her way across the floor and into her mother's arms.

"How are you feeling, sweet angel?" Billie asked as the child settled in between her and Cat.

Skylar just shrugged. "Why is everyone here?" the child asked.

Doc knelt down in front of the little girl. "To see you, kitten," he said, causing Cat to blink rapidly in an attempt to hold back the tears.

Billie squeezed her shoulder slightly in a show of support.

Doc knelt on the floor in front of Skylar and looked closely at the child...at her puffy eyes, pale skin and listless appearance. He kissed her on the forehead. "You're running a fever, little one," he said.

Doc stood and addressed Cat and Billie. "I'm going to drop your mother off at home, then head to the office to make a few phone calls. I'll let you know if I find out anything new. Is there anything I can do for you in the meantime?" he asked.

Cat wearily shook her head then rested it on Billie's shoulder.

Doc glanced meaningfully at Ida.

Ida turned to Laurel and said, "How would you like to come spend the night with us, Laurel? Doc will be at the office for God only knows how long, and besides, we need a chance to get acquainted," she suggested, taking Laurel's hand in hers.

"That sounds like a lovely idea, Ida," Laurel said. She turned to Cat and Billie. "You girls don't mind, do you?"

Cat looked at their mothers and thought, *You two are about as subtle as bird shit on a black car.*

"No, not at all. Go ahead. We'll call you tomorrow when we know more," Cat replied.

A short time later, the three parents left, leaving Jen, Cat and Billie alone with Skylar, who once again, had curled up and fallen asleep in the corner of the couch.

Cat rose to her feet and hugged Jen. "Thank you so much for being here for us, Jen. You know we love you very much. I can't imagine what we'd do without you," she said.

"Well, I don't plan on giving you a chance to find out," replied Jen. "Look, Fred should be getting back from the ball game with the kids soon. Why don't I keep Seth and Tara for the night and let you two have some time alone with Sky, then you won't have to worry about telling them about this until you know more. Okay?" she suggested.

Billie too, rose to her feet and embraced their friend. "You know, it seems lately that our kids spend more time sleeping at your house than in their own beds. Thanks, Jen. We'll call you tomorrow after Sky's appointment," she said before leaning down to kiss Jen on the cheek.

Soon, they were alone with their sick child.

* * *

"Billie?" Cat said as they lay in bed that night.

"Yes, love?"

"Billie, I can't bear the thought of losing her."

Billie took a deep breath to choke back the threat of tears. "Cat, I'm afraid of losing her too," she said as she reached over the small form sleeping between them to touch Cat's face.

Cat started to cry.

Billie started to cry.

Rising from the bed, Billie walked around to the other side and climbed in next to Cat. She gathered Cat into her arms and they cried out their torment as the frail wisp of a child slept beside them.

CHAPTER 8

When Billie, Cat and Skylar arrived at the doctor's office the next morning, a friendly nurse carried Skylar away to actively engage her in play while Dr. Berry took the two women to her office for a chat. As they followed Dr. Berry down the hallway, Billie looked back at Skylar, worry etched on her forehead.

"Relax, Billie. Skylar is safe. She won't even miss you. Carol is wonderful with children. She'll keep Sky entertained while we talk," Dr. Berry said.

Dr. Berry stopped at a door at the end of the hall and held it open to allow Cat and Billie to enter ahead of her.

"Have a seat," she said, gesturing to two chairs facing her desk. Dr. Berry circled around her desk and sat down then opened a drawer to pull out a flip chart to aid in their discussion. Placing it on the desk, she folded her hands on top of it and smiled at the women.

"All right," Dr. Berry said as Cat and Billie sat facing her. "Billie, for your benefit, I will explain exactly what leukemia is and how it is usually treated. Okay? Stop me at any point if you have questions."

Billie nodded as Dr. Berry opened the flipchart.

"Leukemia is a disease that affects the bone marrow. There are three major types of blood cells—red, white, and platelets. All three are produced in the bone marrow, and enter into the bloodstream in a liquid called plasma.

"Red blood cells carry oxygen and carbon dioxide throughout the body. When the bone marrow is functioning normally, the red blood count remains stable. When it isn't, anemia occurs. Anemia is characterized by a shortness of breath, weakness and fatigue. There is a protein in red blood cells called hemoglobin. In a person fighting leukemia, blood transfusions are usually warranted when the hemoglobin level drops below eight.

"White blood cells protect the body from germs, manage the immune system, and help the body fight infection. The Absolute Neutrophil Count, or ANC, is used to measure the amount of white blood cells available for that purpose. If the ANC falls below 500, there is an increased risk of infection. If it falls below 100, there is an extremely high risk.

"Platelets are cells in the blood that cause clotting. Platelet counts in children are normally between 150,000 and 350,000. Anything under 150,000 is considered thrombocytopenia. If the platelet count is less than 50,000, the risk of bleeding is significant. For this reason, anti-inflammatory drugs, such as aspirin must be avoided.

"Any questions?" Dr. Berry asked, pausing to catch her breath, and to turn the chart.

Billie and Cat both shook their heads.

"All right, I'll continue then," she said, pointing once more to the chart.

"Bone marrow is the soft tissue in the center of the bone where blood cells are produced. All blood cells begin in the marrow as blasts or stem cells. Blasts are very immature cells. In a normally functioning immune system, the blasts mature into red or white blood cells or platelets, depending on the need, then travel through the body to carry out their mission. In a leukemic person, the blasts look normal, but they are unable to differentiate between red, white or platelets, so they end up accumulating as islands or mounds in the bone marrow.

"In a nut shell, a leukemic person will appear tired and listless because their body is not producing enough red blood cells. As a result, they become anemic, they are prone to infection and disease because there is a shortage of white blood cells, and they bleed easily, because of a lack of platelets. All of these shortages are due to the blasts' inability to determine which type of blood cell the body needs, thereby accumulating in the bone marrow."

Dr. Berry paused to see if her audience was still with her. "It's a lot to take in. Do you have any questions for me at this point?" she asked.

"Yes, I have one," Billie said. "I guess I can understand what leukemia is, but what I don't understand is how Sky caught it."

"Well, first let me say that leukemia is not contagious, so it isn't a matter of whether Sky contracted it or not. Scientists really don't understand exactly what causes leukemia. Some leukemia in animals is caused by viruses but in humans, there is only one rare virus that can cause it. There might be some genetic predisposition to leukemia, but this requires the presence of certain chromosome damage. We'll test Skylar for this, but I don't really believe it to be the cause.

"Certain environmental factors can cause leukemia, like exposure to high-dose radiation, such as the survivors of Nagasaki and Hiroshima. There is even the belief that people with certain immune deficiencies are predisposed to it, but overall, the examples I have given you account for a very small percentage of all the leukemia cases. For the majority of people with this disease, the cause is completely unknown."

"Great. That's just great." Billie said. She stood up and began to pace across the room. "Our daughter develops a disease and we don't know how or why." She stopped in front of Dr. Berry. "Please don't tell me the treatment is as unknown as the cause."

"Billie, please sit down," Cat said irritably.

"No, that's all right, Cat. It's a good question," Dr. Berry said patiently. "Fortunately, Billie, for most patients, there is a good possibility that the disease can be brought into full remission. Unfortunately, the treatment is not a pleasant one, usually involving chemotherapy and/or bone marrow transplants," the doctor explained.

"You said the disease can be brought into remission. What exactly is remission? Does it mean she'll be cured?" Billie asked.

"Complete remission occurs when all signs and symptoms of the disease disappear and abnormal cells are no longer found in the blood, bone marrow, or cerebrospinal fluid," Dr. Berry explained. "In some cases, remission is permanent. In other cases it is a temporary cancer-free period."

"So does that mean if Skylar goes into remission there will always be a threat of recurrence for the rest of her life?" Billie asked angrily.

"Not necessarily," Dr. Berry replied. "The general rule of thumb is that if a patient is cancer free for five years, they are most probably cured."

Cat leaned toward the doctor. "You said for most patients there is a good possibility of remission. Define *most*," she said.

"Eighty-five percent of children with childhood leukemia survive with proper treatment," Dr. Berry replied.

Cat sat back and pondered the statistics. Looking up at the doctor she said, "So that means there is still a fifteen percent chance that our daughter will die."

Dr. Berry looked at Cat and said softly, "Yes."

A muffled curse was heard coming from the corner of the room as Billie tried very hard to control her temper. Choking back a sob, she reached for the door handle and paused to say over her shoulder, "Cat, I have to leave before I hit something. I'll be outside." Then she was gone.

Cat looked at Dr. Berry. "I'm sorry," she said.

"Don't be, Cat. Actually, Billie's reaction is normal. At least she is expressing her anger. I'm more concerned about you. It's okay to be angry about this, Cat. After all, this is your child we're talking about. The injustice of the situation is very difficult to understand," the doctor explained.

Cat just nodded. "So what do we do now?" she asked. "I suppose we'll need to find an oncologist. Is there someone you can recommend?"

"Actually, my degree is in pediatric oncology, which comes in pretty handy in my pediatrics practice. I'd be happy to treat Skylar, but if you'd feel more comfortable with someone who focuses only on oncology, I'd be happy to recommend someone," Dr. Berry replied.

"No...no, actually I'd just assume stay with you," Cat said. "So, again...what do we do now?" Cat added.

"Well, the blood work we did the other day provided us with Skylar's complete blood counts. What is missing to make the final diagnosis of the type of leukemia she has...and thereby the treatment she'll need...is a bone marrow aspiration and bone marrow biopsy."

Dr. Berry paused before continuing with her explanation.

"Unfortunately, these are very unpleasant procedures—especially for a child to endure. They require the insertion of a needle into the bone marrow of the hipbone to withdraw marrow fluid. The biopsy actually requires a small piece of bone to be removed. These procedures can be made more tolerable by putting the child under anesthesia, but the discomfort of recovery from the procedures cannot be avoided."

Having finished her explanation, Dr. Berry sat back and took a deep breath, watching Cat carefully with a trained eye.

Cat closed her eyes and lowered her chin to her chest. She sat there for long moments without moving a muscle.

"Cat, are you all right?" the doctor asked.

Cat opened her eyes and looked at Dr. Berry. She looked down at her hands folded in her lap, then at the wall behind Dr. Berry's head. Finally, returning her gaze to the doctor's face, she said, "What happens if we do nothing?"

"The disease is already affecting Skylar's immune system. The fever is indicative of some type of infection. The persistent bruise on her shin is a sign that her body lacks platelets. Her fatigue, pallor and listlessness are signs of anemia. If we do nothing, she will continue to decline. It won't be long before she develops an infection that her body won't be able to fight. She would most likely develop sepsis. In her already weakened state, it would not take long for it to overcome her," Dr. Berry said, in a tone that demanded Cat's attention. "Cat, surely you know if we do nothing, she will die."

Cat dropped her head into her hands and started crying. Her shoulders shook under the weight of the emotional burden.

Dr. Berry quietly rose from her chair and left the room.

Several moments later, the door opened and Billie entered. She stood in front of Cat and pulled her to her feet then wrapped her within the circle of her arms.

"I'm here, Cat. I've got you. I've got you," she said as she held the sobbing woman close to her heart.

* * *

Cat and Billie spent the rest of the day at the hospital while Skylar underwent the remaining diagnostic tests, including the bone marrow aspiration and biopsy, spinal tap of her cerebrospinal fluid, and a chest X-ray to detect any potential infection in her lungs prior to the start of treatment. The procedures were grueling and painful for both of them, as well as for Skylar.

Skylar spent most of the time during the procedures, clinging to Billie, and crying out for Cat. Many tears were shed, not all of which came from Skylar's eyes. By the end of the day, the child lay exhausted in Billie's arms as she carried her to the car and gently laid her in Cat's lap in the back seat for the ride home.

Cat was defenseless against her own tears as she cradled her baby daughter in her arms, holding her tight and whispering *I love you* over and over. Billie had all she could do to keep the tears from her own eyes as she watched her wife and daughter in the mirror, straining hard to see the road through the mist, as she maneuvered the car through the streets to their home.

Cat insisted on carrying Skylar into the house herself and putting her to bed after cleaning the insertion wounds from her tests.

Billie stood by and watched, feeling deposed and ousted in her position as Sky's protector.

If truth be known, I don't feel much like a protector at the moment, she thought. *I can't even protect my child from this hideous disease.*

After a few more moments of watching Cat and Skylar, the sudden thought occurred to her.

My God! What would have happened if we hadn't found Dr. Berry? What if we had taken Dr. Sorensen's diagnosis as fact? What is that man doing practicing medicine... especially on children?

Billie turned and left the room while Cat finished preparing Skylar for bed.

Cat looked over her shoulder as Billie walked away, feeling guilty that she had shut her out of this nightly ritual. She rubbed the dull throbbing in her temples.

I'm sorry, Billie, but I don't want to waste one precious moment with her, she thought as she pulled the blankets up to the child's chin and kissed her on the forehead.

Billie had retreated to the living room to call Jen.

The phone was answered on the first ring. "Billie? Cat?" the voice asked frantically from the other end.

"Is that any way to answer the phone, Jen?" Billie asked.

"Billie! Thank God you called. I have been worried about Sky all day. How did things go?" she asked.

Billie took a deep shaky breath. "Not so good, Jen. The doctor spent a great deal of time explaining the details and symptoms of leukemia to us this morning, and everything fits...the behavior, the fever, the bruises...everything fits," Billie explained, her voice choking up near the end. "God, this is hard," she added, trying to continue. "Uhmmm, they spent the afternoon putting my sweet angel through...God, Jen...I'm...ahhh...I'm sorry," Billie said as she fell apart verbally on the phone. "I'm sorry...I'm having a tough time even talking about this. Damn."

Billie took a deep breath to compose herself.

"They, ah...they took bone and fluid samples. Jen, she cried so hard. She clung to me like I could save her from all of it. It tore my heart right out of my chest. She begged us to make them stop. She cried, *Mama, Mommy, make them stop*. Jen, I have never been so heart broken in my life."

Billie took a large gulp of air before continuing.

"My baby girl needed me and I couldn't do anything to help her. Jen, I would give my life if I thought it would save her from all this." Billie was sobbing openly, torturous cries ripping from her chest, her head leaning against the wall next to the phone. "Jen, what are we going to do? I can't bear to lose her."

Little did Billie know, Cat had been standing near the foot of the stairs, just a few feet away during the agonizing phone call. The pain in Billie's voice struck raw nerves in Cat's heart. She approached Billie and placed a hand on the small of her back.

Billie turned abruptly and saw Cat standing there, tears running freely down her own face.

Cat held out her hand for the receiver, which Billie handed over to her.

"Jen, Jen, honey, this is Cat," she said into the mouthpiece while maintaining eye contact with Billie.

"Cat, is there anything I can do? Billie told me about the horrible day you had at the hospital. Cat, she's a mess. She really needs you right now. Are you all right?" The questions seemed to pour out of their friend nonstop.

"Jen, there is one thing you can do for us," Cat said, sniffling slightly.

"Anything, Cat, you know that," Jen vowed, her own voice choked with emotion.

"Can you keep the kids for one more night? I don't think either one of us is in the best shape to deal with them right now," Cat observed.

"Sweetheart, they can stay here for as long as you need them to. Don't worry about Seth and Tara. Fred and I will be there for you...and them," Jen said.

Listening carefully, Jen could hear both women softly crying. She covered her mouth with her hand to muffle the sound of her own sobs as she fought to regain control.

My heart is breaking, knowing the pain they are going through. I love them so much. They own a large piece of my heart. I can only imagine the agony of knowing their child is critically ill. If it was Stevie or Karissa, I don't know if I'd have the will to go on, Jen thought.

Jen's attention was drawn back to the phone when Cat came back on the line.

"Jen, I'm sorry. I'm afraid Billie and I are in quite a state right now. It's been a difficult day...the first of many more to come, I'm afraid," Cat said. "We really appreciate you keeping Seth and Tara. You are a true friend, and we love you dearly," Cat finished.

"Cat, please take care of yourself, and take care of the big guy, okay? She's not as strong as she looks. You know that, don't you?" Jen asked.

Cat smiled slightly at the truth of her friend's words. "I know, Jen. I've known that all along, but thanks for pointing it out to me. Sometimes I forget and expect her to be stronger than what is reasonable," Cat said into the phone as she reached up with her free hand to touch the side of Billie's face.

Billie caught her hand and kissed the palm.

"Take care, Cat. Kiss Billie for me, okay?" she asked.

"Only if you kiss Seth and Tara for us," Cat replied.

"It's a deal, my friend. I love you both. Goodnight," Jen finished before hanging up the phone.

"We love you too Jen," Cat said into a dead phone. Taking a deep breath, she let it out heavily as she replaced the receiver in its cradle.

Cat looked up at Billie, her red-rimmed eyes mirrored on her wife's face.

"Is Sky sleeping?" Billie asked, still holding Cat's hand close to her heart.

Cat nodded.

"Good. She's had a rough day. The poor little angel is worn out," Billie said, trying to force a smile she didn't feel.

"We'll stop in and kiss her goodnight on the way to bed, okay?" Cat suggested.

Billie led Cat toward the stairs by the hand she was still holding. Before moving on to their room, they stopped at Skylar's room and said their tender goodnights to the sleeping child, both promising to do their best to help her get better soon.

Stripping out of their clothes, they climbed into bed together and wrapped themselves around each other's nakedness, both needing to feel close and connected to the other. No merging of bodies or blending of souls occurred on this night, just an attempt at closeness and unity in their sorrow.

Soon, sheer exhaustion and overloaded emotions drove the women into a deep sleep, away from their torturous world, if only for one night.

* * *

The next day was Sunday, and the rising sun found Billie standing in the window, head leaning against the pane, traces of tears having etched tracks on her cheeks. Billie's thoughts tormented her as she imagined a small casket being lowered into the ground.

Looking into the sunrise, she offered herself in place of Skylar.

Take me, her mind pleaded silently, *Sky is just a baby, she has so much life ahead of her. Please take me instead.*

Lowering her chin, she cried softly, unaware that Cat had also risen, until she felt Cat's arms circle her waist, her face pressing against her back.

Billie turned around and took Cat into her embrace, their naked bodies pressing against each other.

"Billie, what time did you get up?" Cat asked.

"I don't know. A few hours ago I guess," she said, placing her cheek on top of Cat's head.

"I couldn't sleep either," Cat said. "I kept praying to whichever god would listen, to take me instead. Billie, she's just a baby. It breaks my heart to think that she may never grow up. Billie, what are we going to do if she dies? I will surely die with her. I know I will," Cat cried.

Billie kissed Cat's head and held her tighter, her intense sorrow mingling with Cat's. "We have to think positively, Cat. We need to give her all the love, support and care we can. Dr. Berry said there is an eighty-five percent survival rate. We need to hold on to the belief that Sky will be one of those survivors," Billie said passionately.

Cat just nodded. "Billie, we need to do something special with Sky today. No tests, no hospital, just something special,"

Cat said, "and, we have to tell Seth and Tara about this," she added.

"I know we do Cat, but I don't know if I can do it. I don't know if I can keep my emotions in check long enough to tell the kids," Billie feared.

"We'll do it together, Billie," Cat said.

* * *

Cat and Billie were sitting at the kitchen table having coffee when the kids came home; Jen right behind them. Tara went immediately into the living room and turned on the TV to her favorite cartoon, while Seth stopped and looked at his mothers.

"Mom, is everything okay?" he asked.

Billie looked at Cat and then at Jen, before turning her eyes to her son.

"No, honey, everything isn't okay. Mama and I have something very serious to tell you and Tara in a few minutes. Why don't you go on into the living and watch TV with your sister while we talk with Jen, then we'll be in to see you," Billie suggested to her son, who did as he was told.

During the exchange between mother and son, Cat had bowed her head and struggled to hold back her tears. With Seth out of the room, she looked up at Billie and allowed the tears to escape down her cheeks.

Billie reached over and wiped the tears away with her thumbs. "Don't cry, Cat. Like you said, we need to be strong to talk to the kids," she said.

Cat nodded and wiped the remaining tears from her face.

Billie looked at Jen and saw their own torment mirrored in their friend's eyes. "You didn't sleep much last night, either, did you, Jen?" Billie asked.

Jen took a deep breath and shook her head. Coming around to stand between her friends, she threw an arm around each of them and pulled them into an embrace they gladly returned. For the next several minutes, all three women shared their pain through the common bond of motherhood.

Several minutes later, Jen broke the embrace and addressed her friends as she wiped the dampness from her face. "Cat, Billie, I want you to know that I will be here for you and the kids. Anything you need, anything—please ask. Please let me help you through this. I love you two so much, it tears my heart out to see you in such pain, and the thought of losing a child...well, it is more than this heart can handle. I can only imagine what it's like for you right now," she said. "Tara and Seth will need a place to go when things get rough. Let them come to me. My house and my arms are open to them, okay? I love them, and Skylar too, like they were my own," Jen added.

Looking at her friends, she realized that she had just reduced them both to a puddle of tears. She once again pulled them into an embrace and said her good-byes, extracting promises from them both that they would call when they needed her.

As Jen was leaving, she passed Laurel, who was just arriving from her two-day visit with Ida. "Good morning, girls," Laurel said as she embraced both women. Neither woman was in any condition to answer coherently after Jen's visit.

Looking back and forth between her daughter and daughter-in-law, she said, "Wanna talk about it?"

Billie looked at her with an expression bordering on hatred, "Our daughter may be dying, Laurel. What's there to talk about?" she said.

"Billie, that was unnecessary," Cat exclaimed as Billie lowered her gaze to the coffee cup in front of her.

"It's all right, Cat. I understand that Billie is confused about how I could possibly care about my granddaughter when I didn't care about *her* all those years ago," Laurel said.

"No, Laurel. Regardless of what unfinished business there is between you and Billie, there is no excuse for rudeness," Cat explained.

"Really, Cat, I understand...," Laurel began.

"No, Cat is right. I'm sorry. I had no right to make that comment," Billie said. "Look, we need to put this aside for now and concentrate on getting Sky well," she added.

"Mom? Sky is dying?" Seth asked from the doorway, tears coursing down his cheeks. Tara was by his side, holding his hand tightly, fear written across her face.

* * *

"Damn! Me, and my big mouth," Billie said. Turning toward the children, she opened her arms to them, gathering them into her embrace. "I'm sorry you heard that. Look, let's go into the living room. Mama and I have a lot to talk to you about. Okay?" Billie asked.

Rising to her feet, she followed the children into the other room, leading Cat by the hand. Laurel followed, making herself inconspicuous in a corner of the room.

Cat sat between the two children on the couch, holding each of their hands, while Billie paced back and forth. The children looked expectantly between their mothers for an explanation.

Cat began. "Seth, Tara, you know your little sister has been ill lately, right?" she asked, seeing both children nod. "Well, Mom and I took her to the doctor, and they discovered that she has leukemia," Cat explained, sounding more controlled than her emotions belied.

"What's that?" Tara asked.

"Sweetheart, leukemia is a blood disease. It's a type of cancer," Cat said, barely able to choke out the C word.

"Cancer?" Seth exclaimed. "Sky has cancer?" he asked incredulously. "Mom, people *die* of cancer," he said in a panic-stricken voice, his eyes wide with fear.

Billie knelt on the floor in front of her son. "Not all people, scout," she said, taking his hands in hers. "A lot of children develop this disease and survive. We have to hope and pray that Sky will too," she finished, hoping she had given her son something to cling to.

"Is Sky in the hospital?" asked Tara.

"No, sweetheart, she's still sleeping. In fact, I should go check on her," Cat said, staring to rise to her feet.

"I'll go, Cat. You stay with the children," Laurel said from the corner of the room.

Cat sat down again and placed an arm around each child beside her.

Seth looked up at Cat. "Will Sky need an operation, Mama?" he asked.

"I'm not sure yet, honey," she said, running her index finger down his cheek. "I imagine they'll try medicine first and if that doesn't work, then maybe she'll need an operation. Mom and I have to meet with her doctor tomorrow to discuss what to do to help Sky get well again," Cat explained.

"If she needs an operation, can I help? Can I give her part of me, like a kidney or something?" Seth asked.

"Me too!" added Tara. "I can give her a kidney too."

Billie and Cat's eyes met and welled up with tears immediately. Billie took her son and daughter's hands in hers and brought them to her lips, allowing her tears to spill over onto them.

"Seth, Tara, that is the most unselfish and loving thing I have ever heard. Sky is so lucky to have a brother and sister like you. And I think Mama and I are very lucky to have such wonderful kids. We love you two and Skylar so much," Billie said.

Cat was too choked up for words. She just wrapped her arms around her children and held them close, whispering *I love you* to each.

Just then, Laurel came down the stairs, carrying a very groggy Skylar in her arms. "Here she is," Laurel said. "She was just waking up when I walked into her room."

Skylar reached out for Billie when she saw her. Taking the child into her arms, she mouthed the words *thank you* to Laurel and went to join Cat and the kids on the couch.

Billie placed Skylar on Cat's lap and her parents and siblings fussed over her, asking how she was feeling and about what she wanted to do that day.

Watching the scene from the far side of the room, Laurel smiled sadly then inconspicuously slipped away, down the hall to her own room.

Billie raised her head and watched her go, a look of intense sadness on her face.

* * *

"So tell me, love bug, what would you like to do today?" Cat asked the sick child.

"I don't know. I'm tired. My leg hurts," Skylar replied without lifting her head from Cat's shoulder.

"Where does it hurt?" Billie asked.

"Right here," Skylar replied, pointing to the insertion wound through which the bone marrow and bone chip had been extracted the previous day.

"Poor sweetling," Billie replied as she leaned in to place a kiss on the wound. "Yesterday was a pretty yucky day at the hospital, huh?" she asked.

Skylar just sniffed and nodded her head.

"Sky," Tara called as the galloped down the stairs from the second story carrying a large basket. Stopping in front of her mothers on the couch, she addressed her little sister once more. "Sky."

Skylar turned around to look at Tara, who promptly turned the basket upside down and sent dozens of paper dolls fluttering to the floor like dried leaves on a light wind.

"Wanna play paper dolls?" Tara offered, her eyes wide with encouragement.

Skylar grinned from ear to ear and nodded enthusiastically. Gingerly climbing off Cat's lap, she scrambled to the floor and along with Tara, began sorting out the dolls and outfits.

After watching their girls play for a few moments, Cat turned to Billie. "Coffee?" she asked.

Billie nodded her head. "Sounds good. Can I help?" she asked.

"No, I think you are needed elsewhere," Cat replied, nodding her head in Seth's direction.

When the girls began to play with the paper dolls, Seth went over to stand by the picture window. With his hands driven deep into his pockets, he stood there with his back to the room and stared out the window.

Billie looked at her son, then back at Cat, nodding at Cat's suggestion. Rising, she carefully stepped over the mound of paper dolls that had been dumped at her feet, and made her way to join her son at the window. Standing next to him, she placed an arm around his shoulder.

Seth looked up at his mother and allowed all the fear and sadness he was feeling in his heart to show on his face before he returned his gaze to the window and leaned his head on her shoulder. "I'm scared, Mom," he admitted softly.

Billie leaned in so that only he could hear her speak. "I am too, scout. I am too."

"Will she die?" he whispered hoarsely.

Billie took a deep breath to compose herself before answering. "We're doing everything we can to stop that from happening, Seth. We cannot give up hope, okay?"

Seth looked at his mother again. "I want to help, Mom. There must be something I can do to help her," he insisted.

Billie smiled at her son and allowed the tears she was fighting to cascade down her face unchecked. With one arm still around his shoulder, she reached up with the other hand and touched his chin. "Seth, you are doing everything you possibly can right now. You are giving your sister your love and support. Right now, there is no better medicine," she explained.

"What if that isn't enough?" he asked with wisdom beyond his years.

"How can it not be enough?" Billie asked. "Sky-baby has so many people that love her...you, Tara, Mom and I...Nana, Grandma and Grandpa...Jen and Fred. All of our love and support and prayers will help. It has to."

Seth just nodded, then sniffed and wiped his eyes with his shirttail as Billie rubbed his back. He glanced over his shoulder at his sisters, who were happily sitting in the middle of a large pile of paper dolls. "I wonder if they'll let me play with them," he said.

Billie's eyes shot open. She took her son by the shoulders and turned him to face her, smiling broadly. "Seth, you are a better person than I am. I hate paper dolls. But I'm willing to bet your sisters would love to have you join them."

Seth smiled back as he turned and approached the girls while Billie looked on.

"Whatcha playing?" he asked.

Tara and Skylar looked up at their brother, twin frowns gracing their brows.

"We're playin' house," Skylar replied.

"So whose doll is the mom and whose is the kid?" he asked.

"Tare's doll is the mom, why?" Skylar asked her brother.

Seth once more drove his hands deep into his pockets. Kicking an imaginary piece of dirt on the rug, he looked down and mumbled, "Well, I guess I thought maybe I could be the dad," he said.

Skylar's eyebrows took up residence high on her forehead as she looked at her sister, who mimicked her expression.

"Cool!" Skylar said as she began rummaging through the pile of paper dolls around them.

Tara looked up at her brother with a genuine smile on her face. "Yeah, very cool," she said sincerely. The pride she had for her brother shone brightly on her face.

"Here, Seth. Here's a boy doll for you to play with," Skylar said, handing the paper doll to her brother who just took the doll and looked at it. "Sit down, Seth. You can't play dolls standin' up!" she added emphatically, reaching for his hand and pulling him down to sit next to her.

It took several moments for Seth to loosen up, but soon, he was in full paper doll mode as he actively role played with his sisters.

Billie inconspicuously made her way around the playing children and into the kitchen where she found Cat pouring coffee. Coming up behind her, she wrapped her long arms around Cat and held her close as a shudder wracked her own body.

Feeling her wife's distress, Cat turned around and looked at Billie. "What is it, love?" she asked.

Billie looked into Cat's eyes and smiled. "Cat, even in times like these, I count our blessings. We are the luckiest mothers in the world," she explained. "Come," Billie added, taking Cat's hand and leading her toward the living room. Stopping in the doorway between the two rooms, Billie whispered, "Look…three angels have alit in our home, and they are ours to keep."

Cat looked in the direction Billie indicated. A sob was caught in her throat as she viewed the surreal scene before her. As Billie had indicated, a tableau of angels lay before her eyes, and whether it was real or not…or whether it was the light playing tricks, Cat could have sworn she saw an illuminant light radiating above the head of her youngest child.

CHAPTER 9

"Well," Dr. Berry said to the two women sitting across from her. "We now know what type of leukemia we are dealing with. Sky has what is commonly referred to as Acute Lymphoblastic Leukemia, ALL for short. It is the most common of childhood cancers and represents about seventy-five percent of all childhood leukemia cases. It is characterized by an overabundance of immature blood cells, which in turn causes a shortage of mature white and red blood cells and platelets," she explained. "Like I said earlier, it has about an eight-five percent survival rate."

Cat and Billie were holding hands as they listened to the diagnosis while Skylar sat on the floor a few feet away, putting a puzzle together.

"We've lost so much time thanks to the incompetence of her previous doctor. Will that affect her chances for recovery, Dr. Berry?" Cat asked.

Dr. Berry smiled. "Look, we're going to be seeing a lot of each other over the next several months. Why don't we drop the formalities? I'd like you to call me Alexis, or Alex, if you'd like," she said pleasantly.

"My grandmother's name is Alex," Cat said absently.

"Mine too," Billie added. Seeing the confused expression on Dr. Berry's face, Billie raised her palm to the doctor and said, "Don't ask."

"All right then, the eighty-five percent overall survival rate is indeed dependent on Skylar getting the right treatment... and if the disease is treated early enough in its cycle. Survival also depends on the individual person's ability to tolerate the treatment program," Dr. Berry explained.

Billie frowned. "What do you mean, tolerate the treatment program?" she asked.

"Some would argue that the treatment is worse than the disease. The most effective treatment for leukemia is chemotherapy, although alternatives such as surgery and radiotherapy do exist," the doctor explained.

Cat's head lowered at the mention of chemotherapy. She had seen the results of the so-called cure on some of its innocent victims. Her medical mind told her that chemo was the best shot Skylar had, but her emotional mind was giving the demolition team directions to her heart as she thought of the potential side effects of the treatment.

Billie noticed the gesture. "Cat, is something wrong?" Billie asked, grasping her hand tighter.

"No...well, it's just that I have seen what chemo does to some people. It is a very difficult treatment," Cat said.

"Difficult, how?" Billie asked.

Dr. Berry answered Billie's question. "There are several side effects to chemotherapy," she began. "The risk of infection is very high. Unfortunately, chemo affects healthy blood cells as well as abnormal ones, so there will be a drop in the white blood cell count almost immediately after starting the treatment.

"Some of the symptoms she is already displaying will continue for a while. These may include fatigue, paleness, listlessness, and general crankiness. Bleeding is also a common symptom, especially bleeding of the gums after brushing, and easy bruising. These are some of the first signs that lead doctors to test for possible leukemia in kids."

Dr. Berry paused to let the information settle with the women before continuing.

"Unfortunately, that is just the beginning. Most patients develop nausea and vomiting from the drugs. There may be bowel irritation, including diarrhea or constipation, sores in the mouth, and weight loss. Probably the most visible side effect is hair loss. She will probably lose it all relatively early in the process."

Billie released Cat's hand and ran her fingers through her own locks, remembering how she felt to lose all her hair to the brain surgery operation more than a year ago. Propping her elbows up on the armrests of the chair, she formed a teepee with her fingertips and rested her chin on them as she intently eyed the doctor and listened to the horrors that her daughter would have to endure...all without a guarantee of survival.

Cat placed her hand on Billie's thigh and gave it a gentle squeeze.

"So how and when do we get started?" Billie asked.

Dr. Berry rose from her chair and walked around her desk, sitting on the edge of it in front of Cat and Billie and crossing both her arms and ankles.

"Well," she began, "for starters, we'll need to admit Sky to the hospital for a while so that we can start treatment and monitor her blood levels on a daily basis."

"How long will she be in the hospital?" asked Cat.

"Depending on her progress, I'd say a couple of weeks," Dr. Berry answered. "Maybe more, maybe less,"

"A couple of weeks?" Billie asked. "My God."

Cat reached again for Billie's hand, shooting a sideways look at her emotional wife. "Why such a long stay?" Cat asked.

"Well, we'd like to keep her at least through one course of treatment. A course begins with the start of chemotherapy, and goes until the blood and bone marrow cell counts are back to normal. As I said earlier, when treatment first begins, her blood cell counts will dramatically reduce. Chemotherapy basically empties both normal and abnormal cells from the bone marrow. When the bone marrow begins to recover, the blood counts will return to normal levels, however, during this process, her neutrophil count may drop low enough to make her extremely vulnerable to infection. It's best to have her here in isolation for that reason, and to make it easier to take her daily blood counts," Dr. Berry explained, giving them a few moments to absorb what she had already said before continuing.

"In addition to what her blood work told us, we found traces of abnormal blood cells in the cerebrospinal fluid sample we took. That means she will also require a treatment called Central Nervous System Prophylaxis, which consists of injecting chemotherapy drugs directly into the cerebrospinal fluid to overcome the natural blood/brain barrier that exists in the body. That treatment will have to be done here at the hospital," Dr. Berry added.

Billie rose from her chair and started to pace. Dr. Berry watched her walk back and forth a few times, before stopping to ask a question.

"What happens then? Will she be cured?" Billie asked hopefully.

"Not exactly. After the first course is complete, and her blood counts are back to normal, she'll be discharged and phase two of the treatment starts. Phase two can be done on an outpatient basis. During this phase, she will be given new combinations of drugs to prevent the reappearance of the disease. At this point, if all traces of the abnormal cells are gone from her blood, marrow and cerebrospinal fluid, she'll be in remission. If all goes well during this phase, she'll enter into maintenance, during which she'll receive daily low doses of chemo drugs to kill any remaining cancer cells. This maintenance period could be as long as two or three years."

Cat sat quietly, her hands folded in her lap and her eyes glued to her hands, while Billie stood in front of Dr. Berry, hands on her hips and pointedly asked "Are you telling us that our daughter will be ill for the next two or three *years*?"

"I am saying that she will be in treatment for the next two or three years, Billie. Will she be ill for that entire length of time? No, I don't think so, not unless she has a relapse," Dr. Berry said.

Cat looked up. "Will she suffer the side effects of chemo throughout the maintenance period?" she asked.

"Generally, the dose is low enough during maintenance, that the side effects are minimal, if they exist at all," the doctor explained.

"You mentioned a relapse. Are you telling us there is no real cure…that it might come back in the future?" Billie asked.

"Like I've said, the five year survival rate for children with ALL is eight-five percent overall. Survival rates are based on the percentage of children who live at least five years after the cancer is found. Of course, several of them live beyond five years. With acute leukemia, children who are found to be free of the disease after five years are likely to have been cured, as it is extremely rare for the cancer to return after that amount of time," Dr. Berry explained.

"That would explain the long-term low dose maintenance period," Cat said. "I would think it would increase the likelihood of her being cancer-free after five years."

"Exactly," Dr. Berry replied.

Billie walked over and reached down for Skylar, who went into her arms eagerly. Kissing her cheek, she held the child close to her heart, feeling the heat of her fever through her clothing.

Skylar put her head on Billie's shoulder and said, "Mommy, I don't feel good. My belly hurts."

Cat and Dr. Berry both rose to their feet to look at the little girl. Lifting Sky's shirt, they noticed that the child's abdomen was somewhat distended.

The two doctors looked at each other knowingly, then at the worried expression on Billie's face.

Dr. Berry spoke. "Her liver and spleen are enlarged. We need to admit her today."

* * *

"Billie, slow down," Cat said as she grabbed for the restraining bar above her door to prevent herself from being thrown across the car.

Billie stared straight ahead, a hard set to her face, jaw clenched, brow creased, as she reluctantly slowed the car. Her knuckles were white as she tightened her grip on the steering wheel in an attempt to maintain control over her emotions.

Cat cast a worried glance at the woman beside her before her attention was drawn to the child sitting in the back seat.

"Mama, where are we going?" Skylar asked.

"We're going to the hospital, sweetie," Cat replied.

Skylar immediately started to cry. "Nooooo! I don't want to go to the hospital. They hurt me there," she wailed, causing Billie to grip the steering wheel even tighter.

Cat reached into the back seat and cupped the side of her daughter's face with her hand. "Love bug, I'm sorry, but you have to go to the hospital. Dr. Berry can't help you feel better if you're not there," she reasoned.

"She can come see me at our house," Skylar suggested in a shaky voice.

"Baby, there isn't the right kind of medicine and equipment at our house to make you better," Cat replied.

"Then bring some home from the hospital when you go to work tomorrow," Skylar demanded.

Cat sighed, wondering how she was going to convince this child that the hospital was the best place for her right now.

Billie had been listening carefully to the exchange, her anger slowing dissipating as she absorbed the child's logical approach to the situation. Seeing the exasperation on Cat's face, she decided to try a little convincing of her own.

"Sky," she said, drawing the child's attention to her. "You really do need to go to the hospital. Do you remember when Mommy was in the hospital?" she asked.

Skylar nodded and grinned. "You were bald, Mommy. You looked funny," she said, giggling.

"Yeah, yeah, yeah," Billie said dryly. "Well, guess what, rugrat, you're gonna be bald too. So take that."

"Really?" Skylar replied, her interest peaked. "Way cool!"

"So, you need to cooperate, okay? No fussing. Deal?" Billie asked.

Skylar considered what her mother had to say. "Are they gonna pick me?" she asked.

Billie exchanged a glance with Cat before answering. "They probably will, love, but Mama and I will be there to kiss it for you when they're done. Okay?" she asked.

"Can I have jello and pudding like you did when you were in the hospital?" Skylar asked hopefully.

"Lots of it," Billie replied.

Billie let the child think about it for a while as she looked at Cat, a hopeful expression on her face that the child would cooperate.

After a moment or two of quiet contemplation, Cat reached into the back seat and nudged her daughter. "So, what do you say? No fussing?"

"Okay, Mama," Skylar said. "But I want lots of jello and pudding," she added.

"It's a deal," Cat said, turning in her seat and extending her hand to Skylar who took it willingly as Cat sent a silent *thank you* to Billie with her eyes.

* * *

"Art, this is Billie. Look, I have a problem that I need to arrange for a couple of weeks off to deal with. I'll take vacation if I have to," Billie said to her boss over the phone.

"I knew something was up with you. Billie, where are you?" he asked.

Billie hesitated. Art really didn't need to be worrying about her.

"Billie, I won't agree to the time off unless you tell me what you're up to. Look, I'm not just your boss, I'm your friend. Now talk to me," he insisted.

"I'm at the hospital, Art," Billie said, her voice cracking with emotion.

"Are you hurt?" was the first question out of his mouth, remembering the two times he had rushed her to the hospital for beatings she had endured at the hands of anti-gay activists, and a would-be rapist.

"No, Art, I'm fine," she said.

"Is it Cat? The kids?" he asked, his voice laced with panic.

"Art, it's Skylar. She...ah...she's real sick." Billie cleared her throat, obviously having a difficult time speaking.

"What is it, Billie? You can tell me. Take your time," he urged.

"She has cancer, Art. My baby has leukemia," Billie managed to get out before covering her mouth with her hand to stifle the tears.

"I'll be there in five minutes, Billie," he said, hanging up the phone before she could object.

Moments later, Billie joined Cat who sat in the waiting room near the hospital's admissions area. Skylar was sitting on her lap, her head resting on Cat's shoulder.

Billie sat down next to her wife and child. Reaching over, she stroked Skylar's hair, then leaned in and kissed her cheek, which was flush with fever.

"What did he say?" Cat asked.

"He said he'd be here in five minutes. He didn't give me the chance to discuss the time off once I told him about Sky," Billie said.

"He's a good friend, Billie," Cat replied.

"Yes, he is. I don't think there'll be a problem with me taking a short leave. One of us can spend the days with Sky here, and the other can spend the nights. That way one of us can also be home with Seth and Tara at night," Billie reasoned.

Cat just nodded her head then looked at her wife. "Did you call your Mom?" she asked.

"Yeah. She said Seth and Tara are worried about Sky, but everything else was fine. She said not to worry about them...that she'd be here for us as long as we needed her," Billie explained.

"Billie, I know you are having a hard time believing her sincerity, but I really do think she cares deeply about Skylar," Cat commented.

Billie sat there clenching her hands in her lap, her right leg bouncing up and down with nervous tension. "Maybe," she replied solemnly.

"Mrs. Charland?" the nurse asked.

Both women looked up at her. "Yes," Cat said.

"Mrs. Charland, come with me. We have Skylar's room ready," she said.

Following the nurse down the hall they passed the main desk and saw Dr. Berry there, talking to a nurse and writing notes on the paper attached to her clipboard. She smiled when she saw them coming. As they approached, she put the clipboard down and reached out her arms to Skylar. The child went to her willingly.

"Hi sweetness," she said to the little girl. "Ready to go see your room?" she asked.

Skylar started to cry and rub her eyes with balled fists. "I don't wanna stay in the hospital," she whined.

Billie started to step forward, but was restrained by Cat's hand on her arm as they watched Dr. Berry walk away from them, still holding Skylar in her arms.

"Sky, honey," the doctor said, walking toward the little girl's room. "You need to stay here for a little while so we can make you feel better. You want to feel better, don't you?" she asked the child.

Skylar shook her head yes.

"Well, then, let's make a deal. If you are a good girl and stay here with all the nice nurses, I'll get permission for your moms to stay with you. Sound good?" she asked.

Skylar's face lit up. "Can Mama and Mommy sleep here too?" she asked hopefully.

"Yes, they can," Dr. Berry said as they entered Skylar's semi-private room.

Skylar looked at the single bed. "I think we need a bigger bed, Dr. Berry," she said in all seriousness, "'Cause me and Mommy and Mama can't fit in it," she observed.

Dr. Berry tilted her head back and laughed. Turning around, she looked at a blushing Cat and Billie before commenting on the child's observation. "Sky, honey, Mama and Mommy will have to take turns staying with you. I'm afraid this is the biggest bed we have. Is that okay?" she asked.

Skylar looked over at Cat and Billie who were grinning and nodding their heads at the child. Looking back at Dr. Berry, she said, "I guess that's okay. Can they have lots of jello and pudding too?" she asked.

"Jello and pudding it is," replied Dr. Berry as she placed the sick child on the bed. "All right, little one, why don't you get out of those clothes and into this hospital gown so I can examine you," she finished, giving the gown to the child.

Cat made a move to help her, but Dr. Berry motioned for her to let Skylar do it herself.

Cat looked a little put out at the doctor's instruction.

"Look, Cat. I know it's a natural instinct for a mother to want to help a sick child, but too much of that, and she'll become dependent on you, then pretty soon, she'll expect you to do everything for her," Dr. Berry explained.

Billie came up behind Cat and wrapped her arms around the woman, pulling her back against her chest, in an effort to soothe hurt feelings. Bending over, she whispered in her ear, "She's right Cat. I know it goes against your nature, but let her keep her independence."

Billie placed a light kiss on Cat's cheek and whispered, *I love you*, before releasing her.

When Dr. Berry finished with her evaluation, she excused herself and left the room to order an IV and the insertion of an implanted catheter for Skylar.

Cat climbed onto the bed next to Skylar and sat with her back against the headboard. Skylar immediately tucked herself in against her mother, while Cat's arms instinctively wrapped around the little girl.

Billie half-reclined across the middle section of the bed, facing her wife and daughter. She rubbed Skylar's leg.

"Sky, honey, Mama and I have been talking about our work schedules, and if I can take the time off from work, I will stay with you during the days, and Mama will stay with you at night," Billie began.

"You've got it, Billie," said a deep voice from the doorway.

"Uncle Art!" Skylar exclaimed in a weakened voice at the sight of the big man.

Art walked over to the bed and scooped Skylar up into his arms. "How's my favorite girl?" Art asked the child, hugging her close and kissing her feverish cheek.

"I gotta bellyache," Skylar said.

"Boy, that's too bad," Art said. "Is that why you're here?" he asked.

"Dr. Berry says I have 'kemia and I hafta stay in the hospital for a little while, but Mama and Mommy can stay here too if they want, and they can even sleep here," Skylar explained, wide eyed.

"Oh, really?" Art asked. "Cool. Sounds like Mom will be spending some time with you during the day for the next couple of weeks, 'cause I don't want to see her at work until you feel better," Art said to the child, but looking sideways at Billie.

"Thank you," Billie mouthed to her friend and employer.

Art looked over to Cat. "Cat, are you able to get time off?" he asked.

"As a matter of fact, I can. I have asked the hospital only to schedule me for surgeries on an emergency basis, at least until Skylar is released and is being treated on an outpatient basis," she explained.

Just then, the technician came in to insert the implanted catheter and start an IV. The minute Billie saw the tray of needles and tubes she turned green and clutched her stomach.

Seeing her wife's reaction, Cat excused herself for a moment and took Billie aside. "Sweetheart, why don't you go to the cafeteria and get us each a coffee while they do this. I'll stay with her. Okay?" she suggested.

Billie looked down at Cat, a worried expression on her face. "Cat, I feel like I'm deserting her," she said.

Cat touched the side of Billie's face. "Billie, it's okay, really. I'll tell you what," she said, grinning, "Why don't you stop at the gift shop downstairs and bring something back for her, all right?"

Billie lowered her head and placed a tender kiss on Cat's mouth, receiving shy grins from the technicians who were readying the equipment for the procedure. "All right, love. Can I bring anything else back for you?" she asked.

"Just coffee and yourself. That's everything I need," Cat replied.

Billie smiled and kissed her once more before kissing Skylar and promising the child that she would be back in a few minutes.

Handing Skylar over to Cat, Art excused himself and followed his friend out for coffee.

* * *

Billie walked with determined strides toward the elevator, Art right behind her, struggling to keep up.

"Charland, will you slow down?" he said irritably.

Billie stopped when she reached the elevator and pushed the down button. She kept her back to Art the whole time.

"Billie," Art said.

No reply.

He tried again, this time placing his large hand on her shoulder. "Billie, talk to me," he said.

Billie lost it. Dropping her chin to her chest, she covered her face with her hands and started to cry.

Oh Great! This is just great, Art said to himself as Billie cried. He was just no good when women cried. Whenever his wife, Marge wanted her way with something, all she had to do was cry. Art didn't know what else to do except open his arms to his friend and hold her. Billie cried in the circle of Art's arms, clinging to him in silent desperation.

Realizing they made quite a spectacle standing there, he gently nudged her into the stairwell near the elevator, where they sat side by side on the stairs, Billie tucked comfortably under Art's arm, her head leaning on his shoulder. Art said nothing as he held her and let her cry out her sorrow.

Finally, when she had exhausted her reserve of tears, she lifted her head off his shoulder and looked at him, wiping the tears from her eyes. "I'm sorry, Art," she said.

"You have nothing to be sorry about, Billie," Art said. "Your child is sick. If that isn't reason enough to be upset, then I don't know what is. Tell me, Billie, is there anything Marge and I can do for you or Skylar?" he asked.

Billie covered her face with both hands and wiped her tears away. "I don't know what anyone can do, Art, short of hoping and praying that the treatment works. God, if she dies...," Billie couldn't go on.

"She won't die, Billie. You're giving her the best medical attention possible. She has you and Cat and the kids praying for her, not to mention your friends and family. She'll make it, Billie, I know she will," he said, hugging her once more.

Billie looked at Art at his mention of *the best medical attention possible*.

"Art, there *is* something you can do for me," she said.

"Anything, Billie, just name it."

"I'd like you to start processing a malpractice suit against one Dr. Carl Sorensen for me," she explained.

"Malpractice suit?" Art asked curiously.

"Yeah," Billie answered, a look of hatred filling her eyes. "Dr. Carl Sorensen. He's the son of a bitch that misdiagnosed Skylar's illness. Cat and I brought Skylar to him nearly two weeks ago with the same symptoms she is experiencing now, and we made a point of stressing the bruise on her leg that has been there for over three weeks with no sign of healing. That bastard diagnosed her with an ear infection. An ear infection! Just a few days after seeing Sorensen, we took Sky to Dr. Berry, and she said there was no recent sign of an ear infection of any kind. Can you imagine that?"

Billie was on her feet during this tirade, pacing back and forth in the stairwell. Stopping, she faced Art once more.

"Art, Dr. Berry said Sky's chances of survival are highly dependent on how well she responds to treatment...*and* if we caught it early enough. Sorensen may have cost us two precious weeks of time. Those two weeks may make all the difference in Skylar's survival. I want to see him loose his license, Art. He can't have the opportunity to do this to another child," Billie finished vehemently.

Art watched his friend and coworker intently while she explained her case, thanking the heavens above that it wasn't him she was going after. Sorensen didn't stand a chance.

"All right, Billie. I understand, and I support you 200%. I'll file the petition tomorrow," he said.

Billie looked at him through misty eyes. "Thanks, Art. I don't know how to thank you for your support. You're a good friend," she said.

"No thanks are necessary, Billie. You'd do the same for me. By the way, you take all the time off you need, no questions asked, all right?" he said.

Forcing a smile, Billie thanked him once more and kissed him on the cheek, causing an attractive blush to spread across his handsome brown-skinned features.

Billie extended her hand to her friend, helping him to his feet.

"Let's go, big guy. I've got to go buy my kid something, not to mention a coffee for her mother. She'll have my hide if I forget that," Billie joked, trying to lighten the mood.

* * *

"Sky, honey, you have to sit still," Cat instructed the child as the technician tried to numb the skin prior to inserting the needle for the implanted catheter.

"Mama, he's gonna hurt me. I don't want that needle," Skylar cried.

"Sweetheart, after this tube is in, they can give you your medicine through it every day," Cat explained. "Would you rather they gave you a needle every day instead?" she asked.

Skylar's eyes grew wide. "No!" she wailed.

"Then, honey, please cooperate. They need to do this to help you feel better, okay, love?" Cat asked.

Skylar had no choice but to cooperate, however, she clung to Cat, crying hysterically during the entire procedure. Cat's heart was both breaking for the child, and unreasonably angry with Billie for leaving her to deal with the situation alone. In her hurt and sorrowful state, she had forgotten that it was *she* who urged Billie to leave the room during the procedure.

By the time the procedure was over, and the technicians had left, Cat was a total wreck. Tears were flowing down her cheeks, as she held the sobbing child in her arms, rocking her back and forth, trying to soothe her fears. Skylar was crying over and over that she wanted to go home. In was in this state that Jen found her when she entered the room.

Approaching the chair, Jen knelt on the floor next to her and placed her hand on Cat's arm. Cat looked at her and allowed all the sorrow, hurt, anger and heartbreak to show in her eyes. Without saying a word, Jen opened her arms and took both Cat and Skylar into them. Cat sobbed violently as Jen held them, rocking back and forth ever so gently.

Finally, the sobbing stopped as Cat repeatedly caught her breath in hiccupping gulps. Skylar had fallen asleep in her mother's arms while being rocked by Jen. Cat pulled her head off Jen's shoulder and looked at her friend.

"Let me have her, Cat. I'll put her to bed," Jen said, lifting the small child out of Cat's arms. Cat sat there in a daze as she watched her friend tuck her sleeping daughter into the hospital bed.

"Cat, what is this tube coming out of Skylar's chest?" Jen asked.

"It's called a Hickman catheter. It allows the chemo drugs to be administered without repeated injections," she said distractedly. "It will also make it easier for them to give her medications for nausea and fluids for hydration."

"Good idea," Jen said as she finished tucking the blankets around the child. Returning to Cat, she once again knelt on the floor and placed her arm around her friend's shoulder. "Wanna talk about it?" she asked.

Cat rose to her feet and walked to the window. Jen followed, wrapping her arms around her friend's waist from behind and pulling her in close. Cat let her head fall back to rest on Jen's shoulder. "Jen, I'm so afraid," she said. "If she dies...," Cat was too choked up to continue.

Jen kissed the side of Cat's head. "She won't die, Cat. We won't let her. She is getting the best medical help available. She'll make it, my friend. I know she will. Look, she's got you, Billie, the kids, and the rest of your friends and family rooting for her. She can't help but make it," she finished.

Cat took a deep shuddering breath. "You think so?" she asked.

"I know so," Jen replied determinedly.

CHAPTER 10

Skylar's chemotherapy treatments started later that evening after dinner, with the injection of four drugs into the implanted catheter. Cat and Billie stood by. Billie wrapped herself around Cat as they watched the technician administer the drugs. Dr. Berry sat on the edge of the bed next to Skylar as they all waited to see if there would be any immediate adverse effects from the treatment. Skylar was looking at a comic book that had been brought in from the nursery, nearly oblivious to the worried and strained expressions around her.

Dr. Berry motioned for Cat and Billie to meet her at the other end of the room by the window.

"How long before we know if she's tolerating the treatment?" Cat asked.

"It varies from person to person, Cat. We'll have to keep an eye on her to see," Dr. Berry explained.

"Maybe she won't have any side effects," Billie said hopefully.

Dr. Berry took a deep breath. "That's possible, of course, but not very probable. At the very least, all her blood cell counts will drop dramatically as the chemo drugs take effect. This will put her at high risk for anemia, infection and bleeding, but as you know, in order to kill the cancer cells, the healthy cells have to go as well. If the treatment works, the healthy cells will multiply and repopulate in a couple of weeks, but the cancer cells won't," she explained.

"Mommy," Skylar whined as all eyes turned to her. "My belly hurts."

Before any of them could reach her, or the container on the nightstand, Skylar vomited all over herself and the bed. Seeing the mess she had made, she started to cry as more spasms wracked her small body.

Cat and Billie reached her at the same time. Skylar immediately climbed into Billie's arms, but continued to retch into the container that Cat was now holding under her chin. Before she was done, she'd managed to soil Billie's clothing as well as her own. Billie lifted Skylar into her arms and brought her over to the chair, holding her trembling body close as the interns came in to change the soiled sheets.

Dr. Berry retrieved a basin of warm water and a cloth and handed them to Cat who proceeded to clean Skylar up and dress her in a clean hospital gown as she sat in Billie's lap. Cat then took the sick child from Billie and lay on the bed with her, wrapping her in her arms as Billie did her best to clean the vomit off her own clothing.

"Cat, I need to go home and change. Is there anything you'd like me to bring back?" Billie asked.

Cat reached her hand out to Billie, who took it and brought it to her lips. "Just yourself, love," she answered.

Billie kissed Cat gently then repeated the gesture on her daughter. "I'll be back soon, sweet pea. Is there anything *you* want from home?" she asked.

"Petey," replied Skylar, referring to the worn out, beat up teddy bear whose fur she had effectively loved off.

Billie smiled and kissed the child again. "Okay, love bug. I won't forget. I'll bet Petey would love to sleep with you here. I'll be back soon," she finished before placing one more kiss on Cat's forehead, then heading out into the hall.

Dr. Berry caught her before she headed to the elevator. "Billie," she said. "Why don't you have your other two children put together a care package for Sky, you know, a collection of her favorite books and toys, and maybe they can make her get well cards to bring back and hang in her room. She's going to be here for a couple of weeks at the very least. She'll be more comfortable surrounded by some of her personal things," Dr. Berry finished.

Billie smiled. "That's a good idea, Alexis. Thanks." Turning, she was soon on her way home.

* * *

When Billie arrived home she was greeted by two children very eager to see how their little sister was. As habit dictated, Tara ran and threw herself into Billie's arms the minute she saw her, that is, until she realized what was all over her mother's clothing.

"Ewwwww, let me down, quick!" Tara exclaimed as she scrambled out of Billie's arms as fast as she could.

"Sorry, squirt. Your sister threw up on me. That's why I'm home. I need to change my clothes and pick up a few things," Billie explained.

"Is Sky gonna be all right, Mom?" Seth asked.

Billie caressed the side of her son's face. "I sure hope so, sweetie." Then, remembering what Dr. Berry had suggested, she said, "Look, Dr. Berry thought it might be a good idea for you two to put together a care package for your sister. You should include some of her favorite toys and games, stuffed animals...you know the things she likes to play with. Oh, and if you hurry, you have time to jump on the computer and make a couple of get well cards for her while I get out of these smelly clothes and take a shower, okay?" Billie said.

The kids were off in a shot, racing to see who would make their card first.

Billie turned to head for the stairs and encountered her mother in the doorway to the living room. "Laurel," she said.

An awkward pause permeated the room.

"Laurel, I want to thank you for staying with Seth and Tara. We didn't realize when we took Skylar to her appointment this morning that they would admit her today. We really appreciate it," Billie said.

"Billie, look at me," Laurel said.

Billie hesitated at first, but finally met her mother's eyes.

"Billie, I know you have every reason in the world to be angry with me. I know I denied you a real mother, a real family, but please let me make that up to you now. I want to help you. Please don't thank me for trying to fit into your life and the lives of my grandchildren," Laurel finished.

Billie just looked down at the floor and nodded her head. Meeting Laurel's eyes again, she said, "Look, I have to take a shower. I need to get back to the hospital. I'm not sure what time I'll be home tonight."

Laurel took Billie by the shoulders. "Billie, I said let me help. It doesn't matter what time you come home, or even *if* you come home. I will be here with Seth and Tara. I won't leave until you tell me to, okay?" she said.

"And what about Jim, Laurel? Won't your husband object to you spending so much time with your gay daughter?" Billie asked, venom lacing her voice.

Laurel sighed deeply. "Billie, I won't allow Jim, or you, to force me to choose between you. There is room in my life for both of you. If you can't accept each other, then that's just too bad. I'm not asking you to accept Jim, nor for Jim to accept you. All I am asking is for you to accept me," Laurel stated.

Billie locked eyes with her mother for several moments then said, "I have to go shower. Excuse me." Brushing past her, Billie headed for the stairs.

* * *

When Billie arrived back at the hospital, she found Skylar asleep in Cat's arms, both of them curled up on the bed. Cat was stroking Skylar's red-gold hair, remnants of tears evident on both their faces. Their eyes met as Billie entered the room.

"Hi," she said.

"Hi, yourself," Cat replied.

Billie approached the bed and kissed Cat gently on the cheek, prompting Cat to roll onto her back and pull Billie down for more. Several kisses later, Billie sat on the edge of the bed and rubbed her hand up and down Cat's arm.

"You look beat. How were things while I was gone?" Billie asked.

"She just barely fell asleep. The poor baby threw up for another hour after you left," Cat said, new tears springing to her eyes as she relayed the events. "She's so weak, Billie. If she continues to throw up everything she eats, I'm afraid they'll have to feed her intravenously."

Billie sighed, having no words to comfort her wife, as she felt no comfort of her own. Instead, she looked at the child sleeping peacefully beside Cat and allowed a rush of sorrow to wash over her. She brushed a stray lock of hair from Skylar's face and watched a small smile cross the little girl's face as the gesture ticked her skin.

"She looks like an angel," Billie observed.

Cat choked up with emotion as she brought her hand to her mouth to stifle a sob. "God willing, she doesn't become one," Cat said softly, causing a sob to catch in Billie's throat as well as she nodded her head in agreement.

Remembering the bag she had brought from home, Billie fished Petey out of it and placed him under one of Skylar's arms. Leaning down, she kissed her daughter affectionately then climbed in behind Cat, spooning her frame behind her wife and wrapping her arms around both her girls. Cat snuggled into Billie, eliminating any space between them.

"Billie, tell me we'll get through this intact," Cat said pleadingly.

"We'll get through this, love. We will. All of us. I just know it," Billie said, kissing the back of Cat's head. "Sleep now, Cat. Tomorrow will be another long day."

Soon, all three were sleeping soundly in the hospital's biggest bed.

* * *

Billie had intended to go home that night to be with Seth and Tara; however, knowing they were being cared for by Laurel, she decided to stay with Cat as she anticipated the difficult night her youngest child would put in.

Skylar tossed and turned all night, alternating between sweating profusely with fever, to vomiting what little remained in her stomach from dinner the night before. Billie and Cat slept very little after their initial nap, spending most of the night trying to convince Skylar to drink water or juice to rehydrate her depleted system. A great deal of crying was done by all three; Cat and Billie during the short periods when Skylar *did* sleep, not wanting to cry in front of their daughter.

Knowing the night would be long, the ladies took turns sleeping when Skylar slept, tending to her when she woke crying or vomiting, and watched over her through the night. When morning came, all three were exhausted.

Dr. Berry said as much when she came in bright and early to check on Skylar while she was eating breakfast.

"You two look like hell," she said, looking back and forth between the two ladies. "Don't tell me you both stayed with her last night," she said in a voice that indicated she already knew the answer. Looking at two guilty faces, she added, "Remind me to talk to you two about this later." Then, turning her attention to Skylar, she picked the child up, cradling her in her arms and said, "Didn't sleep very good last night, huh, pumpkin?"

Skylar shook her head, a pathetic look on her face.

Dr. Berry felt Sky's feverish forehead and frowned. "Still feverish, kiddo. I'm going to order some children's chewables for you to take it down, then we'll need to give you more medicine for the leukemia, okay?" she said to Skylar.

Skylar's bottom lip started to quiver. "I don't wanna throw up no more," she whined, looking at Billie who was leaning with her backside against the windowsill. "Mommy, do I have ta?" she asked.

Billie closed her eyes and sighed. Opening them again, she saw all three of the room's occupants looking at her. Cat and Dr. Berry were warning her with their eyes to say the right thing, while Skylar looked at her hopefully.

Damn it, she thought to herself. *Why do I have to be the one to break her heart?*

Looking at Skylar, she said, "Sweetheart, if Dr. Berry says you need the medicine to make you feel better then you have to do it. I'm sorry, love." Billie was fighting the tears in her own eyes that matched the ones that were now escaping Skylar's.

"But Mommy, I don't feel better when I throw up. It hurts my belly," she cried.

"I'm sorry, baby, but you have to," Billie said again, feeling lower than the belly of a snake.

Skylar lowered her chin to her chest and pouted, crossing her arms in front of her and refusing to look at any of the adults.

Billie usually found this behavior in her daughter amusing, since it reminded her so much of Cat when she pouted, but today she didn't feel like smiling. Looking over at Cat, she saw that her wife too was struggling with the image, biting her lip to prevent the tears. Billie opened her arms to Cat as they watched the technician administer another dose of chemo drugs to their daughter through the catheter. Cat buried her face in Billie's shirt, not wanting to see the hurt in her daughter's eyes for their betrayal.

Again, they watched her for several minutes, ready to react to the vomiting they were sure was to come, only to be surprised when she lay down and drifted off to sleep rather than lose what she had eaten for breakfast.

Dr. Berry took this opportunity to talk to Cat and Billie. Motioning for them to sit on the edge of Skylar's bed, she sat opposite them in a chair and crossed her arms.

Billie placed an arm around Cat in a symbolic attempt to protect her from the tongue-lashing they both knew was coming.

"First, let me say that if both of you insist on staying with her at night, neither of you will make it through the first week. The best scenario would be for one of you to take the day shift, and the other the night shift while sleeping on the shift you're not here. At the very least, take turns so that each of you has every other night off to get some sleep."

Pausing to see how the ladies were taking the lecture, she saw a look of rebellion on Billie's face that she knew she had to address.

"Billie, I'm serious. Skylar will be depending on both of you to be strong for her. You will not be able to support her and help her recover if you are ill yourself."

Knowing Dr. Berry was right, Billie lowered her chin to her chest and nodded in submission.

Dr. Berry rose to her feet and paced back and forth in front of the ladies as she continued.

"Now, I told you earlier that we found traces of abnormal cells in Skylar's cerebrospinal fluid, and that we would have to do a Central Nervous System Prophylaxis. I'd like to do that today, preferably as soon as she wakes up. Administering the drug as soon as possible after the dose she just received will allow the side effects to happen all at once, giving her some relief later in the day," Dr. Berry finished, continuing to pace.

After watching the doctor pace back and forth several times, Billie spoke. "Alexis, what is it you're *not* telling us?" she asked, sensing Dr. Berry's hesitation to continue.

Dr. Berry stopped and looked at the anxious expectation on the ladies' faces. "We need to implant another catheter between two vertebrae in her spine to tap directly into the cerebrospinal fluid. Based on her behavior when the first catheter was inserted, I fully expect her to resist, so I'm nervous about doing this procedure without putting her under anesthesia," Dr. Berry explained. "I would hate to see her thrashing about while we were tapping into her spine," she added.

Cat could feel Billie tense behind her. Turning around in her wife's arms, Cat reached up and placed two fingers on Billie's mouth to silence the tirade she knew was coming. Billie looked down at her, a frown etched into her brow.

Cat turned back to Dr. Berry. "I agree. We can't have Skylar thrashing about during the implant, however," she paused to get Dr. Berry's full attention, "I'll agree only if you allow me to administer the anesthesia myself," she declared.

Dr. Berry looked at her long and hard for several moments, struggling with the medical ethics involved in this decision. Finally, she spoke. "All right, Cat, I'll agree to that."

Cat smiled as Billie visibly relaxed behind her. "Let's do it then," Cat said.

* * *

Allowing Cat to administer the anesthesia turned out to be a blessing in disguise. Cat's presence, hovering closely over her daughter, proved to have a calming effect on the little girl, who went quickly and quietly under sedation. With Skylar under anesthesia, insertion of the spinal catheter went smoothly. Cat sat at the head of the operating table, keeping close tabs on her daughter's vital signs as she administered the anesthesia. A short time later, Skylar was returned to her bed and a dose of chemo drugs injected into the spinal catheter. Again, they waited and watched for adverse effects. They didn't have to wait long.

Within minutes of administering the new drugs, Skylar woke up screaming. Seeing Cat, she reached out to her and clung for dear life as her mother gathered her up into her arms. "Mama, it hurts," she cried. "My head hurts."

Cat looked to Dr. Berry, who indicated that the pain was a normal reaction.

"Mama, it hurts, make it stop," she cried again.

"Sweetheart, calm down, please. Crying will only make it hurt more. Sweetie, please calm down," Cat begged the child.

Skylar was sobbing violently. "Mommy," she said into Cat's shoulder. "I want my Mommy," she said again.

Billie took a step forward, but stopped short when she saw the angry look in Cat's eyes. She was totally taken back by Cat's reaction.

What did I do? she thought. *My God, she looks ready to kill.*

Dr. Berry observed the scene from the far side of the room.

"Mom...Mom...my," Skylar cried again, sobs interjected between syllables.

Cat consciously quelled the green-eyed monster dwelling within her chest, and handed her daughter to Billie.

Skylar clung to Billie, burying her face deep into her shoulder. While maintaining a death lock around her neck, she sobbed out her pain and confusion in her mother's arms. Another look passed between Cat and Billie before Cat excused herself and left the room. Billie watched her go with pain and confusion of her own written across her face.

Dr. Berry approached Billie and placed a hand on her arm. "Billie, this is very hard on all of you, but especially on Cat. I know you love Skylar like your own, but Cat is her birth mother, and to hear the child beg so desperately for you instead

119

of her is breaking her heart. Do you understand?" she asked the tall woman.

Billie looked at Dr. Berry and swallowed hard. "I understand, Alexis," she said, "but what's important right now, is what Sky wants and needs. I won't turn my back on my daughter...our daughter. Cat's *and* mine," she explained.

"I'm not asking you to turn your back on Sky, Billie. What I'm asking is that you try to understand how Cat feels," Dr. Berry explained.

Billie looked at Dr. Berry and then at the empty doorway that Cat had just retreated through. "I'll try," she said, "I'll try."

* * *

Cat returned about an hour after she left, curtly apologizing for leaving so abruptly, but not apologizing for her reaction. When she stepped into the room, the first thing she saw was Billie rocking a sleeping Skylar. She stopped short when she saw them and consciously pushed her momentary anger aside. She sat on the edge of Sky's bed.

Billie looked at Cat. "Hey," she said.

Cat covered her face with her hands and rubbed it vigorously, not acknowledging Billie's greeting. "How is Skylar?" she asked.

"Pretty much the same. The question is, how are you?" Billie replied with a question of her own.

"I'm not the one in trouble here," Cat replied a bit sarcastically.

"I'm not so sure about that," Billie replied under her breath.

Cat's head snapped up. "What did you say?" she asked sharply.

Billie just looked at her wife and opened her mouth to respond with an equally sharp response when Skylar stirred in her arms.

"Mommy?" she asked in a weak voice.

Billie's attention was immediately drawn to her daughter. "Hey, sweetling. How are you feeling?" she asked.

"My belly hurts," the child whined.

Cat was on her feet immediately, grabbing the basin and placing it in front of the child just as she lost the contents of her stomach, putting an end to the hostile banter that set the tone for the day.

* * *

Skylar spent the entire morning vomiting up her breakfast and alternately being held by both her mothers. Billie tried to distance herself from the situation to give Cat more time with Skylar but the child would have none of it, begging to be taken and held by both of them. By lunch, Sky was so weak and tired it was difficult for her to eat, although she did manage to consume a little applesauce and juice for Cat as she sat in Billie's lap. All of this was accomplished with no verbal communication between them.

Cat laid across Skylar's bed as Billie sat back in the chair with the child sprawled across her lap when Dr. Berry came in with her blood work results from that morning. As she entered the room, she could feel the silent tension permeate the atmosphere as she looked back and forth between the ladies.

Dr. Berry perched herself on the end of the bed and addressed both women. "Well, Sky's ANC is at 500. Normal is 1000. This means that the chemo is doing its job emptying the bone marrow of cells. When it reaches a level between zero and 200, it should start to climb again, and if all goes well, over the next two weeks it should be back to normal. At that point, we can start the second phase of treatment," she said.

"And if all doesn't go well?" Cat asked.

"Then we give it more time, and if more time doesn't work, we try an alternate approach," she said, "but we're being a little premature with this discussion. Let's think optimistically," she encouraged.

Walking over to Skylar, Dr. Berry leaned down and kissed the child on the forehead, noting yet again that she was still feverish. "We'll have to do something about that fever real soon, little one," she said before standing again and addressing Billie and Cat. "There is a new drug on the market called Zofran that may help with the nausea and vomiting. I'd like to try that as well. I'll stop at the desk on the way out and order it for her."

Cat simply nodded without responding verbally.

Dr. Berry looked back and forth between the two silent women. "All right then. I'll stop in again later in the day to check on Sky."

Dr. Berry passed Jen on her way out of the room.

"Hi," Jen said cheerfully to both women as she entered the room. She immediately noticed the tension and gave Billie a questioning look as she bent down to kiss Skylar. "How are you feeling, rugrat?" she asked the child.

Skylar, who had been lying with her back against Billie's chest, smiled weakly and said, "My belly hurts, Aunt Jen."

"Well, I'm sure you'll start to feel better soon, love," Jen told her before placing another kiss on her cheek. Then, looking up at Billie, she said, "How are Mommy and Mama doing?"

Billie just sat there silently holding Skylar in her arms.

Cat sat up on the edge of the bed and sighed deeply.

"That good, huh? Wanna tell me what's going on here?" she asked, looking back and forth between the women. Receiving no response from either, she said, "Okay, Cat, since Billie's tied up at the moment, I'll talk to you first. In the hall, *now*," she demanded.

Cat obediently got up and went out into the hall, followed by Jen, who locked arms with her and walked her down to the solarium before starting to talk.

"Okay, spill it," Jen said once they reached the end of the hall.

"Spill what, Jen?" Cat asked innocently.

Jen backed Cat up against the wall and pinned her there with a hand on either side of her. "Don't mess with my head, Cat. You know damned well what I'm talking about. I walked into that room and had to fight my way through the tension, it's so thick. Now, I want a straight answer," she said firmly.

Cat locked eyes with Jen for several moments before they misted over too much for her to see. Closing them, she allowed the tears to flow down her cheeks.

Jen instantly melted and took Cat into her arms.

"Cat, I'm sorry. I didn't mean to be so gruff," Jen apologized.

"No, Jen, it's not you. It's me. I can't help it. Jen, she's my wife. I shouldn't feel this way. She's Sky's mother too. They've always been close. Oh, Jen, I don't know what to do. I can't help feeling this way," Cat cried disjointedly.

"Whoa, wait a minute. Cat, slow down and tell me again. This time, give me just a little more detail, okay?" Jen asked, leading Cat over to the couch at the far end of the solarium.

Cat sat down heavily, with Jen beside her. Jen took her hand and held it between her own as Cat talked.

"I'm jealous, Jen. Jealous of my own wife and child," she said. Seeing the look of confusion on Jen's face, she continued. "Every time Sky is in pain, every time she has a bad reaction to the chemo, every time she wakes up screaming, she calls out for Billie. If I'm the only one there, then she is satisfied, but as soon as Billie enters the room, she wants nothing to do with me. God, Jen, why do I feel this way? Billie is a wonderful mother to all of our children. I have no right to be jealous," Cat explained.

Jen was staring at the floor, nodding her head up and down. Looking at Cat, she said, "You can't help but blame Billie for this, can you?"

Cat nodded then rose to her feet and walked a few paces away, her back still to Jen. "No I can't. I know she's not doing it on purpose, but damn it Jen Skylar is *my* daughter. *I* gave birth to her. *I* endured the heinous rape which conceived her. She's *mine*, Jen," Cat said passionately as she quickly turned around to stress the last point to her friend.

Little did Cat or Jen know, as Cat angrily vented her irrational anger, Billie had made her way to the solarium and was standing well within hearing range as Cat, in no uncertain terms, pulled rank over her as Skylar's biological mother.

Coming unexpectedly and suddenly face to face with the object of her anger caught Cat off guard, as she stood there speechless.

Jen rose to her feet and stood by Cat's side, finding herself caught in the whirlwind brewing between her friends.

Billie was visibly shaken as she looked everywhere but at Cat. "Um…Skylar is sleeping. I put her to bed. I...ah...I'm going home for a while, okay? I'll spend some time with Seth and Tara," she said as she turned to walk away. Stopping after a few feet, she turned around and said, "I'll come by tomorrow morning to see Skylar. Goodnight."

Jen and Cat stood rooted to the spot, paralyzed with regret. Neither of them knew that Billie had been standing there for the better part of Cat's explanation. Neither of them knew until it was too late.

CHAPTER 11

"Billie," Cat exclaimed as she moved to run after her wife.

Jen grabbed her hand and held her back. "No, Cat. Go back to Skylar's room and stay with her. I'll talk to Billie. I think both your emotions are a little too raw right now for a direct confrontation," Jen explained.

Cat's eyes were wild with nervous anxiety. She wanted desperately to run after Billie and tell her she didn't mean it, but if the truth be known, she *was* jealous, and part of her *didn't* want to share her daughter with Billie. She knew it was wrong to feel this way. She knew Billie would give her life for any one of their children, but every time Skylar chose Billie over her, it was like a knife stabbing deep into her heart. Part of her hated Billie for that. The other part of her knew Billie was just being the dependable, loving parent Skylar had always known, and the caring, dedicated, exceptional human being she loved so much. Such were the emotions waging war in her head as she walked arm-in-arm back to Skylar's room with Jen.

Stopping at the doorway, Jen kissed Cat on the forehead and said, "Before I go, I need to know one thing—do you still love her?"

Cat looked at her friend, totally floored by the question.

"Of course I love her, Jen. I love her with all my heart. I know what I'm feeling is just jealousy. I know it's my own foolish heart that is making me feel this way. Jen, that part of my heart which is reserved just for Billie is still intact and still deeply in love with her," Cat said, desperation filling her voice as rapidly as the tears were filling her eyes, "I can't lose her and Skylar too. I'll die from the heartbreak. I know I will."

Jen nodded. "I'll talk to her Cat. I hope it will help," she said. *Damn it. Billie is in tremendous pain right now after what she heard. Why does life have to be so damned hard all the time for these women? Someone up there had better start listening and do something about this before it rips them both apart,* Jen finished in her thoughts as she walked away.

* * *

Billie drove home, struggling to see through the blinding veil of tears. In her mind, she was about to lose everything she loved, except her son of course. That is, unless he chose to stay with Cat.

He chose to stay with Cat before, Billie thought. *Of course, that was when he thought I would harm her,* Billie reminisced, thinking about times past when she was working on the McBride domestic violence case and had argued angrily with Cat over some photographs received in the mail.

She was quite a mess when she finally pulled into the driveway and shut off the engine. She sat there for a long moment, trying to regain her composure before going into the house, all she could think about were Cat's last words.

Skylar is my daughter. I gave birth to her. She's mine.

Billie rested her forehead on the steering wheel and cried her heart out, cried so hard that she didn't hear the car door open and a body slip into the seat beside her, until her friend's arm circled her back.

"Billie," Jen's voice said softly. "Billie, honey, look at me."

When Billie turned her head and looked at her, Jen's heart broke immediately for this woman. Never in her life had she seen such raw emotion and pain on a person's face. All the pain, sorrow, desperation and despair that Billie was feeling was evident in that one look.

Jen's eyes teared at the sight of it as she opened her arms to her friend. Billie fell immediately into them and sobbed violently.

"Jen, I can't do this any longer. My baby is dying. My wife...well, I'm not really sure what Cat thinks. Jen, our lives are falling apart. I'm not strong enough for this. I just can't do it.

I can't sit by and watch Skylar dwindle away like she is...and now I'm losing Cat. It's ripping my heart out. I just want to die," she said, breaking down into sobs once more.

Jen held her close, her own tears mingling with Billie's. Finally, after a time the tears stopped and Billie's trembling began to subside.

"Billie," Jen said, placing a kiss on the side of Billie's head. "You are not losing Cat. She loves you. She is just very confused right now. Confused about Skylar's attachment to you and heartbroken about seeing her child critically ill. Billie, imagine how you would feel if, heaven forbid, it was Seth instead of Skylar, and he cried out for Cat instead of you. How would you feel, Billie?" Jen asked.

Billie sat up and wiped the tears from her face. She didn't want to deal with that right now. She was still angry at Cat's words...*Skylar is my daughter. I gave birth to her*...and at Seth's words well over a year ago as he stood between her and Cat, *I won't let you hurt her, Mom.* As far as she was concerned, her whole life was going down the toilet. She was losing everything she loved.

"Jen, I need to go inside. I haven't seen Seth and Tara since yesterday. I have to try to salvage at least this part of my life," she said, reaching for the door handle.

Jen grabbed her arm before she climbed out of the car. Billie turned her head sharply to look at her.

"Billie," she said, "Don't close the door on Cat. You'll be making a huge mistake if you do. She's in pain right now. Just give her some time, okay?" Jen asked.

"She's not the only one in pain, Jen," Billie said as she climbed out of the car and slammed the door, turning her back on her friend and walking into the house.

Jen sat in Billie's car long after her friend had entered the house, cursing the fates that had led her friends to the brink of destruction.

* * *

Cat spent most of the afternoon holding a weakened Skylar in her arms, rocking her back and forth and humming lullabies, all the while fighting tears of loss and heartfelt sorrow at the rift that had developed between her and Billie.

Billie, I'm so sorry. I can't help the way I feel. I didn't mean to hurt you, she thought to herself as she rocked Skylar, and defensively convinced herself that her feelings were justified. *I know she loves Sky. I know she does, but it is me who shares her blood, not Billie. I should be first. She's my flesh and blood,* Cat reasoned.

It was like this that Dr. Berry found her an hour later. Coming into the room, she sat on the bed opposite Cat and looked at her carefully, worried that she was not holding up well under the duress of Skylar's illness. When Cat's gaze met her eyes, Dr. Berry asked her how the child was doing.

"Alexis," Cat said, fatigue obvious in her voice. "She's still feverish, and cranky. It's breaking my heart not to be able to do more for her."

"Cat, her fever is obviously a sign of infection. I'm also betting her red cell count has dropped, which is common in leukemia patients. I want to do a blood transfusion this evening, followed by a round of antibiotics. I think it will help her," Dr. Berry explained.

"Take mine. We're the same blood type," Cat said.

"All right," Dr. Berry said as she started to rise. "Oh, this is your choice, of course, but generally, family members are eager to help in a situation like this. You might want to ask your friends and family to consider donating blood. We can use it to do transfusions of red or white blood cells, or to use just the platelets through the aphaeresis process," Dr. Berry explained.

"All right, I'll contact everyone right away," Cat replied.

Dr. Berry started walking toward the door then stopped and turned around. "By the way, I don't see Billie here. Did you take my advice and decide to work in shifts?" the doctor asked.

Cat just looked away, fighting the tears that threatened to well up once more.

Seeing Cat's distress, Dr. Berry walked back to her and squatted down on her heels. Placing a hand on her leg she said, "Cat, I know this is an emotional time for both of you, but you have to be strong through this. Strong for Skylar, and for Billie. She is in pain too. I know that Sky is your child biologically, but she is just as much Billie's child psychologically as she is yours. Billie loves her very much, and this is ripping her apart as terribly as it is you. Be sensitive to that, Cat. I would hate to see what you and Billie have together destroyed by Sky's illness," Dr. Berry finished.

Cat looked at Dr. Berry. "I'm afraid the destruction has already begun," she said, finally allowing the tears to escape her lids.

"Destruction can be repaired. Just don't let the damage become too severe before you decide to fix it," she said. Rising to her feet, she added, "I'll go arrange for the transfusion. A technician will be here shortly to collect you and Skylar."

Cat just nodded as she watched Dr. Berry leave the room.

* * *

"This is really good, Nana," Seth said as he ate another large forkful of Sheperd's Pie. "You're a really good cook."

"Thank you, Seth," Laurel said.

"Yeah, with Mama at the hospital with Sky, we'd have to eat Mom's cooking if you weren't here," Tara commented.

Laurel looked at the child with raised eyebrows. "And what's so bad about that?" she asked.

"Everything," Tara exclaimed, nearly causing Laurel to choke on the drink of water she had just taken.

"You can't cook?" Laurel asked her daughter.

"Guilty as charged," Billie volunteered. "Usually when Cat's not home, we go out for dinner. It's less risky than eating my cooking," she added.

"I'll say," the ever-expressive Tara piped in before abruptly changing the subject. "Mom, when can we visit Sky?" Tara asked.

"Not for a few more days, sweetie," Billie replied. "The kind of therapy she is taking right now is making it easy for her to catch things, like colds, from other people, so she can't have too many visitors. Hopefully in a few days she'll be stronger then I'll talk to Dr. Berry about bringing you and your brother for a visit," she explained.

"I'd like to visit too," Laurel said.

Billie looked at her mother and said, "Of course, if you'd like to."

Laurel looked at Billie intently, her eyes saying, *of course I'd like to*, but her voice remaining silent, not wanting to get into a confrontation with her daughter in front of the children. The look she gave Billie, however, clearly indicated that this conversation was not over.

Just then, the phone rang. Billie jumped to her feet in near-panic that the call was about Skylar.

"Hello?" she said cautiously. It was Cat. "Cat! Cat, is Sky all right?" Billie asked quickly. "Yes, yes, of course. That question should have never even crossed your mind," Billie said, anger tingeing her voice. "Yes, all right, I'll ask. Hold on a second."

Billie cradled the receiver on her shoulder as she turned to Laurel. "Laurel, the hospital is looking for blood donors for Skylar's transfusions. Would you...,"

"Absolutely, Billie. I'd be happy to," Laurel replied before Billie could finish asking the question.

Billie turned back to the receiver. "Yes, Cat, count us both in, and I'll give Art and Marge a call as well. I'm sure they'd be happy to help. Do you want me to call Jen and Fred? All right, I'll do that. All right. Kiss Sky for me and tell her I'll see her in the morning. All right. Good night," Billie said, hanging up the receiver.

Laurel raised an eyebrow at her, noting the absence of the words *I love you* before hanging up the phone.

Billie quickly made two more phone calls, one to Art and the other to Jen, all four adults more than willing to donate life's most precious fluid to help the ailing child.

Hanging up the phone, Billie returned to her dinner and chased her food around her plate, eating very little.

"Mom, can we go over to Stevie's to play in the pool?" Seth asked for himself and his sister.

Billie snapped out of her distracted state and looked at her son. "Does Jen know about this?" she asked.

"Yep! Actually Fred was the one who invited us," Seth replied.

Billie smiled. "Okay then, sweetie. Grab a couple of towels, and don't forget to bring them home with you, okay? Oh, and don't track water through Jen's house," she shouted as the two children ran up the stairs to get into their bathing suits. Moments later, they flew past both women, who were still seated at the kitchen table.

Laurel rose from her seat and retrieved the coffeepot, refilling both hers and Billie's cups. She put the pot back on the warmer then sat down again and wrapped both her hands around her cup. She looked at Billie, waiting for the younger woman to start a conversation.

After several long moments of silence, Billie looked at her mother. "What?" she asked.

"You tell me, Billie," Laurel replied.

When Billie didn't respond, Laurel continued. "Billie, something is wrong between you and Cat. I can feel it. From the first moment I laid eyes on the two of you together, I could feel that special something between you. It's missing now. What happened?" she asked.

Billie continued to look down at the table, shaking her head side to side. "I don't know. It's like she doesn't want me involved in Skylar's recovery, Laurel. Skylar cries for me, but yet when I take her, hold her, Cat becomes angry and jealous. I don't know what to do. I am trying to stay away to give Cat more time alone with her, but its breaking my heart."

Billie took a deep breath and held her hand to her chest.

"I feel such tightness here. I feel like I'm losing them both," she explained.

Laurel had a faraway look in her eyes as she listened to her daughter. "Billie," she said, "Thirty-three years ago, when I placed you in your adoptive mother's arms, she looked at you with such love and joy, that it ripped my heart out. I wanted to shout at her that she had no right to love my daughter as much as I did, but you know what? She did have that right, because I gave it to her, just like Cat gave you the right to love Skylar as your own the day you adopted her. Billie, do not walk away from this. You will regret it for the rest of your life. Trust me, I know," she finished, tears in her eyes.

Billie looked at her mother and nodded, looking down once more at the table.

* * *

Cat lay on the bed beside Skylar while she distractedly ran her fingers up and down her daughter's arm. The little girl watched the cartoon that was showing on the wall-mounted TV opposite her bed. The day had been hectic and difficult, not only for her, but for her mothers as well. Unfortunately for all, the day was ending with a large chasm spanning the distance between their damaged hearts.

During a commercial, Skylar turned her head and looked at Cat. "Mama, when is Mommy coming back?" she asked.

"Tomorrow, sweetheart," Cat answered. "She'll be here tomorrow."

Satisfied with the answer, Skylar went back to watching her show.

Several hours later, Cat still laid beside her child, only now, Skylar was sleeping peacefully, oblivious to the tempest of emotions stirring within her mother.

Billie, she thought to herself. *My mind is torn with love and guilt and insecurity. I need your love and support, but I've hurt you so. I don't know how to say I'm sorry. I don't know how to rid my heart of these jealous feelings. I know it is jealousy making me feel this way, but it's anger too. The anger scares me, Billie. I don't know where it is coming from.*

Cat closed her eyes and allowed the tears to escape down the sides of her face.

Cat tried desperately to put herself in Billie's shoes.

God, how would I react if this were Seth instead of Sky? How would I feel if Billie were jealous over my love for Seth?

As much as Cat's rational mind understood the logic behind her thoughts, her emotional mind would not allow her heart to listen.

The emotional impact of Cat's thoughts was too much for her to bear. Throwing her legs over the side of the bed, she sat up and bent over at the waist, holding herself tight as she rocked back and forth while sobs wracked her body. For long moments, she cried until she became too weary to stay awake.

Soon, she joined Skylar in sleep, at least for a short while as she was awakened periodically throughout the night by a screaming Skylar, crying out for Billie and adding fuel to the already raging fire of jealousy in Cat's heart.

* * *

Billie lay in bed, staring at the ceiling. Her stomach clenched tightly as she agonized over the plight she found herself in. Her rational mind felt love and understanding for Cat and what she was going through…what they were *all* going through. Her emotional mind however, was angry and bitter at what she saw as unreasonable jealousy and betrayal on Cat's part.

Damn you, Cat, she thought. *She's my daughter too. Just because I didn't give birth to her, doesn't mean I don't love her. Please don't take her away from me. If she has limited time left, let me share it with her as well.*

Billie's soul cried out in pain as her emotions took over her tortured mind. Rolling onto her side, she pulled her knees up into her chest and hugged them close while she cried out her sorrow.

Moments later, the door to Billie' room opened as small feet made their way across the floor.

"Mom, please don't cry," Tara said as she wrapped her arms around her mother's neck.

Billie unfolded her long frame and gathered her daughter into her arms.

"Are you sad about Sky?" Tara asked.

Billie shook her head. *Oh, sweet love, it's so much more than that,* Billie thought. *I love you and your sister so much. I don't want to lose either of you.*

Thoughts such as these ran through Billie's mind as she cried harder, not hearing Seth enter the room until he crawled in behind her and wrapped his arms around her.

"Mom, please don't cry. Sky will be all right," he said, snuggling in close behind her.

Billie reached back and pulled Seth in closer. "I love you two so much," she said through her tears.

"I love you too, Mom," both children said at once.

Hours later, Billie still lay there, staring at the ceiling, book-ended by two sleeping children. Her mind drifted to Cat.

Cat, I love you so much. Please don't let this tear us apart. I can't help but love her as my own, Cat. Please don't take her away from me.

Finally, after many hours of sleeplessness, Billie drifted off, only to be awakened two hours later by the alarm clock.

CHAPTER 12

Billie arrived at the hospital the next morning just as Skylar was receiving her chemotherapy. As soon as the child saw her, she lunged forward, intending to scramble off the bed to meet her.

"Sky, honey, stay there. I'll come to you," Billie said as she sat down next to the child and wrapped her in her arms, holding her tight as the technician injected the drugs into the catheter.

"Mommy, I missed you," Sky said, clinging to Billie with all her might. Cat stood off to the side, her heart in her throat at the sight.

"I missed you too, love bug," Billie said, kissing the child on the head. She looked at Cat. Intense loved passed between them, but something indiscernible kept them apart.

Cat smiled slightly before looking away.

"Cat, go home and get some rest," Billie said. "I'll stay here with Sky...that is, if you don't mind," she added.

Cat looked around distractedly. "No, no, I don't mind," she said, yawning.

Billie had all she could do to resist taking Cat into her arms and holding her close, but something stopped her.

"All right then, go home," she said. "Laurel is taking Seth and Tara to spend the day with your Mom, so the house is empty. You should be able to get some sleep."

"All right," Cat said, approaching Skylar for a hug and a kiss. "C'mere, sweetie," she said, taking the small child into her arms and holding her close. "I'll be back this afternoon, okay? Mama needs to take a nap and a shower. You be a good girl for Mommy, all right?" she said, stroking the child's cheek, then handing her back to Billie.

Skylar smiled widely. "I'll be good, Mama, I promise," she said, wrapping her arms around Billie's neck.

Cat looked at Billie. Their eyes held for a few moments, causing Cat to catch her breath suddenly at the intensity of the blue pools she so loved to drown in. Then, looking away abruptly, she said, "I'll be back some time this afternoon."

"All right," Billie said, watching her go. Sighing deeply, she looked at Skylar. "Well, love bug, what shall we do today?"

"Mommy...," Skylar whined as she clutched her stomach. Billie reached for the basin just in time as Skylar emptied her breakfast into it.

It was going to be another long day.

* * *

Cat and Billie quickly fell into a pattern of impersonal co-existence. Billie arrived midmorning each day and relieved Cat who went home to sleep, shower and spend time with the other two children while Billie stayed with Skylar at the hospital. Due to the timing, Billie was the one to nurse Skylar through her side effects, while Cat dealt with the nighttime crying spells.

The arrangement seemed to work out well for Skylar, who managed to bask in the attention of both mothers; neither having to vie for equal time, seeing as they were not present at the same time, except to change shifts.

During this week, Skylar's ANC counts bottomed out at zero and then started to climb as expected. Each day, the side effects of the chemo lessened and her strength steadily improved. Early on in the week, after two more blood transfusions, her fever disappeared.

Early in the second week of her stay at the hospital, Billie arrived for her shift change and found a very distraught Cat sitting there, holding a clump of Skylar's red-gold hair in her hand, tears running down her face. Skylar was sitting cross-legged on her bed, contentedly coloring. When Billie walked in on the scene, she had an immediate flash back to her own stay in the hospital more than a year earlier during which she had lost all her hair to brain surgery.

Considering Skylar seemed to be dealing just fine with the situation, Billie approached Cat and knelt on one knee in front of her. "It will grow back, Cat," Billie said, reaching for the hair in Cat's hand.

"No!" Cat said adamantly, snatching the hair away from Billie.

Billie narrowed her eyes at Cat, then stood up and backed away. "All right," she said, throwing her hands up in surrender.

Cat rose from her chair, kissed Skylar and promised to be back that evening, then left without a backward glance at Billie. Three days later, all of Skylar's hair had fallen out, and Cat had collected and saved every bit of it.

Skylar wore her shiny bald scalp with pride.

"I look like you did when you were in the hospital, Mommy," Skylar said, grinning from ear to ear.

"Yes you do," Billie said, rubbing her smooth scalp.

Cat frowned as she shoved the zip-lock bag containing Skylar's locks, into her pocket.

Although the shift changes seemed to work out well for Skylar, they were taking their toll on Cat and Billie. The sum total of their communication consisted of subtle looks that passed between them as well as cursory status reports on Skylar's condition. Occasionally, their encounters were emotional, but that emotion was more often than not, angry rather than loving.

The time they spent together was generally in tense, ten-minute intervals as they said hello and good-bye. Neither was sleeping well, spending several hours lying awake each night agonizing over the loss of their relationship. Both had lost weight and their faces were drawn and tired with worry.

None of this was lost on Laurel or Jen. Early into the second week of Skylar's hospital stay, Laurel confronted Billie on her way out very early one morning.

"Billie," Laurel said to her daughter as Billie filled a travel mug to take with her to the hospital.

"I gotta go, Laurel. I don't have time to talk," Billie replied abruptly.

"Then you'll make the time," Laurel demanded as she stepped into her daughter's path to stop her departure.

Billie looked up at the ceiling and sighed audibly. "Laurel, please don't start. I really need to go," she said firmly as she gently pushed Laurel to the side and walked past her.

"What will you have left if she dies, Billie?" Laurel asked, hoping to shock her daughter to a standstill.

It worked, as Billie suddenly stopped and turned to face her mother. "What did you say?" she asked incredulously.

Laurel put her hands on her hips in an effort to make her point. "I said, what will you have left if she dies? You are throwing away everything of value in your life, Billie. From what I've seen, you and Cat barely talk to each other anymore. You aren't sleeping…yes, I hear you pacing in the middle of the night," Laurel said, answering Billie's unasked question. "You should see yourself from my perspective, Billie. You look like hell."

"Hmph. I love you too, Mother," Billie interjected sarcastically.

"Billie, I'm serious. You look like hell. Your face is drawn, you've lost weight, and it's been nearly two weeks since I've seen a smile grace that beautiful face of yours. Billie, you're killing yourself," Laurel exclaimed.

Billie leaned in so her face was inches from her mother's. "Let's get something straight, Laurel," Billie said in a low, even tone. "Nothing matters more in my life right now than my daughter's health. When we've finally chased death away from her door, then and only then will I worry about the other things. Quite frankly, what doesn't survive this trial probably isn't worth having anyway," she said cynically.

"Does that include your wife, Billie?" Laurel asked pointedly.

"That especially includes my wife," Billie replied.

Laurel was aghast. "How can you say that? How can you throw away what you and Cat have?" she asked.

"I didn't throw away what I had with Cat, Laurel. She took it from me, or at least she's trying to, only Skylar won't let her.

She cut me to the quick when she tried to take my child from me, Laurel. I don't know if I can forgive her for that," Billie explained.

Laurel held Billie's gaze for a long moment, at a total loss for a response.

Finally, Billie broke the stalemate and grabbed her travel mug. "I'll be back later this evening. Kiss the kids for me when they get up, okay?" she asked as she headed to the door, only to stop and turn around. "Oh, by the way, tell Seth and Tara that I'll take them out for pizza when I get home this evening. You're welcome to come along too, of course," she said.

"All right, I'll tell them," Laurel replied as Billie turned to leave again. "Oh, and Billie, kiss Sky for me," she added, watching her daughter nod as she finally exited the kitchen and headed for her car.

Laurel stood at the kitchen door and watched through the window as Billie backed the car out of the driveway and drove down the street.

* * *

Within days, Skylar's ANC count was high enough to make it safe for the other children to visit. After a terse discussion, Cat and Billie agreed that Billie would arrive early, bringing Laurel, Seth and Tara with her, and that Laurel would take them home with her so that Billie would have more time to visit with Skylar before returning home herself.

Laurel immediately agreed to the plan, hoping it would be an opportunity for Billie and Cat to spend more than a few minutes alone together after she left with the older two children.

When the day came, Billie showed up two hours early, with Seth, Tara and Laurel in tow.

The first thing Seth did when he arrived was to take his hat off to show his sister his newly shaved head. She giggled when he told her he did it for her. Then he gave her his hat to wear until her hair grew back in.

"Just like when Mom lost her hair," he said smiling.

Billie was moved to tears by her son's gesture. *He has so much of Cat's gentle nature that you would swear he is her son,* Billie thought.

Tara had a new selection of color books and crayons for her little sister and promptly climbed onto the bed and started coloring with her. As they were coloring, Tara nonchalantly looked at Skylar and said, "Sky, if anyone laughs at you because of your hair, I'll deck'em for you, okay?" to which Skylar vigorously nodded her head.

Tara's comments made Cat smile. *She has so much of Billie's tough-guy attitude, that you would swear she is her daughter,* she thought.

Billie and Cat's eyes met over the heads of their children. For the briefest of moments, a connection was established between the two, across which jolts of emotion and love jumped. However, the connection was short-lived as each quickly retreated into her own cocoon of self-protection.

Just a few minutes into their visit, Jen arrived. It was not unusual for Jen to stop in unannounced, and on this day her arrival was a blessing in disguise as far as Laurel was concerned.

Laurel took Jen aside. "Do you think you can get Cat and Billie out of here together for a while? They need a break from this place. They haven't been together for more than ten minutes at a time for nearly two weeks, and those ten minutes have always been right here in this room. I'm afraid there will be nothing left of their relationship if something drastic doesn't happen soon," Laurel warned.

Jen nodded. "I'll take care of it," she said.

Billie was standing by the window looking out over the city, while Cat sat on the edge of the bed visiting with the children. When each was sure the other wasn't looking, both would steal glances at the other, glances filled with mixed feelings of love, longing, anger and regret.

"All right," Jen said to the general audience in the room. "Billie, Cat, I'd like you to come with me," she said.

Billie and Cat looked at her questioningly, both pairs of eyebrows raised into their hairlines.

"Laurel, would you mind visiting with the kids while I take my friends to dinner?" she asked the older woman, a knowing grin on her face.

"Not at all. We'll be fine here," she said. Looking back and forth between Cat and Billie, she added, "Go on. You both need a break."

Cat and Billie looked at each other, both ready to object, when Jen interrupted.

"I don't want any excuses. Let's go—now," she commanded.

Since the hospital was in the middle of the metropolitan area, they were close enough to the business district to walk to any convenience store or restaurant. This suited Jen just fine, since taking the car would mean that one of them would have to sit in the back seat. By walking, she could make sure that they walked side by side, just by positioning herself on either end.

The walk to the restaurant was tense, with Jen carrying most of the conversation for the three of them. They would answer direct questions, but avoided answers that required more elaborate discussion. The fifteen-minute walk to the restaurant felt more like thirty. Finally, just before entering the eating establishment, Jen confronted her friends.

"Look. This isn't going the way I planned, all right?" she said. "You two need to start talking to each other. Skylar will be going home soon, isn't that right? Well, isn't it?" Jen asked.

Cat and Billie looked at one another, neither one sure which of them Jen was directing the question to. Finally, they looked back at her and said, *yes* together.

"Okay, then, that means the two of you will actually be living under the same roof...at...the...same...time…again, right?" she asked.

Both women nodded.

"Then don't you think you need to start actually talking to each other *before* then?" she finally asked.

Billie looked annoyed. Cat looked amused. Neither looked at the other.

"Damn it. Look at each other. Don't just glance—*look*," Jen said, taking each one's arms and turning them to face the other.

Cat looked up shyly as Billie looked down. Their eyes met and locked, a silent message of love and longing passed between them. Both women smiled slightly, unable to immediately break the gaze.

"Now we're getting somewhere," Jen said, pleased with her efforts as she allowed them more gazing time before urging them into the restaurant.

Jen asked for a small, isolated table so that Billie and Cat would be seated across from one another with her on a third side. The table was in a corner, affording them some sense of privacy in an otherwise crowded restaurant. Sitting down, Jen refused to initiate conversation. Instead she sat back and watched her two friends interact.

Billie reached over the table and asked for Cat's hand, which Cat gave willingly. Bringing it to her lips, Billie kissed each knuckle, never taking her piercing blue eyes from Cat's face.

Cat's eyes closed as a look crossed her face that was almost obscene. Jen squirmed in her seat just watching her. When Cat opened her eyes again, they were mist-filled. "Billie," she said faintly.

Just then, the waitress came for their order.

Jen cursed her silently under her breath.

Cat and Billie seldom took their eyes off each other through the meal. At one point, they both reached for the salt shaker, Cat retracting her hand shyly, blushing slightly under watchful blue eyes as Billie yielded it to her. There was most definitely a seduction going on back and forth across the table and Jen felt like a voyeur taking pleasure in her friends' foreplay.

At one point near the end of the meal, Jen excused herself to use the ladies room, leaving Cat and Billie alone at the table.

Conversation suddenly became awkward without Jen there to mediate it.

"So, Alexis said Sky should be able to go home in a few days," Billie commented.

"Yes she did," Cat replied. "This morning's ANC counts were almost normal."

"I think I want to set a cot up in the corner of our room for her, at least for a little while...you know, so we can keep an eye on her at night," Billie said.

"I don't think that's a good idea, Billie," Cat said. "We can't be treating her differently than when she was healthy."

"What do you mean we can't be treating her differently?" Billie said, her anger starting to rise. "Cat, our daughter has cancer. She could have a relapse. I want her near us," Billie stated adamantly.

"No, Billie. Having her in our room will not make any difference to her health. It just doesn't make sense," Cat explained.

Billie took her napkin off her lap and put it on the table. "You're going to be unreasonable about this, aren't you?" she asked.

"Me? Billie, *you* are the one being unreasonable," she countered.

Billie rose to her feet. "This is neither the place, nor time to argue, Cat. I'm going back to the hospital. Please give Jen my apologies," she said as she threw some money down on the table and left the restaurant.

Moments later, Jen returned from the ladies room to find Cat sitting there alone, eyes cast down at the table, hands in her lap. "Where's Billie?" she asked, afraid to hear the answer.

"She's gone back to the hospital Jen. She left her apologies," Cat replied.

Jen sat back in her chair and sighed, dropping her head back, and closing her eyes for a moment or two. Finally she looked at Cat. "What happened?" she asked.

"We argued about Sky's sleeping arrangements when she comes home in a few days," Cat explained.

"You argued about Sky's sleeping arrangements. Damn it Cat. How did that get started?" Jen asked.

We were having a civil conversation about Sky coming home, when Billie insisted that she sleep on a cot in our room for a while. I didn't agree," Cat simply stated.

Jen propped her elbows on the table and held her head between her hands. Looking back up at Cat, she said, "Cat, would it have hurt to let her have her way for a few days, at least until Sky was sleeping comfortably through the night?"

Now it was Cat's turn to become indignant. "Jen, Skylar is *my* daughter. I know what's best for her," she insisted.

Jen sat back in her chair again. "Oh, I get it," she said, throwing her napkin on the table. "You objected to the sleeping arrangements to make a point...to have the final say about *your* daughter, *not* because you disagreed with Billie."

Cat drew an angry mask across her face and remained quiet.

Jen looked directly into Cat's face. "Cat, until you realize that Billie is this child's mother too, and until you give her equal say, you have no hope of salvaging your marriage. You had better decide what you want more, your pride or your family." With that, Jen got up, threw more money on top of what Billie had placed there, and left Cat to walk back to the hospital alone.

* * *

When Cat returned to the hospital, she found her family waiting to say goodnight to her before Laurel took them home. Skylar had drifted off to sleep shortly before she arrived and was tucked into bed, Seth's baseball cap securely on her head, and Petey tucked under her arm. Billie was sitting on the bed, her back propped against the headboard, while she drew lazy patterns on Skylar's arm with her fingertip. Seth and Tara were sitting on the foot of Skylar's bed watching cartoons, while Laurel stood in front of the window, looking out at the night lights of the surrounding city. Jen had apparently gone home directly from the restaurant.

Cat came in and immediately locked eyes with Billie. A barrage of emotions crossed her face as she looked at her wife, not the least of which was fear...fear of losing her child, fear of losing Billie and her family, fear of the unknown.

On the way back from the restaurant, Cat had detoured into the park and sat for long moments on the swings thinking about what Jen had said to her.

Was Jen right? Was it self-righteous arrogance that was causing the rift?

The phrase, *Pride goeth before the fall*, kept going through her mind.

I'm so confused, Cat thought.

Looking at Billie now, she realized she needed to understand what she was feeling before she could discuss it with her. Finally, breaking her gaze with Billie, she approached the children and kissed them both, extracting promises from them to be good for their grandmother before going over to hug Laurel.

Laurel ushered the children out of the room and told Billie she'd see her later that evening as she left her daughter alone with Cat and Skylar.

Billie continued to sit on the bed, drawing lazy patterns on Skylar's arm.

Cat turned to look at Billie from her position by the window, her hands nervously intertwining. "Billie—" she began.

"Go home, Cat. I'll stay with Sky tonight. I suspect I'll be doing a lot of that when she comes home," Billie said.

"No, Billie. I'll stay," Cat said.

"Go home, Cat. I'm not leaving. So unless you want to spend the entire night maintaining this polite, meaningless façade, I suggest you just go home," Billie said coldly.

Tears sprang immediately to Cat's eyes as she quickly left the room, thinking that maybe Jen was right. Maybe there was little hope of saving her marriage.

CHAPTER 13

Three days later, Skylar was released from the hospital with ANC counts of 950, and strict instructions to keep her living environment as clean as possible to avoid risk of infection while she was undergoing the second phase of chemotherapy.

Skylar's homecoming was a quiet affair, with only her immediately family in attendance, including Doc and Ida. All through the visit, Cat and Billie kept a polite distance between them as Ida and Laurel fretted over the chasm separating their daughters.

"Ida, I don't know what to do to help them," Laurel said. "This entire problem started because of Skylar's attachment to Billie. I can understand why Cat is upset about that. Believe me, I know from personal experience how Cat feels, but both our daughters are being so damned stubborn about this whole thing. So stubborn that their marriage just may fall apart because of it. We can't let that happen," Laurel stated vehemently.

Ida sat and contemplated Laurel's words, thinking of her own childhood, and how Alex had basically provided nearly all the mothering even though Jo was her birth mother. Then it hit her. "Of course," Ida said out loud, placing a hand on her sister's arm.

"What is it, Ida?" Laurel asked.

"I know just the person who can help straighten this mess out," she exclaimed.

"Who?" Laurel asked anxiously.

"Josephine Wycliffe," replied Ida.

Laurel looked at her with wide eyes. "Yes! It's perfect. Ida, you're a genius. Let's call her right now," Laurel suggested.

Both women slipped off to the guestroom to make a phone call to Charleston, South Carolina.

Laurel stood by looking at her sister as Ida made the call.

I would love to have grown up with you, Ida, Laurel thought. *These past few days of getting to know you have been wonderful. Nona and Jo did a good job raising you. I am so glad you have welcomed me into your life.*

Laurel wiped away an errant tear from the corner of her eye as Ida made the call to Charleston.

The phone was answered on the third ring. "SpireClyffe Acres" said a man's voice on the other end of the line.

"Good evening, Chet, this is Ida. Is either of my mothers home?" she asked.

"I'm sorry, Miss Ida, but Miss Alex and Miss Josephine are on an historical lecture circuit in Rome. They aren't due back for another three weeks," he said.

"Damn," Ida swore under her breath.

"Would you care to leave a message, Ma'am?" Chet asked.

"Yes, please have them call me at home, or call Laurel at Billie's when you hear from them. All right. Thank you Chet. Goodbye," Ida said, hanging up the phone. "They're in Rome," she said, looking at her sister.

"Damn," Laurel said.

"Mom?" Cat said from the doorway to Laurel's room.

Ida and Laurel spun around at the sound of Cat's voice, guilty looks on both their faces.

"Cat," Ida exclaimed, seeing her daughter eye them suspiciously.

"We're cutting the cake if you'd like to join us," Cat said.

"Of course, dear, of course. We'll be right there," Ida said.

"Phew. That was close," Laurel said after Cat left the room.

"Phew, is right," Ida said. "Now, let's go welcome our granddaughter home, proper-like as Nona likes to say."

"Proper-like, indeed," repeated Laurel as she locked arms with her sister and headed for the kitchen.

* * *

Laurel decided to go home with Ida for a few days to give Cat and Billie full reign of their home while they became familiar with living as a family under one roof again.

The silence in the house was deafening after the grandparents left and the children had been put to bed.

Billie retreated to the family room where she knelt on one knee in front of the fireplace, poking randomly at the dying embers, staring at the glow, but seeing nothing.

Cat came half way down the stairs and sat on the steps, bending her upper body forward and hugging her legs. She sat there for a long moment watching Billie poke at the fire.

Billie was aware of her presence, but did nothing to initiate conversation.

"Billie," Cat finally said, breaking the silence. "It's very late. You should try to get some sleep."

"I'm not tired, Cat," was all Billie said.

"Well, I'm going to bed. Try not to stay up too late, okay?" she said as she rose to her feet.

"Goodnight, Cat," Billie said, still not turning to look at the woman.

Cat sighed deeply as she turned and climbed the stairs to the kitchen.

It's going to be a long night, she thought sadly.

Hearing her go, Billie dropped down to sit on the floor, letting the poker fall into the ashes and wrapping her long arms around her legs which she had brought up into her chest. Resting her chin on her knees, she blinked away the tears and stifled a yawn.

It's going to be a long night, she thought sadly.

* * *

In the middle of the night, Cat woke suddenly. Sitting up, she looked around in the darkness. "Billie?" she said, feeling around the bed for her wife, but not finding her there.

Cat climbed out of bed and went in search of Billie, heading directly down stairs to the family room. She found the room to be eerily dark, the ashes in the fireplace long since dead and cold. A check of Laurel's room and the couch in the living room also turned up empty. Climbing the stairs to the second story, she checked each child's room, tucking them in as she went. First Seth, then Tara and finally Skylar, where she finally found Billie asleep, wrapped around her youngest daughter.

Cat approached the pair and stood there watching them sleep, tears cascading down her cheeks at the sense of loss she was feeling in her heart.

"Go to bed, Cat," Billie said, startling her.

"Billie?" Cat asked, sobbing. Cat wanted desperately to ask Billie to come to bed, to hold her and comfort her.

"I said go to bed," Billie repeated, making it clear that she planned on staying with Skylar all night.

Cat fled to her room and threw herself down on the bed, crying herself to sleep.

* * *

Billie paused at the end of the driveway the next morning and stretched before starting her run. Like so many other mornings, Jen showed up moments later. Billie waited as her friend approached. She hadn't seen her since she left her with Cat in the restaurant five days ago.

"Good morning," Jen said.

"Good morning, Jen," Billie replied

"You look like hell, big guy," Jen remarked.

"I love you too, Jen," Billie answered as they started their run.

Running side by side, they covered their normal five-mile route without a word of discussion, stopping at their usual place for coffee and half-mile cool-down walk back to their homes.

"Wanna talk about it?" Jen asked as they walked side by side, sipping their coffee.

"Not much to talk about, Jen. Sky is home. She's sleeping in her own room. I'm sleeping with her," Billie said.

"You're sleeping with her?" Jen asked incredulously. "Is that by choice, Billie?" she added.

"Yes," she replied.

"How does Cat feel about that?" she asked.

"I don't care how Cat feels about that," she said coldly.

Jen stopped and placed a hand on Billie's arm, effectively stopping her as well. "You don't care? Why don't I believe that, Billie?"

"Believe what you'd like. That's the way it is. I feel better being close to Sky. Since Cat won't allow her in our room, I'll go to her. It's just that simple," she finished.

"Nothing is just that simple, my friend. Billie, you and Cat have to find a way to work this out or there will be nothing left between you. Don't you see that?" Jen asked.

"Jen, there was a time when I thought Cat and I shared everything...*everything*, right down to our children," Billie said passionately, her eyes becoming moist at the exclamation. "Now, I'm not so sure."

Jen was crying now. Reaching up, she touched the side of her friend's face. "Billie, I can't bear to see you and Cat in so much pain. I love you both so much. I'm so afraid of losing you," she cried.

Billie took Jen into her arms and held her close, crying with her. "Jen, no matter what happens between Cat and me, you will always be my friend. I love you too, Jen. I always will," she said.

Jen suddenly turned macho on Billie. Pulling out of her arms, she said, "Look at us, acting like babies," she said. "I'm not through with you and Cat yet, Billie. I won't give up on the two of you, even if you've given up on yourselves," she said. "Look, the kids will be waking up soon, I've gotta run. Tomorrow morning, same time?" she asked.

"Same time, Jen," Billie replied as they ran to their respective homes.

* * *

Billie showered quickly, wanting to avoid any potential confrontation with Cat. Normally, she would welcome the company and their morning playtime. It was traditionally their favorite way to start the day. Under the present circumstances, however, she was in no mood for such an encounter. As luck would have it, Cat slept through her shower. Billie even managed to rummage through the dresser, collecting her clothes for the day and to clothe herself without waking her. Moments later, she was dressed and had her long wet hair combed out. Slipping her shoes on, she left the room to check on Skylar, looking back one more time at a still-sleeping Cat.

* * *

Cat lay there listening to the shower run. She was tempted to climb in behind Billie and work her into a sexual frenzy like she had so many times before. It was one of their favorite ways to start the day. However, this morning, Cat didn't think Billie would appreciate her company, so she remained in bed, feigning sleep as her wife showered, then moved around the room collecting her clothes and getting dressed. Soon, she heard Billie leave the room. Rolling over, she watched the door close behind her. Cat buried her face in the pillow to stifle the sound of her tears.

* * *

"Sky, honey, sit still, please," Cat instructed her daughter, who was sitting in the kitchen chair, squirming, as Cat was trying to inject the phase-II chemo treatment into the catheter. Billie stood by the counter, sipping coffee as she watched Cat struggle with the child.

"Skylar, do as Mama says," Billie added.

Skylar continued to squirm.

"Sky, please," Cat said again, sending a visual plea for help in Billie's direction.

Billie put her coffee cup on the table and reached down to scoop Skylar into her arms then sat down with the child in her lap. "Hold still," she said as she reached into her pocket for a quarter. Tilting the child's head back, she placed the quarter on her nose. "If it doesn't fall off between now, and the time Mama is done with your medicine, you can keep it, okay?" Billie asked the child.

Skylar grinned, almost causing the quarter to fall as she whispered the word *okay* to her mother. Skylar sat as still as a statue for several moments as Cat injected the treatment into the catheter.

"All finished," Cat said, marveling at Billie's innovative approach to parenting.

"Okay, Mommy?" Skylar asked.

"Okay, rugrat, it's all yours," Billie said, hugging her daughter. "I'm proud of you, sweet pea," she added before putting the child down on the floor to face Cat, who tucked her catheter into the pouch strapped to her back.

"Now, you let us know if you start to feel funny, or if you need to throw up, okay?" Cat said before kissing her daughter on the cheek and sending her into the family room to play with her sister.

"Okay, Mama," Skylar said as she skipped off happily to show her quarter to her big sister.

Cat looked up at Billie and smiled. "Thank you," she said. "You're a good mom, Billie," she added.

"Am I, Cat? You didn't think so about a week ago," she commented.

Cat shook her head from side to side. "Billie, I..."

"Mom! Skylar is throwing up all over the place down here," Tara yelled from the family room.

"Damn," Cat exclaimed as she rose to her feet and headed down the stairs.

Billie detoured to the broom closet for the mop bucket, then headed down behind her, heading back up a few minutes later wearing soiled clothing and carrying a sick Skylar in her arms.

"It's all right, love. I've got you. Mommy's got you, sweetheart," she said soothingly into her daughter's ear as she headed directly to her own room, Skylar in tow.

Stripping them both down, she turned the shower on and slipped under the spray, holding the little girl close to her chest, rocking her back and forth under the warm spray, while humming random tunes to her.

Soon, Skylar was asleep on her mother's shoulder.

Billie turned off the spray then reached out for a warm fluffy towel, which she gingerly wrapped around the sleeping child. Carrying her into their bedroom, she threw the covers back on the bed and placed the towel-wrapped child in the center. After quickly toweling herself dry, Billie slipped a night shift over her own head and crawled in beside her daughter, pulling the blankets up around them.

After ushering the older two children to bed, Cat entered the room, also needing a shower from her cleanup activities. As she entered the room, she locked eyes with Billie, who silently challenged her to object to the sick child sleeping peacefully beside her in their bed. Taking a deep breath, Cat did the unexpected. Instead of losing her temper, she smiled broadly while giving up any attempt to quell the tears that were forming in her eyes.

A short time later, Cat exited the bathroom and approached the bed, a towel wrapped around her still-damp body. She paused by the bed and looked down at Billie and Skylar. Billie made eye contact with Cat as she reached over Skylar's body and grabbed the covers on Cat's side of the bed, yanking them down in invitation. Cat quickly toweled herself dry and slipped a T-shirt over her head, crawling into bed on the other side of Skylar, and pulling the blankets up around herself.

Both women lay on their sides facing each other and their daughter. In a gesture of heartfelt magnanimity, Billie reached her right hand up and held it over Skylar, palm facing Cat. Cat reached her left hand up and interlocked her fingers with Billie's, bringing their entwined hands down to rest on the pillow above Skylar's head. Their eyes locked in silent agreement to keep their daughter safe, even at the cost of their own happiness. Soon, both of them drifted off to sleep, one on each side of their sweet angel.

CHAPTER 14

Life in the Charland home settled into a routine over the next two weeks. Skylar's health remained tentative but stable, allowing both Billie and Cat to return to work, with Laurel staying on to help care for the children who were on summer vacation from school.

Leaving the ailing child each morning was extremely difficult for both mothers.

Cat usually cried all the way to work, trying desperately to regain control over her emotions and professional focus before taking the lives of her patients in her hands under anesthesia.

Billie generally held it together until she arrived at work and had to face Sky's illness all over again by answering Art's inquiries on the little girl's progress. Little did Art know, the reason for Billie's closed door throughout the day was to conceal moments when her attempts to hold it together failed.

By the day's end, both women were anxious to return home, to once more reaffirm their little girl was still in their lives.

Cat continued to give daily injections of phase-II chemotherapy to Skylar through the catheter, and Skylar continued to reject the contents of her stomach shortly after the drugs were administered. Fortunately, this appeared to be the only real side effect, aside from the persistent hair loss. Also fortunate for the little girl was the fact that the upset stomach was short lived, allowing her a mostly normal day after the vomiting had subsided.

During this time, the situation with Billie and Cat was anything but normal. Despite the temporary truce called a few days earlier, Cat continued to object to Billie's desire to have the sick child close to them at night.

"Cat, I don't see what it would hurt, allowing Sky to sleep on a cot in our room," Billie said.

"She needs her independence, Billie. I know she's sick, but coddling her won't make this situation go away any faster."

"Tell me what's really behind your insistence, Cat. Why can't you just admit to yourself that this is nothing but a power struggle over who knows what's best for *your* daughter?"

"That's not fair, Billie."

"Don't tell me what's fair, Cat. What's fair is allowing me equal say in how we care for *our* daughter."

"The problem is, you don't want equal. It's killing you, not being in control for once, isn't it?"

"This isn't about control, Cat. This is about doing what's best for Skylar."

"Well, *I'm* her mother, and *I* know what's best. End of discussion."

The power struggle over Skylar led to frequent confrontations, primarily concerning the children or about their relationship in general...while at the same time, underlying currents of love, regret and longing surfaced between them. One such confrontation was especially explosive.

It was late in the evening, nearly two weeks after Skylar came home from the hospital. The day had passed with relatively little conflict. They even managed to snuggle together while watching a movie with the family after dinner. All was well until it was time to put Skylar to bed for the night. Cat once again insisted she sleep in her own room.

Billie retreated to the family room while Cat tucked the kids in for the night. She squatted before the dying embers and poked at them while waiting for them to die out before joining Skylar for the night. Before long, she sensed Cat's presence on the stairs.

"Go to bed, Cat," she said.

"No, Billie. Not without you," she said.

Billie sighed and dropped her chin to her chest. "Cat, please. I'm in no mood to fight with you tonight," she said.

"Well that's good, because I'm not in the mood to fight either," Cat said, as she moved down the stairs and approached Billie, who was still crouched by the fire.

Billie felt her approach and stood up to her full height, backing up into the mantel to escape Cat's advances.

Cat, however, was not to be deterred as she boldly approached Billie and wrapped her arms around her wife's waist, resting her head between Billie's breasts. "Billie, come to bed. Make love to me," she begged.

Billie grabbed Cat by the arms and pushed her away. "Stop it, Cat. I told you I wasn't in the mood to fight with you tonight," Billie warned.

"This isn't fighting, Billie," Cat reiterated, wrapping her arms around Billie once more, squeezing her bottom with both hands.

Billie fought hard against the sensations that were coursing through her body. "Stop it, Cat, before I do something I'll regret later," she warned the smaller woman.

"The only thing I'll regret, Billie, is living through this night without making love to you. Please Billie. I want you. I need you. Please make love to me. It's been so long," Cat pleaded, reaching behind Billie's neck to pull her head down for a kiss.

"No!" Billie shouted, breaking Cat's hold on her by flinging her arms away, a little harder than she intended.

Cat lost her balance and fell backward, over the coffee table and hit her head on the floor, knocking herself out cold.

Billie stood there, frozen with terror before her senses finally returned to her.

"Cat! Cat!" she exclaimed, lifting Cat off the floor and laying her on the couch. "Oh, my God. Oh, my God," Billie chanted, kneeling beside Cat, unsure of what to do to help her. Luckily for Billie, the commotion was enough to awaken Laurel in the room above them.

"Billie? Billie, what's going on down there?" Laurel called from the kitchen doorway.

Billie ran over to the stairs. "Laurel! Thank God you're awake. Cat is unconscious. I need help," she exclaimed.

Laurel was down the stairs in seconds, leaning over Cat, feeling for injuries. "What happened here, Billie?" Laurel said, suspecting the worse.

Billie was immediately on the defensive. "I didn't hit her, Laurel. Get that out of your mind right away. I would never do that," Billie said adamantly.

"Then tell me what happened," Laurel said pointedly to her daughter.

Billie told her the truth, about her wife's advances and how she had flung Cat's hands away, causing her to stumble backward and fall over the coffee table.

Based on what Billie had said, Laurel found the knot at the back of Cat's head. While she was feeling around the knot, Cat moaned and began to stir. Laurel looked up at Billie. "Do you have an ice pack?" she asked, as she placed a pillow beneath Cat's head.

Billie nodded and quickly ran up the stairs to retrieve it from the kitchen freezer. She returned in seconds and handed it to Laurel, who was talking to a now conscious Cat. She lifted her head and placed the ice pack in the indentation in the pillow, then gently laid her head back down on the couch, right on top of the ice pack.

"Owww," Cat complained.

"Cat...," Billie began, but stopped short when Laurel lifted her hand to silence her.

"Cat," Laurel said. "Cat, can you hear me?"

Cat opened her eyes and nodded.

"Do you know who I am?" she asked.

Cat looked at her mother-in-law. "Laurel," she replied then looking over her shoulder, she saw the target of her earlier amorous affections. "Billie, I'm sorry. I guess no means no, huh?" she said, starting to laugh, but catching herself as her head throbbed at the movement.

Billie was scared to death. "Cat, I'm the one who's sorry. I have never physically hurt you before. I'm so sorry," she said, her voice cracking with emotion.

"It was my fault, Billie. You said no. I didn't listen. I just wanted you to love me," Cat said.

Billie dropped to one knee beside Cat as Laurel moved to stand near the mantel. Taking Cat's hand in her own, she looked directly into Cat's eyes. "Cat, I do love you. I love you more than life itself, but I don't know if I can live with someone who doesn't respect me as an equal," she said. "I thought we had it all, Cat. We had each other, our home, three beautiful children...*our* children, Cat. Not mine, not yours, but *ours*. At least I thought they were. I guess I was wrong. I have learned that with Sky's illness. I'm sorry I presumed the girls to be as much mine as they are yours. I am so sorry for that, Cat, but I love them like they came from my own womb. I always will. For that I will never apologize."

Cat shook her head side to side. "Billie...," she began before Billie rose to her feet and started pacing back and forth, interrupting her before she had a chance to say any more.

"This is worse than divorce," Billie exclaimed. "I feel like I've lost my children as well as my wife, but I know now they were never mine to lose, except for Seth, that is."

Billie stopped to compose herself, looking down at Cat who was a total wreck.

"Cat, I am leaving in the morning," she said, drawing a gasp out of Cat and Laurel.

"Billie, no," Cat said.

"Yes, Cat. Look what I have done to you," she said, motioning to the coffee table. "I've hurt you. I have never done that before tonight. I can't let that happen again," she said.

"Billie, it was my fault. Please don't leave me, Billie. Please," Cat begged while reaching up to grab at Billie's clothing.

Billie took Cat's hands and brought them to her lips. Tears poured from both their eyes as Billie kissed Cat's hands. "I love you, Cat. I always will. Please remember that," she said.

Billie stood and looked at Laurel. "I'm going out. Please see that she makes it to bed. Okay?" she asked.

Seeing Laurel nod, she thanked her mother and climbed the stairs to the kitchen, tears pouring down her face and her heart filled with pain with every plea coming from Cat's mouth as she walked away.

Cat sat on the couch and wrapped her arms tightly around herself, rocking back and forth as she cried out her torment. "Billie, please come back. I'm so sorry...so sorry," she cried.

Laurel's heart was breaking as her head waged battle with her heart. On one hand, she too, was disturbed by Cat's behavior leading to this rift with her daughter. On the other hand, her heart was bleeding and aching for her as she felt her pain. She also felt hurt and confused that Billie had rejected Cat's attempt to make amends. The love between these women was so real, it was tangible, but the chasm that Sky's illness had opened between them was impassable, and no amount of love would close the rift as long as they both allowed their stubbornness to stand in the way.

* * *

Billie didn't go home that night. Instead, she went to work and slept fitfully on the couch in her office. It was there that Art found her the next morning.

"Good morning, Charla...," Art began as he pushed her door open and entered with two cups of coffee. "Holy shit!" he exclaimed when he saw her. Quickly closing and locking her door, he went to sit by her and handed her the extra coffee he had brought.

"Here, strong and black. Looks like you need it this morning. You look like hell, Billie. What in God's name happened?" he asked.

Billie sat on the edge of the couch, her face pale and puffy from crying the night before, her hair a tangled mess, her jeans and T-shirt wrinkled from being slept in. Her head was pounding with a tension headache. "I need drugs," she said, indicating the bottle of pain relievers in her desk.

Art rummaged through her desk it until he found and retrieved the bottle for her. Opening it, she took out four tablets and downed then with a large drink of coffee, burning her throat as she swallowed. She sat on the couch and leaned her head back on the cushion.

"Kill me now, Art, please. Put me out of my misery," she begged.

"How much did you drink last night, Billie?" he asked seriously, looking around for a bottle.

"Nothing," she answered.

"Nothing? Then what were you high on?" he asked.

"I don't do drugs, Art, you know that," she said feeling the beginnings of anger rise in her chest.

"Look, Billie, I'm sorry if my questions are upsetting you, but damn it woman, you've obviously spent the night here…and you look like shit," he exclaimed. "Now tell me what the hell is wrong."

"Thanks for the compliments. You sure know how to make a girl feel good, my friend," she said, running her hand through her hair. "Don't worry about me. I'm fine."

Art grabbed Billie by the arms. "That's enough, Billie. Now I want a straight answer all right? What the hell happened last night?" he demanded.

Billie met Art eye to eye. "Let go of me," she said in a low, angry voice.

"Not until you tell me what's wrong," Art replied, never breaking eye contact with her.

Billie continued to stare at Art unflinchingly, her jaw continuously clenching, causing the muscles in cheeks to contract repeatedly. Just as stubborn, Art held her captive with his large hands clamped tightly on Billie's upper arms.

Suddenly, Billie started to cry. "I left her, Art. I left Cat and the kids," she said, breaking down in her friend's arms and crying her heart out.

Art wrapped strong arms around his friend while she cried into the front of his shirt. Not knowing what to say, he just held her until the crying subsided.

"Tell me what happened, Billie," he whispered into the side of her head as he held the trembling woman.

"I hurt her, Art. I can't believe I did it, but it's true. I had to leave before something worse happened," Billie whimpered.

Once more, Art took her by the arms and held her a short distance away from him. "What do you mean, you hurt her?" he asked suspiciously.

Billie broke free of his grasp and wiped her eyes with the back of her hand. "It was an accident. She wouldn't leave me alone. She was being persistent. I shoved her. I didn't mean to, but I shoved her and she fell over the coffee table and hit her head," she explained, pacing back and forth in front of him. "She was unconscious, Art. I didn't know what to do. Thank God Laurel was there," she added.

"Is she all right?" Art asked.

Billie nodded. "She was okay when I left. Although I'm sure she'll have one hell of a headache this morning," she explained.

Art sat back on the edge of the desk and crossed his arms over his chest. "So how did it happen? I mean, why was she after you?" he asked.

Billie stood in front of her friend with her hands on her hips. "It's a long story, Art," she said.

"We have time. Now spill it," he insisted.

Over the next half-hour, she told Art everything, from her arguments with Cat over Skylar's parentage, to the lack of physical closeness between her and Cat over the past month, to Cat's amorous advances that ended up with Billie injuring the one person she loved more than life itself.

"I had to leave, don't you see, Art? I hurt her. I can't risk that happening again," she said.

"Billie, it was an accident. The real issue here is trust, not the risk of physical harm. Damn it Billie, are you sure you want to leave her and the children at a time like this, I mean, with Skylar sick and everything?" he asked.

"I had to Art. We were miserable. It was just a matter of time before the kids were miserable too. I'm not deserting Sky. I will spend time with her every day. I'll still be there for her if she needs me. I just can't live like that any longer," Billie tried to explain.

Raising her arms in the air to stress her point, she continued. "I feel like a second-class citizen in my own home, Art. I feel like I have no say…no control over anything. Hell, I'm not even sure that my own son would come with me if he was asked to take sides," she explained in a teary voice. "I have lost everything I love, Art. It breaks my heart to see it all within my reach, knowing I am unable to claim any of it."

"You don't know that you've lost them, Billie," Art said. "You said Cat was trying to be affectionate with you. It sounds like she was ready to put all of this behind her. You haven't lost her, Billie."

Cat looked at Art through heavily hooded eyes. "Art, there is a huge difference between being wanted, and being needed. She didn't want me, she needed what I could give her. I will not prostitute myself, Art, not even for Cat," she explained.

Art nodded, understanding the stubborn pride that was keeping his friend from selling herself short. "Is there any hope for a truce?" he asked.

Billie dropped heavily onto the couch and rubbed her face roughly with her hands. "A few days ago I thought we had come to a truce for Skylar's sake, but that very night, I tried again to suggest that Skylar share our room, but Cat immediately pulled rank on me and refused to consider it. The truce went out the window. The momentary closeness we felt was gone. The very foundation of our relationship was shattered, Art, so easily shattered that it makes me wonder if it was ever really strong. She doesn't respect me, and quite frankly, I can't live with that," she said sadly.

Art rose from his seat and paced back and forth, running his hand over his short, curly hair.

"I won't pretend to understand your motives, Billie, but I will give you the support you need to get back on your feet. You're coming home with me. In fact, we'll both take the day off and head home right now. I'll just give Marge a call to make sure the guest room is ready for you," he said as he left her office.

* * *

Cat sat at the kitchen table, her aching head in her hands. Reaching out, she accepted the painkillers and glass of water Laurel handed to her. "Thank you," she said, looking up at her mother-in-law and tearing up at Billie's resemblance to her.

"My God, Billie looks so much like you," she commented as she took the medication.

"I'm not so sure that's a compliment at this point," Laurel commented as she felt the back of Cat's head to see if the lump had subsided from the impact it had suffered the night before.

"Oww, there it is," Cat said quickly as Laurel's deft fingers found the injury.

"It's still a bit swollen. Do you want another ice pack?" Laurel asked.

"No. It'll be all right as soon as the meds kick in," Cat replied, trembling visibly.

Laurel stood behind Cat and wrapped her arms around her. Cat let her head fall back onto Laurel's shoulder and her hand came up to cover the arms wrapped around her neck.

"Are you all right, dear?" Laurel asked.

Cat's shoulders began to shake. "No, I'm not," Cat said. "Laurel, she is my heart, I can't live without her."

Releasing her, Laurel came around and sat in the chair adjacent to Cat. "Do you have any idea where she might have gone?" she asked her daughter-in-law.

"I don't know. Jen's maybe, or Art's," she replied.

"Well, then maybe we need to make a few phone calls," Laurel said, rising to her feet just as the phone began to ring. "I'll get it," she said. "Hello?" she said into the receiver.

"Hello, Cat?" Art asked.

"No this is Laurel, but Cat is right here. May I ask who is calling?" She said politely.

"Art," he replied.

Cat had risen to her feet at the sound of her name and was standing there ready to accept the receiver from Laurel.

"Art," Laurel mouthed while handing it to Cat.

"Art," Cat said eagerly into the phone. "Is Billie with you?" she asked.

"Yes she is. She's in the shower right now. Cat, are you all right? Billie told me what happened last night," he said.

"I'm fine, Art. My head hurts, but other than that, I'm fine. Did Billie tell you it was an accident?" Cat asked.

"The way she described it sure sounded like an accident to me, but you know Billie. She's feeling very guilty about it," he replied.

"Art, has she said anything about coming home?" Cat asked.

Silence.

"Art?" Cat said, fear clutching at her heart, knowing what the silence meant. "Art, please tell me she's coming home," Cat begged, a pathetic quiver tingeing her voice.

"I'm sorry, Cat. She was adamant about that when I found her sleeping in her office this morning. Between the injury and what she keeps referring to as *the loss of her children*, I think she has completely lost hope that you'll ever be a real family again. I'm sorry," he explained.

Cat covered her mouth with her hand to stifle her sobs. "Art, I have been such a fool," she cried. "Please tell her I love her, that we all love her, okay?" Cat asked shakily.

Art's voice cracked on the other end of the line. "Sure Cat," he said, cleaning his throat. "I'll...um, I'll tell her."

"Thanks, Art. Goodbye." Hanging up the phone, Cat collapsed into Laurel's arms.

Art reached over and placed the receiver in the cradle, then with one hand on his hip, and the other rubbing the back of his neck, he took a deep breath to compose himself before delivering Cat's message. He wasn't sure he could do it without breaking down. *Damn, friendships are hard*, he thought as he headed toward the guest room.

* * *

Cat was once again sitting at the kitchen table with her head in her hands when the door opened and Jen stuck her head in. It had been nearly two weeks since their argument in the restaurant, neither having spoken to the other since.

"Truce?" Jen said as she stepped into the room and revealed a bouquet of freshly cut flowers for Cat.

Cat took one look at her friend and broke down crying.

For once, Jen was dumb struck. It was on the tip of her tongue to make some flippant comment about the flowers not being *that* bad, but common sense told her that Cat was in no mood for jokes.

Cat rose from her chair, putting her arms out for Jen to hold her.

Jen immediately put the flowers on the counter and rushed to her friend, taking her into her arms and holding her close, rubbing her back and cooing soothing words of friendship and love to her. At one point, Jen reached up and put her hand behind Cat's head to hold her closer.

Cat winced as Jen's hand contacted the bump from the accident the night before.

Jen released her immediately and spun her around to check out the source of the pain, finding a large egg on the back of Cat's head.

"Cat, how did this happen?" she demanded angrily, "Did Billie—"

Cat broke away from her friend and took a defensive stance. "No, Jen. It wasn't like that. Why does everyone automatically assume that Billie knocks me around?" Cat asked incredulously. "It was an accident. I was pushing her into something she wasn't ready for. When she objected, I stumbled, lost my balance, and fell over the coffee table. She did not intentionally hurt me, Jen," Cat explained.

Jen was seething with anger. "Where is she, Cat?" Jen asked, wanting to hear the explanation from Billie herself.

"She's gone. She left us last night, after *this* happened," she said, referring to the injury. "I'm afraid I've lost her for good this time," Cat said, starting to cry once more as she dropped into the kitchen chair.

Cat's tears immediately extinguished Jen's anger as she pulled up a chair beside Cat. "Cat, she didn't leave because of the injury. She left because of the way she's been made to feel.

She left because she doesn't think she belongs here anymore. In her mind, the intense sense of family that the two of you have worked so hard to build over the past several years is gone," Jen pointed out.

Cat narrowed her eyes at her friend. "Well obviously Billie feels pretty comfortable airing our dirty laundry in front of you," she said sharply.

Jen leaned forward. "Well who else is she supposed to talk to, Cat? *You* obviously haven't been listening to her lately," she returned hotly.

Cat looked down at her hands. "I...I don't know what you mean," she said softly while avoiding Jen's eyes.

"Cat, when was the last time the two of you actually talked about something other than Sky's illness? When have you spent time with each other lately just to renew who you are as a couple? When was the last time you looked at Billie and really considered her your equal, your partner...the other half of your soul?" Jen asked pointedly.

Cat was unable to answer.

Jen continued. "She feels displaced, Cat. For the past seven years she has been the mother of *three* children. You need to work something out or you will surely lose her for good. Cat, in her heart, the girls are very much her own. I have never met anyone before who has such capacity to love another woman's children as much as she does. You must know that she loves the girls with everything she is," Jen explained. "Her place in this family has become so fragile, that she is now even questioning whether she'll lose the only one of three children that is biologically hers," she added.

"She's afraid of losing Seth? Why? I don't understand," Cat said truthfully.

"Cat, whether you know it or not, you hold incredible power in this family. The sharp tongue and quick anger you have wielded against Billie since Skylar took sick has stripped her of her position and reduced her to a level of insignificance...all because you are afraid of losing the very thing you have stripped from her—her position as mother, protector and hero to a very ill six-year-old child. It may not have been intentional, Cat," Jen said as she saw her friend start to object, "but Billie has seen it. *I* have seen it, and I know Laurel has as well."

Cat made eye contact with Jen for several long moments as the truth of her friend's words sank in. Closing her eyes, she physically deflated right where she sat. Closing her eyes tightly, she allowed the tears to escape that had been threatening to mutiny all morning.

"Jen, I've been such a jealous fool, and I may have lost everything because of it," Cat said, lowering her forehead to rest on the arms she had crossed on the table before her.

Jen reached over and rubbed Cat's back. "Do you still love her, Cat?" she asked.

Cat looked at her friend. "I love her with everything that I am, Jen. I am nothing without her."

Jen smiled through tears of her own. "Well, I think it's time you tell her that," she suggested as Cat nodded in response.

"Mama?" came a tiny voice from the doorway to the living room.

Cat and Jen both turned in the direction of the voice and found Skylar standing there, holding Petey in one hand and rubbing her eye with the balled fist of the other hand. Her pajamas were hanging on her loosely and askew, exposing her rounded belly, her skin pale and pasty.

Jen became alarmed, not having seen the child in nearly two weeks. "God, Cat, she's so thin and pale," she commented without thinking.

Cat looked at her friend with a startled expression on her face, then at her daughter. Having not been around her for so long, Jen saw things that those who saw her daily overlooked. Cat forced herself to look at her daughter with an unbiased, professional eye. Jen was right. She was thin and pale, and her lack of hair and protruding belly gave her the appearance of a third world refugee. Cat gasped when she let herself realize the extent of her daughter's condition.

"Sky, honey, come here," Cat said, reaching out her arms to the child.

Sky walked clumsily to her mother, falling down once between the doorway and the kitchen table, a distance that was a mere ten feet. When she finally reached Cat, she climbed into her mother's arms and cuddled deeply into her neck.

Cat noticed immediately that she was feverish again. "Oh, my God, no," Cat exclaimed as she held her daughter close and cast fearful eyes at her friend.

"Tell me what to do, Cat," Jen said, ready to help.

"Jen, Laurel is reading in her room. Please ask her to keep an eye on Seth and Tara when they get up. I'm taking Sky to the hospital," Cat replied.

Jen ran off to do as she was asked while Cat carried Skylar to her own room and gently placed her on the bed then called Dr. Berry. She threw on a pair of shorts and T-shirt, and was just slipping her feet into her sneakers when Jen and Laurel appeared in her doorway.

"Cat, the baby is ill again?" Laurel asked, fear and concern in her eyes.

"She's pale and feverish, Laurel. Dr. Berry is meeting us at the hospital in fifteen minutes," Cat said, looking at her watch. "I need you to stay with Seth and Tara. Please explain to them what has happened, but don't alarm them until we know more," Cat said.

"Of course, Cat. Do you want me to call Billie?" Laurel asked.

Cat paused for a moment then shook her head. "No. I'll call her if it turns out to be something serious. Until I know what's going on, there's no need to alarm her either," Cat reasoned.

Jen looked at her friend as she tied her shoes. "I don't know if keeping Billie in the dark is wise, Cat," Jen said.

Cat stood up and ran her hands through her hair. "Look," she said impatiently. "My daughter is sick. I don't have time to deal with this. I need to get her to the hospital."

Jen grabbed Cat's arm and got right into her face. "This attitude is what caused Billie to leave in the first place, Cat. You *really* need to decide whether you want her in your life, because with this attitude, it will never happen," Jen warned.

"Thank you so much for the advice, Dr. Ruth," Cat said sarcastically. "Now, if you'll excuse me, I have a sick child to tend to."

"I'm going with you, Cat," Jen said.

Cat looked at her friend. "Suit yourself," she said, lifting Skylar into her arms and heading out to the car with her.

Laurel observed the interaction between Cat and Jen with interest.

I really like this neighbor of yours, Cat. It is obvious how much she cares about you and Billie. Don't give up on her, Jen. Don't give up on them, she thought as she went back downstairs to wait for the other children to rise.

CHAPTER 15

Cat sat in the examination room with Skylar on her lap, waiting for Dr. Berry to return with the blood counts. Jen paced back and forth across the room behind them.

"What is taking them so long?" Jen asked as she continued to pace.

Without thinking, Cat said, "You sound just like Billie."

Realizing what she had said, Cat made eye contact with Jen and gasped. Just then, Dr. Berry entered the room.

Dr. Berry pulled up the stool in front of them and sat down. She looked into Cat's face. "Her ANC count is dropping. It's down to 850, but so far, no sign of abnormal cells," she explained, seeing the relief of Cat's face.

Jen stepped forward. "What does that mean?" she asked.

Dr. Berry looked at Cat for permission to divulge her daughter's condition to this woman. Cat nodded her head.

"What it means, is that the level of red and white blood cells and platelets has dropped, making it hard for her body to fight infection. That explains the fever and paleness," she said. "Before you leave today, I want to do another blood transfusion. Are you up to donating a pint?" she asked Cat.

"It's been less than eight weeks since I last gave her blood," Cat said.

"I'll give her a pint," Jen said. "I'm O-negative."

Dr. Berry looked at Jen and smiled at this woman's willingness to help her friend. "That would be great. Thank you for offering," Dr. Berry replied.

"What could be causing the blood levels to drop, Alexis?" Cat asked.

"Well, the phase-II therapy, perhaps. It's possible that the therapy is too aggressive and is killing off healthy blood cells.

We'll change the combination of drugs today and see what happens," she said.

"Should she be hospitalized again?" Cat asked.

"No, I don't think so. She will have to be kept pretty much isolated from large groups of people though, especially in confined places, at least until her ANC is back near 1000. Oh, and be sure to keep people away from her that have pre-existing infections like colds, chicken pox, measles, you know, things like that," Dr. Berry explained.

"All right," Cat said, beginning to rise.

"I'll get you a week's supply of the new phase-II treatment combo to take home with you before you leave. You'll need to call me the minute you see anything different, good or bad, okay?" Dr. Berry instructed. Seeing Cat shake her head, she said, "All right, let's go draw that blood and make this little girl's fever go away."

* * *

Laurel sat at the kitchen table nursing a cup of coffee while Billie paced the floor behind her.

"Billie, please sit. Have a cup of coffee with me. You're making me nervous pacing like that," Laurel said.

"I don't want coffee, Laurel," Billie replied. "What I want is for Cat to get her ass home. I have a few things I need to say to her."

"Billie, I'm sure she didn't want to alarm you until she knew what was causing Skylar's fever," Laurel suggested.

Billie continued to pace. "Laurel, we've been over this. I have a right to know when one of my children is ill, especially when that child has cancer. There is no excuse for Cat's behavior this time, and I plan to tell her so," she said vehemently.

Laurel wanted more than anything for this rift between Cat and Billie to heal, but she had to admit in her heart of hearts that Billie was right this time. She and Jen had both warned Cat before she left that Billie should be notified. She had even volunteered to make the call, but Cat insisted she would take care of it if Sky's fever turned out to be something serious.

The more Billie paced, the angrier she became. By the time Cat and Jen arrived home with Skylar, she was seething, the anger overtly evident on her face when she met them at the door.

"Billie! What are you doing here? Have you come back home?" Cat asked hopefully.

Billie reached out and took a sleeping Skylar out of Cat's arms. She leaned into Cat's personal space and said in a low, angry voice, "Don't you dare move a muscle. I'm going to put our daughter to bed then we need to talk." She turned on her heel and headed up the stairs to tuck Skylar into bed.

Cat watched her go then looked at her mother-in law with a confused, worried expression on her face.

"She called this morning to talk to the kids, Cat. She totally freaked out when Seth told her you had brought Skylar to the hospital. She's very angry that you didn't call her," Laurel said. "I knew she would be."

Cat looked at Jen who had followed her into the house, and was met with an *I told you so* expression. Turning back to Laurel, she asked, "Where are Seth and Tara?"

"At Jen's house, playing in the pool," Laurel answered, looking at Jen.

"Look, Cat. I'm going to head home and keep the kids there until the coast is clear. Good luck, my friend. Just remember that she really does love you and the kids, okay?" Jen said, placing a kiss on Cat's cheek then beating a hasty retreat before Billie returned.

Just as Jen closed the door, Billie walked purposefully into the kitchen, an angry and determined look on her face. Stopping short when she saw her mother still sitting at the table, she said, "Laurel, could I please talk to my wife alone?"

Laurel rose to her full height, nearly equal to that of her daughter, and looked Billie in the eye.

"I'll leave, Billie, but don't give me reason to come back in here. Do you understand?" she asked firmly.

Billie's eyes narrowed. "I won't hurt her, if that's what you're concerned about, Laurel. I would never do that on purpose," she said angrily.

Laurel just nodded and retreated to her room.

Billie was so angry she took a moment to compose herself before speaking.

Cat watched her curiously as she paced back and forth, running a hand through her hair and obviously trying to quell her anger.

Finally, she stopped with her back to Cat and took a deep breath. "Why, Cat?" she asked.

"Why, what, Billie?" Cat replied.

Billie turned around abruptly. "You know exactly what I'm asking Cat. Why the hell didn't you call me?" she yelled loudly, causing Cat to cringe.

"It was nothing, Billie," Cat said almost flippantly.

Billie slammed her hands down onto the table, making a loud banging noise. "Don't tell me it was nothing, Cat," Billie exclaimed in a loud voice. "A cold is nothing. A scraped knee is nothing. A black eye is nothing, but when your child has cancer, a fever and pale skin is *definitely* something! Damn it, Cat. Don't shut me out. I know you find it hard to believe, but I love her like she is my own. I love all three of them equally Cat. The kids are the only things I have left in my life, please don't take them away from me too," Billie pleaded, the anger fading from her voice to be replaced by heartfelt anguish as she sunk into the kitchen chair and dropped her head into her hands.

Cat never felt so low in her life. Jen was right. She should have called Billie.

"I'm sorry, Billie," Cat said. "You are right. I should have called you. I'm sorry," she said again.

Billie lifted her head and looked at Cat, sorrow and heartache filling her eyes. She closed her eyes once more and rubbed her face with both hands before returning her gaze to Cat's face. "What did Alexis say?" she asked calmly, voiding her voice of all emotion.

Cat thought to herself that Billie looked beaten and allowed a wave of shame and regret to wash over her once more before answering.

"Her ANC has dropped to 850. She's not sure why, but she suspects the phase-II meds were too aggressive, killing off healthy blood cells. She said they saw no traces of abnormal cells in the sample they took this morning. She gave me a new combination of meds to try starting tomorrow," Cat finished.

"Anything else?" Billie asked.

"Yes, Sky was feverish, so they gave her another transfusion before we left. They used Jen's blood," she explained.

Billie shook her head side to side in defeat. "My child needs blood and you don't even allow me the opportunity to give her that. Instead, she has to rely on our friend. Our friend, Cat. I should have been there," she exclaimed.

"You're right, Billie. I was wrong. I would say I'm sorry again, but my words can't take back the pain I have caused," Cat replied sadly.

Billie nodded her head then rose to her feet.

"Where are you going?" Cat asked.

"To lie down with my daughter. I want to be there when she wakes up. Is that all right with you?" she asked sarcastically.

Cat just nodded as Billie headed for the living room. Watching her walk away, Cat felt like a total fool.

Why? Why have I done this to her? she asked herself.

Unable to answer her own question, she dropped her face into her hands and cried out her sorrow and regret for the bad decisions she had made that morning.

Having been summoned from her room by the loud banging on the kitchen table, Laurel remained hidden just beyond the doorway to the living room during the exchange between her daughter and Cat, ready to interfere in the event the confrontation in the kitchen became violent. As Billie announced her intention to lie down with Skylar, Laurel slipped away to her room once more to pray to whoever would listen, to heal the wounds that were slowing killing the love that this family was built on.

* * *

Cat was still sitting at the table a half-hour later with her head in her hands when the phone rang. Cat made no attempt to answer it, knowing Laurel was in the house and would probably pick it up. She was right. A moment later, Laurel appeared in the doorway carrying the portable phone.

"It's for you," she said. "You might want to take it in my room where you'll have more privacy," Laurel suggested.

Cat looked at Laurel suspiciously as she accepted the cordless phone from her. Walking into her mother-in-law's room, she sat on the edge of the bed and clicked the phone on. "Hello, this is Cat," she said into the receiver.

"Cat, this is Jo," the voice on the other end announced.

"Grandma Jo!" Cat exclaimed.

"Don't you, *Grandma Jo* me, young lady," Jo said, making Cat sit back a bit startled. "What the hell are you doing, woman?" Josephine asked.

"I…I don't know what you mean," Cat said, confused about why her grandmother would be yelling at her.

"I've been talking to your mother, girl, and I know all about what's been going on in that thick skull of yours. Must be the Wycliffe blood you inherited. Christ, Cat, do you have any idea what you're doing to Billie?" she scolded.

Cat was getting angry…angry with both her mother and grandmother for interfering. "Look, Grandma Jo," she began.

"Don't interrupt me, Caitlain," she said.

Cat knew she was in trouble when Jo used her real name. Grandma Jo *never* used her real name.

"Now you listen to me, and you listen good. When your mother was born, I knew what kind of parent I would be. I knew I wasn't capable of giving her the type of love and affection that normally comes from a mother. I loved her. I loved her very much, but it was a fatherly type of love, Cat. Without Alex there to provide a woman's touch, your mother would have turned out very differently. I thank God daily for that woman of mine.

"I intentionally set out to get pregnant so that Alex could have a child, Cat, and I knew right from the beginning that this child would only get the kind of mothering it needed from Alex. I was grateful every day for her presence in my life, and her role in our daughter's life. We complement each other Cat...just like you and Billie.

"You cannot provide everything your children need. That is nearly impossible for one person to do. Let her help you, Cat. You gave her that right when you allowed her to put a ring on your finger, and when you gave your children her name. Don't take away what's rightfully hers. If you do, you'll regret it until the day you die," Jo finally finished.

Several moments of silence passed before Jo spoke again.

"Cat, are you still there?" she asked.

"I'm here," Cat said emotionally.

"Good. I hope you heard and understood everything I said, girl. Your future happiness and the happiness of your children depend on it," Jo said.

"I understand, Grandma Jo," Cat said, crying steadily now. "I've been a fool. Do you think she'll forgive me?" Cat asked.

"Well, you won't know until you ask, will you? Don't put it off, Cat. It will only get harder the longer you wait," she advised.

"I love you, Grandma Jo," Cat said.

"Ditto, little one. Kiss the babies for me, okay? Keep your chin up, sweetheart. Sky will be fine. I can feel it in these old bones. She can't help but be a survivor. She has Wycliffe blood running through her veins after all," Jo said.

"Thank you, Grandma Jo. Kiss Grams for me too, okay? I love you both, Bye," Cat said, clicking off the cordless.

Cat sat there for several moments looking at the floor before she allowed herself to fall onto Laurel's bed and cry herself to sleep.

* * *

Skylar woke up before Billie. Opening her eyes, she saw her beloved Mommy lying next to her. Grinning ear to ear, the little girl rolled onto her side and started playing a game they had developed over the past few weeks of sleeping together.

Very delicately, Skylar started touching Billie's face. The object of the game was to see how many times they could touch without waking their victim up. Skylar learned early on that the lighter the touch, the more successful she was. Eight touches later, Billie suddenly grabbed Skylar's hand, causing the child to squeal in delight.

Rolling her onto her back and pinning her to the mattress, Billie kissed the child on the nose and asked, "How many touches this time?"

"Eight," she said proudly, grinning ear to ear.

"A new record, dumpling. I'm proud of you," she said, kissing the child once more.

Skylar reached up and placed both hands on either side of Billie's face. "Mommy, you were gone when I woke up this morning. Where were you?" she asked seriously. "Did you sleep with Mama last night?"

Billie smiled crookedly as she looked down on her daughter. "No, sweetheart, I had some things to take care of," she said.

"Will you sleep with me tonight?" she asked.

"I don't know, baby, we'll see," Billie said. "How are you feeling, Sky?" Billie asked, feeling the child's forehead for fever and finding it cool.

"Dr. Berry made my hot go away," Skylar said.

"That's good. Hey, are you hungry?" Billie asked.

"Can I have some ice cream?" the child inquired.

"You know, I just was thinking about how good an ice cream cone would taste right about now," Billie exclaimed picking the child up and hefting her onto her back for a horsey ride down the stairs to the kitchen.

Billie and Skylar entered the kitchen at the same time Seth and Tara came home from Jen's. Both children walked into the house wrapped in towels, dripping wet from their swim in Jen's pool.

"Hey, rugrats," Billie exclaimed. "We were just thinking about scooping up some ice cream cones. You interested?" she asked.

Wide grins appeared on the older children's faces.

"Cool!" said Seth.

"Count me in," exclaimed Tara.

"Good. Why don't you get out of those wet bathing suits while I dish it up? Oh, and don't forget to bring your suits and towels back down stairs and throw them over the line," she said to two retreating backs.

Billie sat Skylar on the counter top and put her in charge of handing her sugar cones while she filled each one. Soon, all three children were sitting happily around the kitchen table eating ice cream. Cat came upon the scene as Billie was dishing up a cone for herself. Looking at her wife and then at the children, she offered the cone to Cat.

"Interested in an ice cream cone, Mama?" Billie said to Cat.

Cat looked at Billie with pain etched into her brow. She knew the offer was for the children's benefit, so she accepted the cone, thanking Billie with a genuine smile. Their eyes locked for a long moment before Billie looked away to fix another cone.

Cat and Billie stood side by side, leaning against the counter watching the children's animated conversation while they ate their ice cream. When they were finished, Cat retrieved a damp face cloth from the bathroom and washed the ice cream from Skylar's face and hands before sending her into the family room to watch movies with her brother and sister.

Suddenly, they were alone in the kitchen. An uncomfortable silence settled over them as they avoided looking at each other. Finally, Cat broke the silence.

"Thank you for including me in the ice cream treat, Billie," she said.

Billie just nodded and looked at the floor. An uncomfortable tension filled the air.

Suddenly, both women spoke at once.

"Billie."

"Cat."

Cat giggled nervously. "Go ahead, Billie, you first," she said.

"No, Cat. What were you going to say?" Billie insisted.

Cat took a deep breath and faced her wife. Reaching out, she touched Billie's arm before speaking. "Billie, I have been a fool," she said. "Honey, I'm sorry. You are right. The children are *ours*. They always have been. You give them something I can't. We complement each other Billie. They need you as much as they need me," Cat admitted. "My jealous heart wasn't allowing me to see that before. I love you with everything I am, Billie. We need you. I need you, and the children need you. Please forgive me, Billie. Come home to us, love—please," Cat finished, hopeful tears running down her face.

Billie looked at Cat and swallowed hard. *Does she really mean it?* she thought. *God, I need some time to think. I need space. I want this desperately, but I need it to be real. I need it to be permanent.*

Billie took a few steps away from Cat then turned around to look at her. She raised her arms to the sides. "Cat, I don't know what to say."

"Say yes, Billie. Say you'll come home. Say we will love and cherish each other again forever. Please say we can put this behind us and start over," Cat pleaded.

Billie was terrified of being hurt again. Her heart was telling her to take Cat into her arms and never let her go, but her head was raising red flag after red flag. Unfortunately for Cat, her head won the tug of war with her heart.

"I can't, Cat. I need time to think. I'm sorry," she said, heading for the door. Stopping just before she left, she turned and said, "I'll be at Art's if you need me, Cat. I'm sorry."

Cat crumbled to the floor crying, as the door shut behind Billie.

On the porch just outside the window, close to where Billie and Cat were having their discussion, Laurel sat in a lawn chair, reading a book. The book closed sharply as she heard her daughter reject Cat's plea for forgiveness.

CHAPTER 16

Cat sat alone in the dark family room, save the light from the dying fireplace. Staring straight ahead, she agonized over a future without Billie.

I can't blame her for rejecting me, Cat thought. *Look at the way I have treated her for the past month. There is only so much pain a person can endure before they build a wall around their heart. God, Billie, I'm so sorry for being the architect of that wall. Please forgive me, my love.*

"Cat, are you all right?" Laurel asked from her position at the bottom of the stairs.

Cat turned to look at her mother-in-law. Feigning a weak smile, she replied, "I'm fine, Laurel."

Laurel approached her and kissed her on the forehead. "You don't seem fine, Cat," she said, sitting down next to her.

Cat reached out and placed her hand in Laurel's. "I'm a survivor, Laurel. As Grandma Jo is fond of saying, *I have Wycliffe blood in my veins after all*. I'll get through this, one way or another," she said, returning her gaze to the fire.

"Do you think she'll come home?" Laurel asked.

Cat wiped a tear from the corner of her eye. Taking a deep breath and putting on a brave front, she looked at Laurel. "I don't know," she replied. "I can only hope and pray that she will."

Suddenly, the damn broken, and the front Cat tried so hard to maintain crumbled against the pressure. Covering her eyes with her hands, she sobbed violently, taking gasping breaths as she fought to control her emotions.

Laurel wrapped her arms around Cat and held her close as she cried. "Billie loves you, Cat. I know she does," the older woman said in soothing tones.

"No, Laurel. I've lost her," Cat whimpered. "To tell you the truth, I don't blame her for not wanting to come home. I have been so horrible to her over the past several weeks. I don't know what's wrong with me. She deserves so much better," Cat added between sobs.

"No she doesn't, Cat. Everyone has faults, even Billie. Heaven knows I have my share. In the short time I've been here, I can see how stubborn she can be," Laurel said, expressing her opinion.

"She's being true to herself and to the kids, Laurel. I am the one who has betrayed her. I deserve whatever stubbornness she chooses to dish out," Cat replied.

Laurel looked at Cat intently, watching the reflection of the fire dance across her china doll features. Even though she didn't fully understand the gay lifestyle, she could clearly see what it was about Cat that Billie loved so much.

My daughter is a fool for rejecting this beautiful woman, and I intend to tell her as much, Laurel decided.

"Neither of you deserves to be as miserable as you both are. Cat, I know she loves you, and she needs you. You need each other. Don't give up hope, okay?" Laurel said, leaning over to kiss Cat on the cheek. "Well, dear, I'm beat. Those grandchildren of mine wear me out. Don't stay up too long, all right?" she said, rising and excusing herself.

"Laurel?" Cat said as her mother-in-law headed for the stairs.

Laurel stopped short and looked at Cat. "Yes dear?" she replied.

"Thank you for being here," Cat expressed. "I can't tell you how much your presence has helped."

Laurel approached Cat once more and kissed her on top of the head. "No Cat," she said, "I should be thanking you for allowing me to be a part of your lives…yours and my grandchildren's. I will always be grateful for that. Goodnight, dear," she said before finally leaving Cat alone to stare at the fire.

Cat remained on the couch for several more hours, watching the fire and wiping the tears from her eyes.

* * *

"Jimmy, this is Billie. Have you had any luck with that missing persons report I asked for yesterday? Yes, that's the one. All right, tomorrow is soon enough. Okay. Thanks Jimmy. I'll talk to you later then, bye,"

Billie hung up her office phone. Turning to the stack of paper in front of her, she began to organize the brief that was spread out all over her desk. The deposition was in two days, and there was still a lot of work to do on the case.

Not for the first time that morning, she congratulated herself on getting to work early that morning. Rising early had not been difficult given the tossing and turning she had done all night as she was totally unable to sleep after her confrontation with Cat.

Just as she was beginning to make sense of the disorganized mess in front of her, the buzzer sounded on her intercom. Pressing the message button, she said, "Yes Deb?"

"Billie, there is someone here to see you. She says she's your mother," the secretary's voice said over the speaker.

Laurel? Billie thought. "Does she look like me, Deb?" Billie asked.

"She looks exactly like you, Billie," Deb replied.

"Send her in," she responded into the phone.

A moment later, Laurel walked in and perched on the corner of Billie's desk. She was dressed in a very elegant blue suit, which hugged her still firm curves and shapely legs. "Do you always screen your calls like that, Billie?" she asked.

"Sometimes," Billie answered, walking over to the coffee machine and refilling her mug, but not offering a cup to her mother. "What brings you here today, Laurel?" she asked.

Setting her clutch down on the edge of Billie's desk, she looked directly at her daughter and said, "I've come to tell you what a fool you are, Billie."

Billie raised her eyebrows into her hairline. "Excuse me?" she said.

"What part of that didn't you understand? Do you have any idea what you did to Cat yesterday?" Laurel asked.

Billie put her coffee cup down on the table and crossed her arms in front of her. "I fail to see where this is any of your business, Laurel," Billie said.

"Oh, this is definitely my business, Billie," Laurel replied.

"How so?" Billie asked.

"Because I've been there. Cat begged for your forgiveness yesterday, and you flat out rejected her. Don't walk out on your wife and children, Billie. It will be the biggest mistake of your life," Laurel warned her.

Billie approached her mother, stopping within inches of her. Leaning down, Billie said directly into her face, "You had no problem walking out on me, Laurel. You sold me for drug money. Remember? Why did you do that, Laurel? Did you think selling your child was easier than spreading your legs for drugs?"

Slap!

Billie found herself sprawled out on the couch behind her, holding her face, an angry Laurel standing over her.

"I am sick to death of hearing you throw that in my face, Billie," Laurel shouted angrily. "I *know* what I did was wrong. Believe me, I live with it every single day of my life. Can't you see I'm trying to help you avoid the same mistake? Damn it, Billie, put aside that goddamned pride of yours and go home. Cat needs you. Sky needs you. They all do. You will never be needed more by anyone else in your entire life as you are right now. Don't you know that? For Christ's sake Billie, don't let your daughter die thinking her mother has deserted her!"

Laurel walked back to the desk and picked up her clutch. Approaching a dazed Billie once more, she said, "I will never get the chance to right my wrong, Billie—you are certainly seeing to that, but God willing, you have the chance to avoid yours. Don't blow it. I am going home now to take the children to the park for a few hours. You need to decide for yourself what to do, but it had better be a decision you can live with for the rest of your life."

That said, she turned on her heel and left, slamming the office door behind her.

* * *

Billie sat there, holding the side of her face which was developing into a warm red welt. She couldn't believe Laurel had slapped her. She was even more amazed that she didn't see it coming.

You're getting old, Charland, a voice taunted her, *or maybe you let her do it because you know she's right,* said another voice.

Billie stared straight ahead, replaying her mother's words over and over in her mind.

Cat needs you, Sky needs you. They all do. You will never be needed more by anyone else in your entire life as you are right now. Don't you know that?...It had better be a decision you can live with for the rest of your life...You know she's right...you know she's right...you know she's right.

Billie jumped to her feet and headed for the door. Walking quickly through the outer office, she said to Deb as she passed her desk, "Cancel all my meetings. I'll be gone for the rest of the day." Moments later, she was in her car, desperate to get home to Cat.

Billie pulled the car to a screeching halt in the driveway then jumped out and ran into the house. Cat was in the kitchen putting the milk back into the refrigerator.

"Billie!" she said, surprised to see her there. "You just missed the kids. Laurel..."

"Laurel took them to the park. I know. Cat, I'm here to see you," Billie said, stopping directly in front of Cat.

Cat looked up at her, a mixture of love, anxiety and expectation on her face. "Billie?" she said reaching up, "What happened to your face?"

Billie placed her hands on both sides of Cat's face and looked into the emerald green pools. "I ran into someone smarter than me, Cat," she began. "But never mind that for now. Cat, I have been such a fool. You begged for my love and forgiveness last night and I let my pride get in the way of accepting your apology. Cat, I couldn't let myself forgive you so fast. I was afraid of being hurt again, afraid of sending the message that it's okay to step on my heart."

Cat took a step forward and reached out with her hand. "Billie...I'm..."

"No, Cat. I have so much that needs to be said. Please..." Billie interrupted, wanting desperately to address the issues head on.

Billie took a few steps away from Cat and ran her left hand through her hair; her right hand perched on her hip before continuing.

"Damn it Cat, I love the girls like they are my own. When you pulled rank on me over Skylar...God, Cat, I thought I had lost everything I loved in this world. It tore my heart out," she said, lowering her hands and turning her back on Cat in an attempt to compose herself.

She turned back to face Cat. "I will accept nothing less than equal parentage. Tara was only four when we met. She stole my heart the minute I laid eyes on her. I have been there from the beginning with Sky. I saw you through the pregnancy, I cut the cord. I have been there for her from the first breath she took. I love her, Cat. I love her *and* Tara like they came from me.

"And Seth...Seth may be mine biologically, but in all other respects, he is yours. He is so much like you, Cat it is so easy to forget he didn't come from you. I would never dream of taking him from you. If I walked out that door today and he opted to stay with you, it would rip my heart from my chest, but I would leave knowing he would be loved and cared for."

Turning to face Cat again, Billie almost lost her resolve as she saw the regret and anguish on Cat's face. She closed her eyes for a moment to compose herself and replenished her resolve before continuing.

"I love you Cat. I love you with all my heart, but I need to feel that this family is mine. I don't know any other way to explain it. They are *my* children too. If you can't understand that, then there is no hope for us," Billie concluded, just barely able to get the last words out before losing her voice in a cascade of emotions.

Cat lowered her chin to her chest, feeling very low and unworthy of Billie's love. She wrapped her arms around her midsection and walked across the kitchen, stopping at the door to stare out the window. Shame prevented her from looking directly at Billie.

"Billie, I'm sorry," she said without turning around. "I don't know what came over me. No. No, that's not true. I *do* know," she said.

"Cat, please look at me. I need to see your eyes," Billie asked softly from her position across the room.

Cat slowly turned around and looked directly at Billie, making and maintaining eye contact. She approached Billie tentatively, not know how she would react, but threw hesitation to the wind when Billie opened her arms to her.

Going willingly to Billie, she wrapped her arms around her wife's waist and rested her head on Billie's chest as Billie enveloped her in a warm embrace. She felt herself melt into Billie's arms as she absorbed all the love radiating from her.

For a long moment, they held each other and allowed love to weld their broken hearts back together again. Finally, Cat spoke.

"Billie, I'm so sorry. I was jealous. Do you believe it? I was jealous of my own daughter. Jealous of the time and attention you gave her. And I was scared as well. I felt so out of control. Other people were making decisions about Sky...the doctors...you. I felt like I had no control and so I put my foot down. Unfortunately, I put it down on the wrong person."

Cat turned her head and placed a delicate kiss in the hollow of Billie's throat where her collarbones met. Looking into Billie's face once more, she continued.

"I was wrong, Billie. I know now that I could no more ask you to give up the children, than to ask you to stop breathing. Your love and devotion to *our* three children is a big part of why I love you so much. I was wrong, Billie, please forgive me," she said.

Billie drew Cat close to her and lowered her forehead to hers. "Cat, I *do* forgive you. I love you and the children so much. I want to come home, Cat," she said passionately.

Cat placed her hands on both sides of Billie's face. Fighting the tears, she said, "Look around you Billie. You *are* home. Please don't ever leave again, love."

Billie's lips met and held Cat's in a fiery kiss that left them both breathless and wanting more. Within seconds, Billie had backed Cat up against the refrigerator, pressing her into the door.

"Billie, I need you," Cat panted. "Make love to me, please. I have missed you so much."

Lowering her head once more, Billie planted tiny kisses across Cat's mouth, jaw and neck, causing little moans and whines to escape her throat...each sound fueling the fire burning within Billie's core.

"Cat," she said hoarsely into her wife's neck, "I want you, and I've missed you so much."

"Make love to me...please," Cat begged.

Reaching under Cat's knees, Billie scooped her up and made her way through the living room and up the stairs to their bedroom, kicking the door shut behind them.

Billie laid her precious cargo gently on the bed and lowered the entire length of her body on top of her. Cat's chin was lifted toward the ceiling, head pressed back into the mattress as she gave Billie access to her neck. Loud moans of pleasure escaped her lips as Billie nipped and sucked on her sensual pleasure points.

"Oh...God....Billie. Please, I can't wait," Cat pleaded as she tried to forcefully remove Billie's clothing.

Billie grabbed her hands and pinned them to the bed above her head. "Oh, no, no, no, no, no. Patience, my love, patience," she said to the squirming woman. "I want to see you, to feel you. I have missed being close to you, Cat."

While holding Cat's hands captive with her own, Billie proceeded to undress her wife using just her teeth, making little growling noises like a puppy playing with a rag doll. She shook her head side to side as she captured Cat's T-shirt between her teeth and somehow managed to pull it over her head. Placing both of Cat's hands in one of hers, Billie reached beneath the frustrated woman and released the catch on her bra, allowing two generous mounds to escape from their prison.

Cat was so turned on she couldn't stand it. Becoming frustrated at the length of time it was taking to reach fulfillment, she shouted at Billie, "Damn it, Billie. Please, I need you!"

Billie lifted her head and looked at Cat, suddenly amused by the depth of desire and desperation in her wife's voice. With her free hand, she took Cat's chin and turned her face toward her. Cat eyes were closed.

"Cat," Billie whispered. "Open your eyes for me love. I want you to see the depth of my love while I make love to you," she said as she placed delicate kisses across her lips.

Cat's eyes remained closed.

Smiling at her wife's stubbornness, Billie slid her hands down the length of Cat's arms and across her breasts, cupping their fullness in her palms and gently squeezing the nipples while she continued to rain kisses across Cat's mouth and neck.

Cat arched herself forward, moaning at the slight pain caused by the vice-like movement. "God, Billie," Cat said in a hoarse whisper as a sensual spasm wracked her body.

Cat's hands found their way to the sides of Billie's head, threading her fingers into the dark hair and pulling her lover closer.

Pulling her head back slightly, Billie freed it from Cat's grasp. "Cat," she whispered again. "Open your eyes for me, love. See the burning desire I have for you in my eyes."

Cat's eyes still remained closed.

Billie leaned down and suddenly took one swollen nub into her mouth, biting it gently.

The suddenness and intensity of the movement was so startling, Cat cried out, "Oh, God! Aahhh, Billie, please!" as a shudder ran through her body.

Cat was quivering with pent up desire, and nearly toppled over the edge when Billie repeated the gesture on the other breast. Cat arched her body upward, moaning loudly while Billie worshiped at her breasts.

"Harder," Cat screamed as Billie more than happily accommodated her lover's request, sending her even higher into the realms of sexual ecstasy.

Billie wasn't sure how much longer Cat would last. She had never seen her in this much need. She herself was near the edge just witnessing the pleasure she was bringing to Cat.

"Open your eyes for me, love. Look into my heart and see how much I love you," Billie whispered once more.

Eyes still closed, Cat strained to raise her upper body toward Billie, wanting desperately to be touched and caressed. Her body was out of control, wild with desire as her hips bucked up and down against the woman above her.

"Billie, please, I need you. Take me, please," she begged.

Billie sat up, momentarily releasing Cat's hands as she peeled off her own blouse and bra, with more than a little help from Cat's roaming hands. Her slacks and panties followed.

Cat's hands were everywhere, desperate to touch, to feel, to connect. They had been apart for so long, all she wanted was to love and feel loved.

Billie captured Cat's hands once more and held them close to her heart and she returned to her position above Cat.

"Billie, let me touch you," Cat begged. "I need to feel you. I need to know this is real."

Billie lowered her mouth to Cat's ear. "Open your eyes for me, love. See what you are doing to me, body and soul," Billie whispered.

Cat still refused to open her eyes.

Billie sat up and smiled once more. *I will win yet, my love,* she thought.

Reaching down, she removed Cat's shorts and panties, placing butterfly kisses across Cat's abdomen, causing Cat to arch herself closer to Billie's mouth.

"Billie, please," Cat begged, her body convulsing with pre-orgasmic spasms. "I can't wait any longer," she said, tears of frustration running down the sides of her face.

Billie lowered herself between Cat's legs. Looking up at Cat, she whispered hoarsely, "Open your eyes for me, love. Watch me worship at your altar as I devour your love."

Cat's eyes snapped open, upon which, Billie immediately dove into her core with wild abandon, teasing Cat's pleasure point while filling her completely with three long digits.

Within seconds of entry, Cat was screaming Billie's name, her body convulsing out of control. Tears streamed down her face as a second wave of orgasmic pleasure ripped through her body, long before the first had a chance to subside.

"Billie, please. Turn around for me, love. Let me love you," Cat begged as soon as she had regained enough coherence to speak.

Billie positioned herself above Cat. She was so near the edge from the pure enjoyment she had brought to Cat, that her climax was nearly self-induced as Cat buried three of her own fingers deep within Billie's core, capturing her pleasure point between her teeth, and sucking it deeply into her mouth. Adding a fourth sent Billie over the edge. The convulsions that wracked Billie's body were stronger than any she had felt in her life as Cat's name rang from her lips, over and over again in a chorus of love.

Moments later, they lay spent as Billie gathered Cat into her arms. Reaching down, she pulled the sheet over their sweat-soaked bodies.

Cat lifted her head and kissed Billie gently. "I love you," she said weakly. "Welcome home."

"I love you too, kitten," Billie said as she planted a tender kiss on Cat's forehead and drifted off to sleep.

* * *

Billie was awakened by a small body sitting on top of her.

"What the h...," Billie started to exclaim until she saw the intruder was Skylar.

"Sweetheart," she said, "Be careful not to wake Mama. She's really, really tired," Billie whispered to the child.

"Sky!" a voice said from the doorway. "Skylar, come out of there," the voice said again.

Billie lifted herself onto her elbows and looked toward the door, the movement causing the sheet to fall to a spot just above her breasts.

Laurel was standing there, gesturing for the six-year-old to come with her, giving her mothers some much needed rest and privacy.

Billie smiled as Skylar kissed her then scrambled off the bed to join her grandmother.

"Sorry," Laurel said as she pulled the door shut.

"Mom," Billie said, effectively stopping the door from closing.

Laurel looked back into the room, smiling ear to ear, acknowledging Billie's choice of monikers for her.

"Thank you," Billie said, rubbing her cheek, "For everything," she added before lying down and gathering Cat into her arms once more.

"You're welcome, baby, you're welcome," Laurel said as she closed the door.

CHAPTER 17

Cat and Billie were awakened the next morning by a piercing scream coming from Skylar's room. Jumping out of bed and throwing T-shirts and boxers over their naked bodies, the two women ran to their daughter's room, only to be confronted by a nightmare. Skylar was sitting in the middle of her bed, covered in blood. There was blood everywhere...on the bed, the pillow, on Skylar's clothing, and all over their daughter's face and arms.

"Oh, my God, Cat! What do we do?" Billie asked, near hysterics.

"Billie, fill the tub with warm water. We need to find out where the blood is coming from," Cat shouted as she tried to calm the screaming child.

By this time, the rest of the household was awake and gathering in Skylar's room. Tara started to cry at the sight, clinging to Seth, who just stood there in wide-eyed horror.

Laurel was the last one to join them, having come from down stairs. "Dear Lord," she said when she entered the room.

Billie came back from the bathroom across the hall and saw the mortified gathering in Skylar's room. Turning to Laurel, she said, "Mom, please take Seth and Tara downstairs. They don't need to see this."

Laurel acknowledged that Billie was right as she led her two older grandchildren out of the room.

Cat had stripped Skylar of her pajamas and quickly examined her, not finding the source of the bleeding beneath her clothing. Scooping her up in strong arms, Billie carried the naked child across the hall and gently lowered her into the tub of warm water, where both she and Cat started to wash away the blood, hoping to find the source quickly. After another quick examination, it was obvious that the bleeding was coming from the upper body, so Billie reached over and turned the shower on to allow the spray to gently rinse the blood from Skylar's face and hair. It soon became apparent that the bleeding was coming from Skylar's nose and mouth.

Grabbing a clean white towel, Cat held it to Skylar's nose and tilted the child's head back. "Billie, call Alexis, quickly," she said. "Tell her what's happened. I'll dress Sky. We're going to the hospital," she added.

Moments later, Cat, Billie and Skylar were on their way to the emergency room, to be met there by Dr. Berry.

* * *

Several hours later, Skylar was tucked into a hospital bed, sedated to keep her from thrashing about and reopening the clots in her nose and gums. They had to perform platelet aphaeresis on Cat in order to collect enough platelets quickly to stop the bleeding. For two hours, Cat sat connected to a blood cell separator, while blood was drawn from one arm and spun through the machine, during which platelets were collected before returning the plasma to Cat's other arm. Upon collection of the platelets from Cat's blood, they were able to use them immediately to stem the flow of blood from Skylar's nose and mouth.

Billie and Cat stayed with their daughter throughout the aphaeresis procedure and were now waiting, not so patiently, in Skylar's room for Dr. Berry to arrive with the child's test results. Cat sat by Skylar's bedside, holding her hand, as Billie paced back and forth across the room.

"Damn. Where is she?" Billie swore impatiently.

Just then, Dr. Berry entered the room.

"Alexis," Billie said, approaching her. "What the hell happened here?" she asked desperately.

Dr. Berry looked sadly at Billie, then took her arm and led her to a chair next to Cat. Sitting down in a chair opposite them, she looked at the women and said, "The leukemia is back."

"No!" Cat exclaimed.

"What do you mean, it's back?" Billie demanded.

"Billie, please calm down. It appears that the leukemia has relapsed. The nosebleed was due to a lack of platelets. She's feverish again, indicating another infection. Her ANC count is at 250. The leukemia is back. I'm sorry," Dr. Berry said.

Cat reached for Billie's hand. "What about abnormal cell growth, Dr. Berry?" Cat asked, expecting, but not wanting to hear the worse.

Dr. Berry nodded her head. "Rapid," she answered. "Not only is the leukemia back, but it is aggressively attacking her system. I'm sorry," she said again.

Billie rose to her feet. "You're sorry? You're sorry? Is that it? Just, you're sorry? Our child is dying and you're sorry?" Billie exclaimed.

"Billie, please," Cat said, pulling her back down into her seat.

Reaching out, Cat touched Dr. Berry's arm. "Alexis, there must be something we can do," she said.

Dr. Berry looked back and forth between the two women. "There is one thing we can do, but it takes time...time I'm not sure we have," she said.

"What is it?" Cat asked, trying desperately to keep a very tense Billie under control by squeezing her hand.

"Bone marrow transplant," Dr. Berry replied. "It may work, but only if we can find a compatible donor in time."

"Compatible donor? Do you mean someone genetically compatible?" Cat asked.

"Yes, we need a donor whose human leukocyte antigens, or HLA typing is genetically matched, or at the very least, similar," Dr. Berry explained.

"Shouldn't Cat's be similar? She *is* her mother, after all," Billie suggested.

"Cat is certainly a potential donor, Billie, but it's rare that a parent is suitable. Siblings are more likely choices, and if she had an identical twin, it would be a perfect match," Dr. Berry said.

"So, Seth or Tara could be matches?" Cat asked.

Dr. Berry nodded. "It's possible, Cat...at least with Tara." Looking at Billie, Dr. Berry asked, "Seth is *your* son, right Billie?"

"Yes he is, but before you rule him out as being just a step brother, you need to know that Seth and Sky have the same father," Billie explained.

Dr. Berry raised her eyebrows in question. "Let me get this straight," she said. "Tara and Skylar belong to you, right, Cat?"

Cat responded by nodding.

"And Seth belongs to you, Billie. However, Sky and Seth have the same father. What am I missing here?" she asked.

Cat spoke up. "Let's just say that Seth's father and I had an encounter, the likes of which, I'd rather forget. The only good thing to come of it was Skylar," she explained.

"Well, this lessens the odds," Dr. Berry said, rising to her feet and pacing back and forth.

"What do you mean?" Cat asked.

"Well, I thought Sky and Tara were full blooded siblings. It appears that she is only a half sister to both Tara and Seth. That lessens the chance that Tara will be a close enough match," she explained.

Billie frowned. "But it *is* still possible that Seth or Tara could be matches, right?" she asked.

"Yes, it is possible," the doctor replied.

Billie jumped to her feet. "Then let's stop wasting time and do whatever is necessary to find out," she insisted, Cat nodding in agreement.

Dr. Berry looked back and forth between the two women.

Cat reached out once more for Billie's hand and pulled her back down next to her. "What is it you're *not* telling us, Alexis?" Cat asked the doctor.

Dr. Berry stood and started to pace back and forth. "Well, you need to know that it's not a pleasant procedure for the donor. This is an issue you need to discuss with Seth and Tara. I'll explain the entire procedure to you before you leave so they will understand what they will be going through if they choose to donate...and make no mistake about it, this needs to be *their* decision, not yours," the doctor explained.

Cat and Billie exchanged looks, each one sure Seth and Tara would be more than willing to help their sister.

"If they agree, when can you have the children here for testing?" Dr. Berry asked.

"I'll go home to get them now, if that's soon enough," Billie replied eagerly.

"That's perfect," Dr. Berry replied. "Oh, you need to know there will be some risk involved in being a donor. I want to make sure that both you and your children understand that, and are willing to endure it," she warned.

Billie and Cat exchanged worried glances. "Risks?" Cat asked.

"Minor risks, such as infection, or potential health issues if the donor is not clinically healthy enough to donate," the doctor explained.

Cat maintained eye contact with Dr. Berry as she spoke over her shoulder to Billie. "Billie," she said. "Please go get the children. Alexis can explain the procedure to me then we will discuss it with them when they get here. Okay, love?" she added, turning her head to face her wife.

Billie leaned down to place a tender kiss on Cat's lips. "I'll be back within a half hour, all right? See you in a bit," she added before hastily leaving the room.

* * *

Billie ran into the kitchen calling out the children's names. "Seth, Tara, where are you?"

Seth was the first one to arrive, followed by Tara and Laurel.

"Mom, where's Sky?" Seth ran to the doorway and looked outside. "Mom, please tell me she didn't die," he begged, not even attempting to check the tears that were flowing down his face.

Tara clung to Laurel. "Mom, is Sky okay?" she asked in a weak voice.

Billie placed a hand on the shoulder of each of her children. "Seth, Tara, Your sister is very sick and she needs special help to get better." She looked at Seth. "Seth, you said you wanted to do something to help her get better. There may be a way you can do that. There may be a way one...or both of you can help."

"Whatever it is, Mom, I'll do it," Seth said.

"Me too, Mommy," Tara agreed.

"Dr. Berry said it might hurt."

"I don't care. We can't let Sky die," Seth said adamantly.

"What is the procedure, Billie?" Laurel asked.

"Bone marrow transplant," Billie replied.

"We need to give Sky our bones?" Tara asked, incredulously?

Billie smiled at her daughter's innocence. "No sweetie. Look, I need to get you to the hospital as soon as possible, so get yourselves ready to go and we can talk more about it on the way. Okay?"

* * *

Cat lay down on her side next to her baby girl as she waited for Billie and the kids to return. Skylar slept peacefully in a sedated haze, oblivious to the gut wrenching decisions being made around her. Cat had one arm stretched out across the pillow above Skylar's head, her own head resting on her bicep as she reached over with the other hand and traced a pattern down the side of her daughter's cheek.

Cat kissed her tenderly then whispered in her ear, "Fight, little one. Fight to stay with us. Mommy and I need you, love bug. Brother and sister need you too. Our lives would be empty without our baby girl. Please fight, sweetheart. We love you so much, my little Sky-bird. Please don't fly away from us."

Cat leaned in once more, kissing the child's cheek and watching a tear fall into Skylar's face. Reaching up, she wiped her tears dry then kissed away the errant drop that had fallen on the baby's cheek.

"Cat," said a voice from the doorway.

Cat looked up to see Billie, Seth, and Tara standing there, watching the tender scene before them. Cat looked at them through misty eyes. "How long have you been standing there?" she asked, clearing her throat.

"Mama, Skylar won't fly away. We won't let her, right, Seth?" Tara said, looking up at her brother.

Seth placed an arm around his little sister. "No, we won't let her," he agreed, his eyes never leaving Cat's.

Cat sat up on the bed and opened her arms to her children. Both of them ran into them and held her tight, promising to do whatever they could to help Skylar, while Billie leaned against the door frame, one hand covering her mouth to stifle the sobs that shook her shoulders.

* * *

"All right," Dr. Berry said to Seth and Tara. "Both of you need to understand what will happen to you, and to your baby sister during these tests."

Seth and Tara sat side by side on the edge of Skylar's bed, listening intently as Dr. Berry explained the procedure to them.

"Being a bone marrow donor is a big responsibility. We have to do many tests to see if your blood matches Sky's before we can use it, but first, we have to be sure that you are healthy. Do you understand so far?" Dr. Berry asked.

Tara raised her hand.

Alexis smiled at the automatic arm raising response so many children learned in school. "Do you have a question, Tara?" she asked.

Tara nodded vigorously. "Will it hurt?" she asked.

Cat and Billie exchanged a nervous look in reaction to their daughter's question.

Alexis took Tara's hand. "Well, to be truthful, parts of the testing will hurt a little bit. But it won't hurt for long, and the hurt will go away quickly," she explained.

Tara just nodded as she acknowledged what Dr. Berry was telling her.

"Any more questions before I continue?" Dr. Berry asked.

Seeing the children shaking their heads, she continued. "Okay. We'll have to give you a physical, including a chest X-ray, blood work and urinalysis," she explained.

"Your-in-al-is-sis? What's that?" Tara asked.

Seth looked at his sister with a typical *what a dumb girl* expression and said, "They need to check your pee."

"Ewwwwww!" Tara exclaimed, causing the three adults in the room to grin.

Forcing the grin from her face, Dr. Berry continued. "Now, we'll have to take several tubes of blood from both of you to see if either of you matches Skylar. That means there will be needles involved. Think you can handle that?" she asked.

Seth puffed his chest out, very macho-like and nodded confidently. "If it helps Sky, then I can take a little pain."

Tara sat there, a little green, her normal tough guy attitude escaping her for the moment, but agreeing anyway, not wanting her brother to best her. "I guess so," she said.

"Good," Dr. Berry said, thinking to herself that Cat and Billie were blessed with two very special children. "All right," she continued. "It will take a few days before we have the results, but if either of you is a match for Skylar, you will have to have a small operation. A needle will be inserted into your hip bone and some of your bone marrow will be taken out."

Dr. Berry had retrieved a teaching aid from the hospital library on bone structure and was now showing the children where bone marrow was located, and just where on the body the needle would be inserted to extract the marrow.

"When we have enough bone marrow, the needle will be taken out, and a bandage will be put over the wound. I won't lie to you and say it doesn't hurt, because it will, but only for a little while," she finished.

"Can we go home then?" Tara asked, a little green around the edges at Dr. Berry's explanation.

"You'll have to stay in the hospital overnight, but you'll be able to go home the next day," Dr. Berry explained.

"Do you have to cut Sky open to put the bone marrow in her?" Seth asked.

"No sweetie. The bone marrow will be injected into Sky's catheter tube, just like when Mama gives her the chemo medicine. She won't feel a thing," Dr. Berry said.

Looking back and forth between the children, she asked, "Do either of you have any more questions?"

"I do," Tara said. "Can we catch leukemia too if we give Sky our bone marrow?"

Cat's eyes closed as she leaned into Billie, weak-kneed at her daughter's question.

Billie's arm tightened around Cat's shoulder as they awaited Dr. Berry's answer.

"No, sweetheart. You will not catch leukemia by donating your bone marrow," Dr. Berry said before standing up and admiring both children.

"I want you to know that what you are doing for your sister is a very brave and generous thing. You must love her very much to volunteer for this," she said, seeing both children nod their heads vigorously. "Well, Sky is very lucky to have such a wonderful brother and sister. You should be very proud of yourselves. I know your moms are proud of you," she finished.

Seth and Tara both looked at Cat and Billie, who were smiling and nodding their agreement, love filling their hearts and minds for these two brave children.

Just then, two technicians arrived in Skylar's room. Looking over at them, then back and the children, Dr. Berry reached her hands out and said, "Okay then. I guess it's time to rock and roll."

Seth and Tara jumped off the edge of the bed and took Dr. Berry's hands. Looking at Billie and Cat, Dr. Berry said, "One of you should come along for this."

Cat immediately rose to her feet. "I'll go," she said. Bending over, she kissed Billie and said, "Skylar needs her Mommy right now, and besides, I need to be tested as well. We'll be back soon, love."

Billie smiled and pulled Cat down for another kiss before letting her go. "Thank you Cat," she said under her breath as they left the room. Then, looking at her daughter lying helplessly on the bed, she reached out and took her hand, bringing it to her mouth and kissing it gently.

"I think it's more like, Mommy needs her Sky," she said to the sedated child.

* * *

Two hours later, Cat returned to Skylar's room with Seth and Tara in tow, all three of them sporting gauze bandages in the hollow of their elbow from the blood work. Stepping into Skylar's room, she found Billie fast asleep, stretched out next to the little girl, and holding the child in her arms. Motioning for them to be quiet, she directed Seth and Tara out of the room. After placing a gentle kiss on both her girls' cheeks, she left to take them home.

Cat stopped at the local ice cream stand on the way home, treating the children to banana splits, all the while praising them for their efforts and bravery. "Have I told you guys how much I love you?" Cat asked.

"You mean in the last five minutes?" Seth said, sarcastically.

"Ah, come on. I'm not that bad, am I? Well, am I?" she asked.

"Worse," responded Tara, causing all three of them to laugh.

"Mom," Seth said suddenly. "What happens if none of us match Sky?"

Cat's brow drew into a frown. "Let's hope that doesn't happen, honey, but if it does, there is a National Marrow Donor Program that we can use to find a match. In fact, I think Alexis...I mean, Dr. Berry is already checking into it, just in case," she explained.

"Why don't we use them in the first place?" Tara asked, scooping a large spoonful of ice cream into her mouth.

"Because it takes a long time to find a donor from a program like that, and Dr. Berry is worried that Skylar is too sick to wait," Cat explained as delicately as she could.

"You mean Sky might die before we can find a donor?" Seth said, ever so perceptively.

Cat put her spoon down on the table and placed her hands in her lap. Looking at her son, she said, "We need to pray that it doesn't happen, Seth, but yes, it is possible that Sky...," Cat said, breaking down before she could finish the sentence.

Seth reached out and covered Cat's hand with his own. "Ma, I said we won't let her fly away. I meant it. One of us will catch her, I just know we will," he said encouragingly.

* * *

When Cat arrived home with the children, she was met at the door not by Laurel, but by Jen.

Before Cat could speak, the kids barraged Jen with questions about where Stevie and Karissa were. Having asked and gained permission from Cat and Jen to spend the afternoon at Jen's they kissed their mother and quickly exited, both anxious to show off their new hero status and battle scars from the trip to the hospital.

"Jen, what are you doing here?" Cat asked, surprised to see her friend. "Where's Laurel?" she added.

"I called to see how things were going and Laurel told me about the nightmarish scene you woke up to this morning and about the bone marrow testing with Seth and Tara. Laurel is at your mom's. I knew you'd come home eventually, so I came over to wait," Jen explained. "So how is Skylar?" she asked.

Cat held eye contact with her friend in silence for a long moment...a thousand unspoken words communicated in that brief amount of time.

Jen's eyes filled with such sympathy that Cat was unable to hold back the tears, as she fell into the open arms of her friend.

"Jen, I am so afraid. My baby is dying. I don't know how I will go on living if we lose her," Cat said in a quivering voice.

"Don't you *dare* give up hope, Cat. She will make it. I know she will. She has so many people rooting for her. She has an entire life ahead of her. Please don't give up hope," Jen pleaded. "Tell me what I can do. Tell me, Cat. I will do anything I can to help."

"There is one thing you can do, Jen," Cat replied.

"Anything. Just name it," Jen said.

"Kick my ass for me the next time I give in to self-pity, okay? I have so much to be thankful for, Jen. Sometimes tragic events in our lives can overwhelm all the good that is there. A reminder now and again really helps," Cat said.

"You got it, my friend. Now get your butt back to the hospital and help your daughter get well. Don't worry about the kids. I'll leave a note for Laurel to let her know where they are. They can stay with Fred and me for as long as they want. Okay?" Jen replied.

Cat forced a smile onto her face. "Okay," she replied as she turned for the door, pausing to say to her friend, "I love you Jen. You know that don't you?" she asked.

"Ditto, Cat...ditto to both you and Billie. Now go before you turn me into a blubbering idiot," Jen joked.

Cat smiled through her tears and blew a heartfelt kiss to her friend before leaving.

* * *

Cat returned to the hospital two hours later and found Billie sitting in a chair by the side of Skylar's bed with the chair turned so that she could rest her elbows on the bed and hold Skylar's small hand in both of hers. Billie was staring at the child's face, deep in thought when Cat walked in.

Cat approached Billie and kissed the top of her head. "How is she?" she asked softly.

Without taking her eyes off Skylar, Billie addressed Cat. "They want to put her in isolation starting tomorrow, Cat," she said. "Alexis left just a few minutes ago after explaining what will happen over the next few weeks if one of you is a match for Sky. She left those papers for you to read," Billie said, indicating the pamphlet of papers on the bedside table.

Cat reached for the papers, but not before wrapping her arms around Billie and kissing her once more. "I love you," she whispered as she took the papers and sat on the arm of Billie's chair to scan them. Cat nodded her head repeatedly as she read.

"It says here that she'll be in protective isolation. That means she'll be confined to a room, and that visitors will have to be limited in number, and wear facemasks to prevent the spread of germs. We also need to keep anyone away who has a cold, flu or other infectious disease," she said, continuing to read.

"Oh, wow, I guess we've got a start on this one," she commented, referencing the information on the next page. "Listen, *before transplantation, your child will receive a conditioning treatment. This includes chemotherapy to destroy any remaining cancer cells, to suppress the immune system, and to prevent rejection of an allogeneic transplant.* Billie, that may speed up the treatment process. Sky has been receiving chemo treatments for several weeks now," she said hopefully.

"Cat, I suspect if anything delays treatment, it will be the search for a compatible donor," Billie commented.

Reaching out to touch the side of Billie's face with her palm, Cat said, "Billie, I am praying that one of us is a match. I'm so worried about being too late to save her," Cat said, starting to choke up. "Do you know what Seth said on the way home? He said, *Ma, we won't let her fly away. One of us will catch her, I just know we will.* God, Billie, I want so desperately to believe that, but at the same time, I'm so worried," Cat cried.

Billie pulled Cat down across her lap, sitting back in the chair and holding the smaller woman close to her heart. Lowering her cheek to rest on top of Cat's head, she allowed herself to cry with Cat, watching her baby sleep through the veil of tears that ran freely down her face.

CHAPTER 18

Billie stood in the window of Skylar's hospital room and looked out over the flickering lights of the city. Cat was sleeping in the reclining chair nearby. She turned around and leaned her backside against the window sill, arms crossed in front of her. She looked at the clock on the wall of Skylar's hospital room. One a.m. Billie closed her eyes and lowered her chin to her chest, nearly dozing off until a moaning sound snapped her awake.

"Sky?" She approached Skylar's bedside and placed a hand on her forehead. "Son of a bitch!" she cursed. In three large steps, she crossed the room and shook Cat awake.

"Cat. Cat, wake up. Skylar is burning up."

"Wha...what?" Cat said groggily.

"Sky is burning up. She's running a high fever," Billie replied.

Cat was awake immediately and hurried to Skylar's bedside. She kissed the little girl on the forehead and immediately reached for the call-button.

A moment later, the night nurse entered the room. "Is everything okay in here?" she asked.

"Our daughter is running a high fever. She needs medication to bring it down," Cat said.

"Let's take a look at her," the nurse said.

A few moments later, a reading of one hundred and four registered on the thermometer. The nurse looked nervously at Cat. "I'll be right back," she said before she ran out of the room, only to return two minutes later with the night shift doctor, Dr. Caldwell.

Dr. Caldwell listened to Skylar's lungs and took her temperature once more. He picked up her chart and recorded her vital signs and several other notes.

"Julie," he said, addressing the nurse. "Call the pharmacy and ask them to deliver several IV doses of Affirmev. I want them administered at six-hour intervals to get her temperature down and keep it there. Oh, and apply cool cloths to her forehead as well." He looked at Cat. "I assume you're her mother?"

"We both are," Cat replied.

Dr. Caldwell looked back and forth between Cat and Billie. "Very well, then. If you don't mind assisting the nursing staff with the cold cloths, that would be much appreciated. I will be back to check on her after my rounds."

Half an hour later, Julie returned with her first dose of acetaminophen and a monitor which electronically tracked Skylar's body temperature.

Cat and Billie spent the next hour continuously applying cold cloths to Skylar's forehead, but despite their efforts and despite the medication, the temperature displayed on the monitor averaged above one hundred and three degrees.

Skylar remained relatively un-reactive, lying limply in the hospital bed like a rag doll, oblivious to the scurry of activity around her. Her skin was pale and waxy in appearance, the look of death already settling in on her tiny features.

"Where the hell is Dr. Berry?" Billie asked under her breath.

"Billie, she has to sleep sometime. Look, Dr. Caldwell is doing everything he can, given the circumstances. He has an entire wing of patients to tend to throughout the night. We can't expect him to spend all his time with Skylar," Cat explained.

"Well, I can," Billie said a little more gruffly than intended.

Billie saw the hurt expression on Cat's face. "Cat, I'm sorry," she said, wrapping her arms around her wife and resting her chin on her head. "I'm just so tired, and so scared. I'm saying things I don't mean," she said.

Dr. Caldwell returned as promised and collected another set of vital signs, then abruptly left after adding more notes to Skylar's chart. Cat took the clipboard down from the hook on the wall and looked at the most recent entries, shaking her head side to side as she read it aloud.

"Motrin every four hours...rotate Affirmev and motrin...increase IV fluids... cold compresses. Billie, they haven't touched her fever," she said.

Cat returned Skylar's chart to the hook and approached her bedside. She leaned over the child and brushed her bangs aside and to kiss her daughter on the forehead. That's when she noticed something wasn't quite right. Cat's head snapped up as she frowned at Billie before lowering her ear to Skylar's chest.

"What is it, Cat?" Billie asked, anxiety immediately paralyzing her to the spot as she noticed Cat's reaction.

Cat held up her hand to temporarily silence Billie as she leaned in close to the child's face once more. A look of panic masked her features as she quickly stood erect. "Oh, my God," she said, looking around frantically for a stethoscope, finally finding one hanging with the blood pressure cuff. Raising Skylar's gown, she listened carefully to the child's chest.

"Cat, please tell me what going on," Billie said frantically.

"Billie, get me the clipboard, please," she said without taking her eyes from Skylar. Within seconds, it was in her hands as she shuffled through the pages.

"Damn it, Cat! What is it?" Billie asked, her mind in a near-panic state.

Checking the entries made throughout the night, Cat found what she was looking for. "Shit! Billie, it says right here...rapid breathing, fever, chest congestion, glossy eyes," she read before looking up at her wife. "Billie, call Dr. Berry. I don't care if you have to get her out of bed. Skylar has pneumonia. With her low blood cell counts, the infection will kill her if we don't deal with this immediately," Cat exclaimed, listening to Skylar's chest once more while Billie ran out of the room and down the hall to the nurse's station.

Cat could hear the commotion down the hall as Billie argued with the head nurse about calling Dr. Berry. Finally, under the threat of bodily harm, she did just that, connecting Dr. Berry through the phone lines into Skylar's room. Billie ran into Skylar's room just as the phone rang. "That's Alexis," Billie said as Cat reached for the phone.

"Alexis," Cat said as she picked up the phone.

"Cat, I know you wouldn't be calling me at this ungodly hour unless it was important. What's wrong?" Dr. Berry asked.

"Sky has pneumonia," Cat informed her.

"Shit!" Dr. Berry said—an unexpected response from the normally composed doctor. "I'll be right there," she said.

Cat replaced the receiver and looked at Billie. "She's on her way," Cat said. "I only hope it's not too late."

Billie's brow crinkled into a frown as she fought to hold back the fear that threatened to spill from her eyes. Opening her arms to accept Cat into them, she held her close and whispered, "Don't say that, Cat. Please don't give up hope."

Not more than fifteen minutes later, Dr. Berry flew into the room, still wearing pieces of her bed clothes. Taking the stethoscope from Cat, she listened to Skylar's chest then quickly flipped through the entries on her chart. Throwing the chart down on the foot of the bed, she said, "God damn it!" then rushed out of the room.

"Cat, what's happening?" Billie asked frantically.

"Alexis is happening, Billie," Cat said. "She'll straighten this out."

Moments later, two technicians appeared and started wheeling Skylar's bed out of the room.

"Where are you taking her?" Billie demanded gruffly.

"Intensive Care. Dr. Berry's orders," he said.

Cat and Billie followed Skylar's bed down the hall, but were stopped short at the entrance to the ICU. Dr. Berry approached them from her position at the nurses' desk.

"I'm sorry, but considering Sky's suppressed immune system, and present state of health, I can't allow you to go in there," she said.

"Not go in there? Alexis, how can you expect us to honor that?" Cat asked.

Dr. Berry took Cat by the shoulders. "Cat, you may have saved her life tonight buy discovering the pneumonia. Don't be foolish enough to take her chances away again by going in there and bringing germs with you. She's very susceptible to catching anything that comes her way right now. Look, I've ordered an intensive regime of antibiotics to fight the infection. We'll see how she is later, then maybe you can see her. Until then, we'll keep her sedated so she's unaware of your absence. Both of you have to promise me that you'll get no closer than this window until it is safe for her again, okay?" Dr. Berry finished, looking back and forth between the women.

"Listen to her, Cat," Billie said, stepping up behind Cat and wrapping her arms around her wife. Cat nodded her head to the doctor as they stood and watched her daughter being hooked up to various life-support monitors.

"Alexis," Cat said, suddenly becoming alarmed again. "That's a ventilator they're hooking her up to. Is she that congested?" she demanded.

"Cat, when you diagnosed pneumonia a while ago, she was very close to taking her last few unassisted breaths. She'll need help breathing for a while. Even with the antibiotics, there is no reason to force her body to work so hard to stay alive," Dr. Berry explained to the crestfallen women.

"Who is doing the intubations? I want to be sure she's sufficiently sedated. I'll do it myself if I have to," Cat said.

"No. You know better than most that's not proper protocol. Don't worry, Cat. She's in good hands," Dr. Berry said.

Seeing the heart-stricken looks on the faces of the two women before her, Dr. Berry reached out and rubbed Cat's arm. "Cat," she said. "We are doing all we can for her. It's pretty much up to her now. If she's half as feisty as her two moms she'll put up a damned good fight. The power of hope is pretty strong. Don't give up on her."

"Never," was all Billie could force from her constricted throat as emotions overcame her. Wrapping her arms a little tighter around the woman she held, she added, "Right, Cat?"

Unable to speak, Cat just nodded her head and closed her eyes as the tears rolled down her face. Finally, the beehive of activity around Skylar died down as each technician left the room. Soon, Skylar was alone, behind the glass wall, breathing with the help of a machine, hooked up to various hoses and wires...all designed to alert the nurses in the event her frail body decided to give up the fight.

Cat and Billie stood there outside the room with their faces pressed up against the glass, hearts tearing from their chests at the sight of their baby so helplessly ill.

* * *

"Daddy. Daddy, my baby is dying and I can't do anything to stop it," Cat cried into her cell phone as she leaned against Billie's shoulder. They sat on the floor outside the intensive care unit...their backs against the wall. Billie sat, knees bent and supporting her elbows, which were in turn supporting her head in her hands. She was crying as she listened to Cat talk to her father.

"Daddy, I can't. I can't call. Please don't ask me to," Cat begged.

Billie looked up at her, confusion etched into her face.

"All right, Billie and I will be right here. No! We're not leaving, Daddy. I don't care that we haven't slept or eaten. Damn it! Skylar is dying. Don't you understand? Nothing else matters...nothing else. All right. Goodbye," Cat said as she hung up the phone.

Billie pulled Cat into her arms. "What did he want you to do, Cat. Who can't you call?" Billie asked, her voice hoarse with emotion.

Cat covered her mouth with both hands and began to cry uncontrollably.

Billie held her closer. "Cat, baby, talk to me. Please," Billie begged.

"Billie, he wanted me to call...oh, God...he wanted me to call a priest to administer the last rights," Cat said. "He was crying, Billie. He said he wanted to be sure his baby angel went to heaven. Billie, I can't call...I can't."

"No." Billie said loudly and adamantly. "No. She's still with us Cat, please don't," Billie begged, tears now falling uncontrollably from her own eyes.

Cat wrapped her arms around Billie's head and drew it in close to her heart. Kissing her dark hair, Cat said, "I won't, Billie. I promise."

It was in this condition that Jen found them when she stepped off the elevator on the pediatrics floor. Stopping dead in her tracks at the sight of them, she took a deep breath to compose herself before approaching her friends. She had cried all the way to the hospital after calling Laurel that morning to check on Skylar's progress. Wiping the still-evident tears from her face, she walked toward the two ladies.

Neither Cat, nor Billie noticed Jen until she stopped directly in front of them. Looking up at their friend, the ladies allowed all the pain and anguish they were feeling to show on their faces, which was way more than Jen's tender emotions could take as she dropped to her knees and wrapped her arms around both her friends.

Literally incapable of speech, the three ladies held each other and shared their pain, bodies quivering with emotion as they shared the unspoken possibility of life without the little girl who had captured their hearts.

* * *

Billie sat on the bench outside the ICU, feet planted firmly on the floor, eyes staring straight ahead. Cat lay on the bench beside her...her head resting on Billie's thigh as Billie's hand randomly rubbed her back while she slept. Billie had yet to sleep since Skylar was moved into intensive care two days earlier. Her troubled heart refused to allow her one moment of peace lest something horrible should happen to their baby daughter while she was asleep. Instead, she sat on the bench outside Skylar's room and listened to the hum and repetitive whooshing sounds coming from the equipment that was keeping Skylar alive as she watched the minutes click by on the clock mounted above the nurse's station. Never before had she felt so helpless...so powerless.

Over the past two days, several friends and family members lent moral support. Jen spent almost as much time at the hospital as they did, bringing food and coffee to her friends, and just spending time holding their hands and providing a shoulder to lean on and a place for their tears to fall. Laurel, Doc and Ida also lent their support through frequent visits and caring for the two older children. Although seldom alone, they were totally isolated in their anguish.

Dr. Berry approached the nurse's desk just as Billie watched the clock strike eight a.m. Noticing the ladies were still standing guard at the window by their daughter's room, Dr. Berry approached them and squatted down on her heels beside Billie. Looking up, she saw Billie's tortured soul mirrored in her eyes before glancing at Cat who was sleeping by Billie's side.

"Billie, you need some rest too. Go home. I'll call you the second Sky's condition changes for the better or worse," she suggested.

Billie blinked once and looked at Dr. Berry. "No," she said. "I can't leave her,"

"You'll be no good for her if you're dead on your feet, Billie," Dr. Berry pointed out.

"I can't leave her, Alexis. I can't," Billie repeated.

Dr. Berry nodded and stood up again. "Will you drink a cup of coffee if I bring it to you?" she asked.

Billie nodded. "Bring one for Cat too. She'll be awake soon," Billie said.

"All right. I'll be back in a jiff," Dr. Berry said as she walked away, worried about these two women who had become more like friends than clients to her. She worried that they had not left the hospital in several days. Worried that the only help they allowed themselves was the presence of their mothers and their friend Jen who came to sit with and comfort them on a periodic basis. In fact, Alex was convinced that without their help, these women would have lost their minds by now. Cat and Billie had a network of strong women around them…women who willingly shared their pain and suffering, strictly out of love for them. Dr. Berry envied them such warm, loving relationships.

Cat stirred beside Billie. Looking down, Billie noted the dark shallow look to Cat's eyes. "Hi," she said. "Did you sleep well?" Billie asked.

Cat looked up at her blankly for a moment then nodded. Forcing herself into a seated position she leaned into Billie and rested her head on her shoulder.

"Billie, you need to sleep too. I'm worried about you," Cat said as she rubbed the sleep from her own eyes.

"I'm okay," Billie replied. "I couldn't sleep if I tried."

Cat sighed deeply, then rose to her feet to begin her ritual pacing back and forth in front of their bench, one hand on her hip, the other worrying the bangs on her forehead. With each pass across the room, she stopped to look at her frail helpless daughter through the window.

Billie rested the back of her head against the wall behind the bench and stared up at the ceiling, counting, for the hundredth time, the hole pattern decorating the ceiling tile.

Finally, Cat stopped pacing and turned to face Billie. Crossing her arms in front of her, she released a frustrated sigh.

"I'm so tired, Billie. Tired of the waiting, Tired of not being able to touch her and hold her. Damn it, Billie, it's been three days since they confined her to ICU. I can't take much more of this," she admitted.

Billie reached out for Cat's hand and pulled her onto her lap, wrapping weary arms around her wife before kissing her on the temple. "I know, love. I know," she said. "I feel the same way."

Soon, Dr. Berry returned carrying two cups of hot coffee. Seeing the gift their new friend was bearing, Cat climbed off Billie's lap and sat beside her, gratefully accepting the coffee the doctor handed to her and whispering a *thank you* for the much needed caffeine boost.

After thanking the doctor for the coffee, Cat looked at her and asked. "What are her stats this morning Alexis? We are anxious for some improvement...for the chance to see her. I need to hold her...to touch her. Please," Cat pleaded.

Dr. Berry sat next to the women on the bench and tried to think of a way to tell these women that their daughter's condition was not improving, that her fever was still high, and her blood counts were still dangerously low. They had been through so much heartache over the last few days she wasn't sure how much more they could take.

Before Dr. Berry could reply, a nurse approached her with a folder. "Thank you," Dr. Berry told the nurse as she opened the folder in her lap and proceeded to read the lab report on top as Cat and Billie waited patiently, albeit a bit impatient that the nurse had intruded on their briefing.

After several moments reviewing the file in front of her, Dr. Berry closed the folder then surprised herself when tears threatened to form at the corners of her eyes. She chastised herself for becoming personally involved in this case, but these women were so endearing, and their love for each other and their children was so tangible, she couldn't help herself. Taking a deep breath, she looked at the two women.

"This is Skylar's file," she said, watching as Cat and Billie immediately became animated.

Cat reached for Billie's hand for moral support as they waited for Dr. Berry to continue.

Dr. Berry tried hard to keep the emotion from her voice as she gave them the test results. "I'm not sure which God or Gods you pray to, but someone was listening. We have a match— Seth," she said.

"Oh, my God," Cat said, starting to shake uncontrollably.

Dr. Berry had all she could do to get the two cups of coffee out of the women's hands before they flew into each other's arms, clinging to this one hope for dear life.

Dr. Berry hated to burst their bubble, but she didn't want them to hold on to false hope either.

"Cat, Billie, you need to know something," she said, finally getting their attention. "Skylar's condition is critical. Her body has not been able to fight off infection for a long time now. The level of toxicity is high. We normally do not introduce healthy bone marrow tissue into such a damaged body, but we have no choice with Sky. If we don't do something soon, the life support systems she is currently on will fail to do their jobs. However, in her weakened condition, this treatment may not work either. I am telling you this because I want to be honest with you. I don't want you to think this is a cure-all. In her condition, there is a high probability that it may fail," Dr. Berry explained.

Cat sat up straight and wiped her eyes. "Alexis, are you telling us that there's no hope. That Sky will probably die anyway?" she asked.

"No, Cat. There is always hope," Dr. Berry said as Billie rose from the bench and headed down the hall.

"Billie, where are you going?" Cat asked.

"I'm going home to get Seth," she said. "He has a Sky-bird to catch."

Cat completely broke down and lost it at her wife's words, falling into Dr. Berry's arms and crying like a baby while Billie continued to walk down the hall.

CHAPTER 19

Seth followed Billie down the hall of the hospital corridor to where Cat was still sitting outside the ICU. Cat rose from her bench and took her son into her arms.

"Seth, I am so proud of you for being willing to help your sister," she said.

"I won't let her die, Mama," was all he said.

Dr. Berry approached with Seth's blood test results in her hand. "Well, young man," she said. "Are you ready for this?"

Seth looked from Dr. Berry to the window of Skylar's hospital room. "Will she die without all those machines?" he asked.

"I'm afraid so," Dr. Berry replied.

"Then yes—I'm ready for this. I won't let her die—not if there is something I can do about it."

Dr. Berry looked warily at Cat and Billie, then focused her gaze on Seth. She put her hand on Seth's shoulder. "Sweetie, you need to know that your sister is very, very sick. You are her best chance at survival, but she's so sick that it may not work. Do you understand that?"

"But she'll die for sure if we don't try—right?" he asked.

"That's right," Dr. Berry confirmed.

"Then let's do this. Let's do this right now."

* * *

Billie paced back and forth across the waiting room while Jen sat in a nearby chair.

"Billie, you're going to wear the carpet down to the bare floor if you don't stop pacing," Jen said.

"I can't help it, Jen. Not only do I have to worry about Skylar, but now Seth is going under the knife as well."

"Yes, but Seth isn't sick."

Billie sat in the chair beside Jen. "I know, but surgery is surgery. I can't help but worry."

Jen reached out for Billie's hand and held it firmly as they waited.

* * *

Dr. Berry glanced at the anesthesiologist sitting at the head of the operating table. "How is he doing?" she asked, looking at Seth lying face down on the table.

"He's stable, and good to go," the anesthesiologist said.

"All right then, we'll begin on his right hip," Dr. Berry said as she inserted the aspiration needle through his skin and into his right hipbone.

An hour later, successful aspiration of about a quart of bone marrow was harvested from each of Seth's hipbones, along with a significant amount of red blood cells. When the aspiration was complete, Dr. Berry turned the remaining part of the operation over to the assisting physician.

"I need to prepare Skylar to accept her brother's bone marrow. I'll ask you to bandage the puncture sites and see this young man through the anesthesia recovery process. I have already ordered a unit of blood cells for him once he's settled into the recovery room," Dr. Berry said to her colleague.

* * *

Billie jumped to her feet as soon as Dr. Berry exited the operating room suite.

"Alexis?" she said.

"He came through it like a trooper, Billie. He's a strong kid. We were able to harvest about two quarts of marrow."

"Two quarts? That sounds like a lot," Billie said.

"Yes it does, but in reality, it represents only about five percent of the bone marrow in your body."

"So, what's next?" Billie asked.

"For Seth or for Skylar?" Dr. Berry asked.

"Both, actually."

"Well, for Seth, he'll spend about an hour in the recovery room during which he'll receive a unit of red blood cells to replace the ones we harvested along with his marrow. He'll most likely be tired…and of course, there will be discomfort in his hips for the next few days. If he were an adult, we'd send him home today, but considering his age, I recommend keeping him overnight."

"Of course, of course," Billie said. "And for Skylar?"

"Skylar is being prepped right now to receive Seth's marrow, but first, the marrow needs to be filtered by the lab to remove any fat or bone fragments. It should be ready by the time Skylar is. I'm on my way to see her now."

"Can I see Seth?" Billie asked.

"He'll most likely sleep for the next hour or so, but yes— there are no restrictions on visitation for him. I'll ask the nurse to page you when he's settled into a room."

* * *

"Okay, little one," Dr. Berry said. "Let's get you better."

Dr. Berry stood by as a line was connected to Skylar's central venous catheter through which Seth's filtered bone marrow would pass. "Infuse it slowly. We don't need fluid overload. Her kidneys and other internal organs are already compromised."

Dr. Berry watched as the flow of marrow began. She watched both Skylar's physical reaction, as well as the data flashing on the monitors reflecting the child's vital signs and overall stability. When she was satisfied the procedure was going as planned, she walked over to the glass windows separating Skylar's room from the hallway where Cat and Billie were pressed against the pane.

Dr. Berry removed her gloves and placed her left hand flat on the window. On the other side of the pane, Cat placed her hand against Dr. Berry's, and Billie placed hers over Cat's.

They remained this way through the remainder of the infusion process.

* * *

"How did she do?" Cat asked as Dr. Berry exited Skylar's room.

"As well as can be expected, considering her condition. I'm pleased her body didn't immediately reject the marrow," Dr. Berry said.

"How can you tell? I mean, she's sedated, so I wouldn't expect a reaction from her," Billie pointed out.

"We would have seen a change in the readout on the monitors, Billie. So far, there has been no significant change in any of the readings, good or bad. That means she's tolerating the infusion," Dr. Berry explained.

"Now we wait to see if her body actually *accepts* the transplant—not just tolerates it," Cat added.

"Exactly," Dr. Berry concluded.

"How long will that take?" Billie asked.

"That's hard to say, exactly. If the graft worked, the stem cells will begin to multiply and make new blood cells. The amount of time it takes to return to normal blood counts varies with each patient, but it could happen as early as two weeks, or as long as six."

"Are you telling me she'll be hooked up to those machines for possibly another six weeks?" Billie asked incredulously.

"I hope not," Dr. Berry said. "If all goes well, her body will begin to bounce back over the next few days. During that time, we'll give her antibiotics to fight any current infections and stave off any new ones. We'll also give her anti-bacterial, anti-fungal and anti-viral drugs until her white blood cells are high enough to take over. Finally, to give her new immune system a boost, we'll transfuse red blood cells and platelets until her own marrow is producing them again."

"In the meantime, it's all a waiting game," Cat said as she stood in front of the windows, intently staring at her daughter. "All of this will be for naught if we can't get her fever down and get her breathing on her own. Hopefully, Seth's stem cells will be the catalyst she needs to get the ball rolling in the right direction."

"That is indeed our hope," Dr. Berry said. She turned to Cat and Billie. "As for you two...go home and get some sleep. Skylar will be sedated for at least the next twenty-four to forty-eight hours."

"No can do, Alexis," Billie said. "I will, however, take some time out to go see my son. He should be awake by now. Thank God, Jen volunteered to stay with him until we get there."

"I'll go with you, Billie," Cat said before turning to Dr. Berry. "Alexis, I don't have the words to tell you how much we appreciate everything you've done for Skylar. Thank you."

"You can thank me by taking care of yourselves. We still have a long road ahead of us and you'll need your strength to travel down it. You'll be of no use to Skylar...or to Seth or Tara if you don't get enough sleep and nourishment. Doctor's orders."

* * *

Two days later, Cat and Billie heeded Dr. Berry's orders and went to the hospital cafeteria for a light lunch. When they returned to the ICU they found Skylar's room empty.

"What the hell?" Billie said. "Where is she?"

"I'll get to the bottom of this," Cat said as she approached the nurses' station with Billie in tow. "Could you tell me where our daughter is?" she asked.

"What's her name?" the nurse said.

"Skylar Jean Charland."

"Skylar...she's been transferred out of ICU. She's in isolation on Baird 6, room 690."

"Thank you. Come on, Billie. Let's go find our daughter." Cat said.

"What did she mean by isolation, Cat?" Billie asked as they made their way to Baird 6.

"It means she's in a private room where no one can enter without wearing a mask, and maybe protective outer wear."

"Why?"

"Usually so the patient doesn't infect their visitors or the staff...or so their visitors don't infect them. In this case, it would be the latter."

"That's a good thing, isn't it? I mean, the fact that she's out of ICU?" Billie asked.

"I would think so, love. Here's Baird 6. Now, to find room 690."

"There it is, Cat. Fourth room on the left," Billie said.

"Here, put this on," Cat said, pulling two masks out of the box on the wall outside the door.

Cat and Billie stepped inside the room and immediately saw Dr. Berry standing beside the bed with her back to them. She was blocking their view of the patient in the bed.

"Alexis?" Cat said.

Dr. Berry swung around. "Cat! Billie!" she said.

"Mama? Mommy?" said a small voice from behind Dr. Berry.

"Sky? Sky-baby, are you awake?" Cat said.

Dr. Berry stepped aside so Skylar could see her mothers.

Skylar giggled. "You look funny in those masks," she said in a soft raspy voice.

Cat covered her mouth with one hand while grabbing Billie's arm with the other. Tears clouded her vision as she looked at Billie. Billie smiled back at her through her own veil of tears.

"She's awake," Billie whispered hoarsely. "Our baby is awake."

They cautiously moved forward, parting like the Red Sea so they could each approach from opposite sides of the bed. In turn, they leaned over the little girl and kissed her on the forehead as she smiled up at them.

"She's still warm, but not hot," Cat said, glancing at Dr. Berry.

"Her temp has come down considerably since the infusion. Some of that is due to the antibiotics and anti-viral meds, but I choose to believe it is also an early sign that the stem cells are beginning to do their job. It will be a few days before we actually know for sure. The biggest improvement though is in her breathing. You'll notice she's off the ventilator."

"Hey, sweet angel," Billie cooed. "How are you feeling?"

"I'm hungry, Mommy. Can I have some jello?"

Billie smiled broadly and looked at Dr. Berry. "Can she?"

Dr. Berry approached the foot of the bed and squeezed Skylar's foot. "I'll tell you what...it's too early for you to have solids, but I think I might be able to find you a juice box. Does that sound okay? I promise you can have jello in a day or two."

Skylar frowned. "I guess so," she pouted.

Billie chuckled. "She so looks like you when she pouts, Cat."

Cat looked at Billie, prepared to refute her statement, but when their eyes met, an amazing rush of love filled her every pore. She was totally unprepared for such an intense feeling as her eyes filled with tears and her breath caught in her throat. She reached forward and touched the side of Billie's face.

"I love you, Billie," she whispered.

Billie closed her eyes and pressed her cheek into Cat's hand. She inhaled deeply and allowed the tears to escape her lids.

"I love you too, Cat, with everything that I am."

Just then, Dr. Berry came back into the room carrying a box of fruit punch. She inserted the plastic straw and gave it to Billie.

"Here you go, dumpling. It's not jello, but it's the next best thing," Billie said as she held the straw to Skylar's mouth.

Cat came around the bed to talk to Dr. Berry while Billie fed the fruit juice to Skylar.

"She looks so much better than she did two days ago, Alexis," Cat said.

"Yes she does, but we're not out of the woods yet. As you mentioned, she continues to run a fever. That means there is still an infection raging inside her. Once we get that under control, we should see a marked improvement in her responsiveness. We won't know if the stem cells are actually working for another week."

"But there's reason to hope?" Cat asked.

"There is always reason to hope," Dr. Berry said.

"We can't thank you enough for all you've done for Skylar," Cat said.

"You're welcome. Now go spend a little time with her then I want both of you to go home and get some sleep. Forgive me for saying this, but you look like hell. Call in a family member to sit with her while you take some time for yourselves if that makes you feel better, but go home and get some rest."

"I couldn't agree more," a male voice said from the doorway.

"Daddy!" Cat said as she ran into her father's arms.

Doc held her close. "Alexis is right. You'll be of no use to your daughter if you fall sick from neglecting your own health."

"Grandpa?" Skylar said softly.

Doc looked across the room to the small figure lying in the bed. "We're not finished here, Caitlain. Give me a minute with my granddaughter."

Doc walked toward the bed and embraced Billie, then shooed her away so he could spend time with Skylar. He stood by the bedside and crossed his arms. In a firm voice, he said, "Someone told me there was a sick little girl in this room. I had to come see for myself...and what do I find? I find my own granddaughter lying there. What do you have to say for yourself, little one?"

Skylar lifted her hands out to the sides and shook her head side to side. "I'm tryin' to get better, Grandpa. I'm tryin' real hard."

"Well that's good, because I'm planning a backyard camping trip, complete with bonfire and s'mores, and I'd sure hate for you to miss it." He grinned broadly at her.

"Really? Can we cook hot dogs in the fire too?"

"Of course. It wouldn't be camping without them."

Doc sat on the edge of Skylar's bed and took her hand. "You need to work really hard to get better, kitten. Do everything Dr. Berry tells you to do, without an argument. Okay?"

"Okay, Grandpa. I will."

Doc placed a tender kiss on Skylar's forehead. "That's a good girl. Now, I have a few patients to see, but I will be back to visit with you while your moms go home to get some sleep. Is that okay with you?"

"Can you read to me?" Skylar asked.

"You betcha."

"Okay."

Doc walked back to where Cat and Billie were standing. He looked at them sternly. "You have one hour to spend with your daughter. After that, you are to go home and sleep for at least six hours. Do you understand? I will call both your mothers, and between the three of us we will stay with Skylar while you're gone."

Cat and Billie exchanged nervous glances.

"No argument, daughters. Do you understand?" he said again, gruffly.

"But...," Cat began.

"But, nothing. Both of you are on the verge of collapsing right where you stand. Enough is enough. One hour."

Doc glanced at Dr. Berry, who tried very hard to hide a smile at the scolding. "Alexis, I'd like to chat about Skylar's progress when I return."

"I'd like that," Dr. Berry said.

Cat looked at Billie. "I guess we have one hour," she said.

"I guess so," Billie replied.

"Mama," Skylar said from her bed. "Grandpa will put you in timeout if you're not a good girl."

"I think he just did, sweetling. I think he just did."

CHAPTER 20

Within a week, Skylar was out of bed and taking short walks down the hallway while wearing a mask and pushing a child-sized walker in front of her. Her color was beginning to return, as well as a dusting of red-blonde peach fuzz on her head. Billie or Cat...or sometimes both, would accompany her on her walks, while pushing her IV along with them.

Near the end of the first week after her infusion of bone marrow, Billie, Cat and Skylar were about to embark on their walk, when Dr. Berry came into the room.

"Hey there, scamp," Dr. Berry said to the little girl.

"I'm goin' for a walk. Wanna come?" Skylar said.

"Actually, I'd like to talk to one of your moms about your progress while you're gone for a walk. Is that okay?" she asked.

"Which one?" Skylar asked.

Dr. Berry looked between Billie and Cat. Billie was the first to speak. "Cat, why don't you stay? If there are any questions, you're more qualified to ask them. You can fill me in later."

"Okay," Cat said. She kissed Skylar's cheek, then Billie's. "Enjoy your walk."

After Billie and Skylar left the room, Dr. Berry turned to Cat. "I have to say that you and Billie are looking much more rested than I've seen you in weeks. I was worried about the two of you."

"You have small children, Alexis. Would you have done it any differently?" Cat asked.

"Busted!"

"Busted is right. A mom is a mom. We just can't help ourselves," Cat said.

"You're right. Okay, so let's talk about Skylar," Dr. Berry said. "First let me say that I am very pleased with her progress over the past week."

"We are too, but I'm still a little concerned that she's not eating well. I mean, her color is better and she has more energy, but she's just not eating much yet."

"That's to be expected. The antibiotics and anti-fungal meds we have her on tend to suppress appetite. One of the things I want to talk to you about is weaning her off those meds. It needs to be done slowly in order to be sure we're not inhibiting the grafting in any way."

"What do you mean?" Cat asked.

"It's been a week since the infusion and just this morning, I received the preliminary blood results monitoring her hemoglobin, ANC, and platelets. You will recall, a week or so ago, her levels were 8, 500 and 20,000 respectively. As I'm sure you also know, the average hemoglobin is 13.5 for a child her age. Normal ANC is between 3,000 and 5,000, and normal platelets are between 150,000 and 400,000. Comparatively, her numbers a week ago were critical. It's no wonder she was feverish and lethargic."

"So, what are her numbers now?" Cat asked.

"Keep in mind, it's only been a week since the transplant, but her hemoglobin is at 10, ANC is at 1,000 and platelets are hovering around 100,000. They're not where they need to be yet, but they are definitely improving. My concern about reducing the antibiotics and anti-fungal meds, is not knowing whether these two drugs are helping the grafting progress along. I won't know unless we discontinue the drugs," Dr. Berry explained."

"You started her on the drugs to begin with to bring her fever down. You were obviously targeting the infection that was in her body. Do you have any idea yet what caused the infection…or better yet, is the infection gone?" Cat asked.

"Good question, but one I don't know how to answer at this point. I'm not completely sure if her numbers are up because the grafting is working, or if they're up because the drugs are ridding her body of the infection. The easiest way to find out is by discontinuing the drugs and keeping a close eye on her numbers. If they continue to go up, the grafting is most likely working and the drugs may no longer be needed. If they go down, it may only be the drugs that are making her feel better and the grafting may not have worked at all."

Cat's eyes grew wide. "Don't say that, Alexis. I can't imagine putting our sweet angel through this only to have it fail."

"As critical as she was when we infused her, Cat, you knew there was a chance it wouldn't work. Let's hope that's not the case, but it *is* a possibility we need to be prepared for."

"So, where do we go from here?" Cat asked.

"Plan A is to slowly reduce the levels of meds in her system over the next few days, then to watch her numbers daily. If they level out or rise, we're good. If they fall, we'll need to put her back on the meds and hope she survives long enough for us to come up with a plan B."

* * *

Cat sat across Billie's lap on the one reclining chair in Skylar's room while Skylar slept peacefully on the bed. Cat's head was on Billie's shoulder. Billie stroked Cat's arm as she stared at the little girl on the bed.

"She's making such good progress. Maybe it's a bad idea to take her off the meds," Billie said.

"Alexis implied it was the only good way to know if the transplant is working. I don't see where we have any choice," Cat replied. "She'll begin by giving her half doses for the next two days, then quarter doses for two more before stopping them altogether."

"She's come so far in the past week. I'd hate to see her take even one step backward, Cat."

"I agree."

Billie kissed the side of Cat's head. "It's nearly eight o'clock, love. You should head home and spend some time with Seth and Tara before they go to bed. I think Skylar is pretty much out for the night."

Cat sat up and kissed Billie tenderly on the lips. "I will see you in the morning, then. I hope you sleep well, my love."

"I'll slip in beside Sky in a few minutes. Kiss the kids and mom for me, will you?" Billie asked.

"Of course."

Cat walked to the bed and kissed Skylar on the cheek.

"Sleep well, sweet angel," she said, then turned back to Billie. "Good night, Billie."

"Good night, Cat. I love you."

"I love you more."

* * *

Five days later, Dr. Berry entered Skylar's room carrying a folder of test results.

"Okay, yesterday was her last day of meds. The blood work we drew this morning will be used as a baseline for determining whether the graft is taking hold." Dr. Berry opened the folder and extracted a piece of paper. "For the record, her baseline numbers are 10.5 for hemoglobin, 1,500 for ANC and 125,000 for platelets."

Cat's eyebrows arched. "Those numbers are higher than they were five days ago," she said.

"Yes they are, albeit, slightly," Dr. Berry said. "That's a good sign, considering we have been steadily lowering her dose of meds for the past four days."

"How long before we know for sure?" Billie asked.

"I'm guessing we'll know in the next few days."

"Any idea when she might be able to go home?" Billie asked again.

"If the graft is working, I'd say, by the middle of next week. If it's not—" Dr. Berry left the sentence hanging.

* * *

A week later, Laurel ran the vacuum cleaner over the rug in the living room while Jen dusted the furniture. Seth, Stevie,

Tara and Karissa worked feverishly to pick up the toys in the bedrooms and make the beds. All four kids ran down the stairs into the living room when they had finished their task.

"Okay, what's next?" Seth asked.

"I'd like the four of you to tackle the family room downstairs," Laurel said. "Girls, there are paper towels and anti-bacterial cleaners under the kitchen sink. Please wipe down all the furniture while the boys clean up the toys and vacuum the rugs...including the stairs."

A chorus of *okay, Nana* rang out from all four children as they set off to complete their tasks.

"Sheesh, I've never seen my kids so excited about cleaning," Jen joked.

"I think what they're excited about is Skylar coming home," Laurel said.

Jen stopped dusting and approached Laurel. She stood in front of her and placed her palm on the side of Laurel's face. "Thank you for being here, Laurel. I know Billie and Cat appreciate everything you've done."

Laurel opened her arms and hugged Jen close for a long moment before releasing her.

"It's the least I can do to make up for all the lost time, Jen. Heaven knows, I can never get those years back." Laurel's eyes misted over.

"No you can't, but the good Lord willing, the years ahead will be long and plentiful."

"The girls are lucky to have a friend like you," Laurel said.

"*I* am lucky to have *them*. I love them with all my heart." Jen said. "My life would not be as wonderful as it is today if they hadn't moved into the neighborhood nearly seven years ago."

Just then, the sound of a car pulling into the driveway drew their attention.

"Holy shit! They're home," Jen exclaimed as she quickly wound the cord on the vacuum cleaner and pushed it into the hall broom closet.

"Kids," Laurel yelled down the cellar stairs. "They're here. Skylar is home."

A commotion louder than a herd of elephants could be heard as all four kids ran up the stairs.

Jen grabbed a box from the kitchen counter and passed it around. Each one pulled out a surgical mask and put it on before Cat, Billie and Skylar stepped into the kitchen.

"Welcome home, Sky!" everyone shouted as the door opened and the little girl stepped in, wearing a mask of her own.

Skylar was immediately surrounded by the four older children, each one hugging her and offering to play with her while Cat and Billie stood in the doorway sporting broad smiles.

Seth beamed with pride when he realized she was wearing his ball cap. He looked at his mothers and smiled, nodding his head.

Billie went to her son and wrapped her arms around him. "You did good, Seth. You did good," she said. "Thank you."

"I told you we would catch her mom. I told you we wouldn't let her fly away," Seth reminded her.

"That you did, scout...that you did."

"Hey, where's my hug," Cat asked as she took Seth into her arms. "You are my hero," she whispered, causing him to blush.

A little uncomfortable with all the attention, Seth hugged Cat, then broke away to suggest they all watch a movie in the family room.

"Mama, can you make popcorn for us?" Skylar asked. "I'm hungry."

"Coming right up," Cat said, smiling through her tears as all five kids ran down the stairs into the family room.

Cat looked at Billie and said in an emotionally tinged voice. "She's hungry! She said she's hungry!"

"C'mere you," Jen said as she hugged Cat tight. "I'm so glad to see you all home."

"We're happy to be home, Jen. The good news is that her numbers are rising...but she has a long road ahead of her yet before we can claim victory."

"But at least we're heading *toward* the finish line and not away from it," Jen pointed out.

"Yes we are," Cat replied.

"Mama, where's the popcorn?" Skylar yelled from downstairs.

Jen laughed. "Come on, I'll give you a hand making it."

Billie turned to Laurel while Cat and Jen made popcorn. She opened her arms and wrapped them around her mother. "I love you, Mom."

Laurel shuddered. "I have waited for so long to hear you say that, Billie. Thank you."

"No...thank you." Billie released her and held her at arm's length. "I have been awful to you for a long time, and for that I am very sorry. I couldn't see beyond my anger to the wonderful, loving woman you are. I will never be able to thank you enough for what you have done for us...and for your grandchildren."

"I would do it again in a heartbeat, Billie. Please know that I never stopped loving you over all those years. Not a day went by that I didn't think about you," Laurel said.

"I may never understand what drove your decisions thirty-three years ago, Mom, but I accept that you did what you thought was best for me. Life is much too fragile and too short to live it angry. I want to put all of that behind us and look forward to the future together."

"I'd like that too, Billie. I'd like that more than anything in the world."

CHAPTER 21

A few days after Skylar came home from the hospital, Laurel returned to Michigan amid a barrage of tears and sad goodbyes at the airport. Before leaving, they made plans to organize a family reunion so that Laurel could meet her four nieces...Cat's sisters, and their families. Billie and Cat both hoped Dylan and Laurel's husband, Jim, would be able to attend that event as well.

Life in the Charland household soon settled into a routine. With summer only half over, mornings once again turned chaotic as Skylar and Tara dressed, ate breakfast and organized back packs for daycare while Cat and Billie prepared for work. Seth, at the ripe old age of twelve, was old enough to stay home alone, with Jen as his emergency go-to person. Billie dropped the girls off at the gym daycare on her way to work, while Cat collected them on her way home in the late afternoon.

Once a week, Cat took Skylar to the hospital with her in the morning where the lab took a blood sample to test her hemoglobin, ANC and platelet levels. The report was then sent to Dr. Berry who closely monitored Skylar's recovery. Cat would then drive her to the daycare before starting her own day at the hospital.

Cat and Billie were on pins and needles every time the phone rang in the first few days after the weekly lab visits, anticipating potentially negative results. In the full month after Skylar's release from the hospital, the lab results came back positive, four consecutive times, with Skylar's blood levels rising to near normal. In addition, Skylar was eating well, sleeping well, and her energy levels had rebounded to pre-leukemia levels.

On this particular morning, Cat managed to be ready for work early and had time to sit with a cup of coffee while the girls ate their breakfast. She was thumbing through a website on her tablet when Billie came into the kitchen.

Billie stopped to kiss Cat and the girls before pouring herself a cup of coffee. She stood behind Cat and read over her shoulder.

"What are you reading?" she asked.

Cat held her tablet so Billie could see. "One of my coworkers recommended a summer camp for children who have, or have had leukemia. I thought Sky might enjoy going," she said. "It's called Camp Kwinisaki, and it's relatively local."

"Is it a day camp?" Billie asked.

"Actually, no. It's a two week program. The parents are allowed to visit on the weekend in between," Cat explained.

"Ah, Cat...I don't know about that," she said, eyeing Skylar over Cat's head.

Cat looked up at Billie. "Why not? I think she'd enjoy it. Look here...there's horse riding, boating, swimming. It sounds like fun."

"Do you think she's ready for that? I mean, what about her blood tests?"

"The camp runs during the last two weeks of August, just before school starts. She's had four positive lab tests in a row. There'd be two or three more before she goes to camp. I'll talk to Alexis about it before I make reservations."

"She's only six, Cat."

"It says here that campers as young as five are accepted into the camp." Cat looked at the worry etched on Billie's brown.

She stood up and took Billie's hand then walked her over to the sink, out of earshot of the girls.

"Billie, I know you're worried about her, but we can't treat her like she's some fragile crystal that might break. There will be other kids at the camp with the same issues she has dealt with. I think she'll enjoy it."

"I don't like the idea of not seeing her for a whole week at a time."

"Look, I'll talk to the camp counselors, and maybe they'll allow phone calls in the evening, or maybe she can take the tablet and we can do video calls with her so you can actually see her, if that makes you feel better."

Billie frowned and took a deep breath. "Wow! I just realized how crazy that sounds. Sending a six-year-old to camp with a tablet so she can do video calls with her paranoid mother. Sheesh, Cat. What's wrong with me? You're right—we can't treat her like she's breakable. Go ahead and talk to Alexis. I trust your judgment."

Cat stood on tiptoe and kissed Billie full on the lips. "Thank you love." She then walked over to the table and kissed the girls on the head. "I hope you two have a great day today. Tara, keep an eye on sissy for us, okay? Sky, be sure to take your nap, and don't give your teachers a hard time about it. You need your rest to stay strong."

"Okay, mama," the two girls said together.

"I'll see you tonight, my love," Cat said, kissing Billie once more.

Billie smiled and watched Cat leave, then turned to the girls.

"All right rugrats, grab your backpacks and lunch bags and head for the car," Billie said.

* * *

Cat picked the girls up after work and headed home. On the way, she glanced into the rear-view mirror and noticed Skylar scratching her arm.

"Bug-bite, sweetie?" she asked.

"It itches, mama," Skylar said.

"Did you play outside today?"

"I played with Missy in the sand box."

"I'll look at it when we get home. It's probably just sand fleas or mosquitoes."

"Okay, mama."

Cat pulled Skylar's shirt off over her head and looked at the rash covering her torso. "Hmmm, I wonder what's causing this." She ran her hand over the rash. "Sky, did your teacher put sunscreen on you today before you went outside?"

"No."

"I'll have to talk to her about that. Your treatments might make your skin ultra-sensitive to sunlight. In the meantime, I'm going to put some hydrocortisone cream on it to stop the itch."

"Will it hurt?" Skylar asked.

"I don't think so, sweetie." Cat liberally rubbed the cream across Skylar's chest and back. "Does that feel better, love?" she asked.

"My arms and legs itch too," Skylar complained.

Moments later, Skylar stood in front of Cat with just her panties on while Cat coated all four of her limbs with the hydrocortisone cream. "If this isn't better by morning, I'm going to take you to see Dr. Berry. There you go, sweetie. All finished."

"Thanks, mama. It feels better now. Can I have a snack?" Skylar asked.

* * *

Later that evening, after the kids were in bed, Cat and Billie snuggled on the living room couch and talked about their day. Cat told Billie about Skylar's rash.

"Maybe you should take her in to see Alexis," Billie suggested.

"That's just what I plan to do if it's not improved by morning."

"Do you think it might be an allergic reaction to her meds?" Billie asked.

"Anything is possible, but she's been taking the same meds for what...six weeks now? I would think we'd have seen it before now if that was the case."

"You're probably right."

Their alone time was suddenly interrupted by a cry from upstairs. "Mama, my belly hurts," Skylar cried.

"Oh, no," Billie said, fearing the worse. She was on her feet in an instant, and running up the stairs with Cat directly behind her.

They found Skylar standing in the bathroom, throwing up into the toilet. Unfortunately, she had also soiled herself.

"Oh, my God. Billie, call Alexis. Tell her Skylar is both vomiting and has diarrhea. Oh, and tell her about the rash too," Cat said.

Billie ran back down the stairs and into the living room while Cat tended to the now-crying Skylar.

"It's okay, sweetheart. Mama is here," Cat said as she waited for her daughter to finish vomiting. "I'm going to start the shower, sweetie, and when you're done, we're going to put you right in there and clean you up, okay?"

Cat felt Skylar's head and noted she was feverish. *Please don't let the leukemia be back,* she prayed. *Our poor baby has been through enough.*

Billie reappeared in the doorway. "Cat, Alexis said to bring her to the emergency room and she'll meet us there."

"Mom?"

Both women turned at the sound of Seth's voice behind them.

"Mom, is Sky okay?" he asked.

"We hope so, honey. Please go back to bed and try not to worry, love," Billie said. "I'm going to call Jen to see if she can come over to stay with you and your sister while we take her to the hospital."

"I want to go with you," Seth said.

"I don't know how long we'll be there, Seth. Please do as Mom says and go back to bed," Cat said as she helped Skylar into the shower then proceeded to remove her soiled clothing. "Billie, I'll need clean pajamas for her."

"I'll be right back," Billie said. On her way back to the bathroom, she stopped in Seth's room and saw that he was sitting on the edge of the bed, holding his head between his hands. Billie sat on the bed beside her son and placed her arm around him. She kissed him on the head.

"She's sick again, isn't she?" Seth asked.

"I don't know, scout. Dr. Berry will meet us at the hospital. She'll be in good hands. We'll do everything we can for her."

"She's just a baby, mom. She's just a baby."

Billie's throat choked closed. "I know, love. Why don't you say a few prayers for her. Maybe that will help."

Seth nodded.

"I've got to get these clean clothes to mama, then we'll head to the hospital with your sister. Jen should be here soon. Okay?"

"Okay, mom."

Billie rose to leave.

"Mom?"

"Yes, love?"

"Tell Sky that her big brother loves her, okay?"

"You bet," Billie said, barely escaping the room before she totally lost control of her emotions.

* * *

Cat and Billie stood beside Dr. Berry as she examined Skylar.

"Alexis, what's wrong with her?" Billie asked.

"I don't know yet, Billie. I've ordered a few tests, including a full LFT series that I hope will diagnose this for us."

"LFT series?" Billie said.

"Liver function tests," Cat supplied. "Alexis, why would you order liver function tests?"

"Because the whites of her eyes are yellowing."

Cat leaned in to look for herself. "Damn," she said.

"While we're waiting for the test results, I'm going to order an IV to keep her hydrated. The poor child has lost a lot of fluid between the vomiting and diarrhea. How has her appetite been?"

"She's been eating fine," Cat said. "In fact, everything was perfect until she complained of her skin itching today. When I took her clothing off, I found this rash covering her body. Then, this evening, the vomiting and diarrhea started."

Dr. Berry frowned.

"What? What is it you're not telling us, Alexis?" Billie asked.

"I need to wait for the lab results before making a definitive diagnosis," Dr. Berry said. "In the mean time, I want to admit her to the hospital."

"Really? Are you serious?" Billie asked.

"I couldn't be more serious, Billie," Dr. Berry said

* * *

For the next two hours, Billie paced back and forth across the emergency room floor while Cat calmed a very upset Skylar. In that span of time, Skylar vomited and soiled herself two more times.

Finally, Dr. Berry returned and threw a folder down onto the foot of Skylar's bed. She ran a hand through her hair and looked at Billie and Cat.

Billie felt like her insides were liquefying as she read the distress in Dr. Berry's face.

Cat clung to Billie's hand. "Alexis, what is it? Tell me, please."

"Skylar has GVHD—Graft Versus Host Disease."

"What the hell is that?" Billie demanded.

"It's a complication that sometimes happens with a bone marrow transplant," Dr. Berry said.

Cat released Billie's hand and went to stand at the window, her back to the room.

Billie watched her walk away and noted the defeated slope of her shoulders. "Cat?" she said.

Without turning around, Cat spoke in a quivering voice. "GVHD occurs when the donated tissue reacts against the recipient's tissue. Seth's cells don't recognize Skylar's body."

"What does that mean, Cat? Alexis?" Billie's voice was choked with emotion.

"It means her newly transplanted immune system is attacking the major organs in her body from within, specifically, her skin, GI tract, liver and lungs," Dr. Berry explained."

"Is it fatal?" Billie asked.

Dr. Berry looked down at a sleeping Skylar. "It can be," she said.

EPILOGUE

Billie sat on the front porch steps, looking out over the lawn.

The grass needs cutting again, she thought. *There never seems to be enough time to enjoy life before it's gone, swept away, forever lost.*

She looked around again and tried hard to convince herself to get the lawn mower out.

Ah, what's the point anyway? It will just grow back again - twice as fast.

"Billie," Cat called out from the screen door. "I thought you were going to mow the lawn."

Billie hung her head. She just had no motivation lately. No desire to do anything but sit and feel sorry for herself.

I have to learn to take each day as it comes, she thought. *Life's too short to worry about things like mowing the grass, clipping the hedges and paying the bills.*

"Billie!" Cat scolded.

"All right, all right, I'll do it," Billie said, rising to her feet.

"And when you're finished, please fix the swing set. You've been meaning to do that for a couple of weeks now," Cat reminded her.

Mow the lawn. Fix the swing set. Cat, you're becoming quite the...no, Billie, don't go there. You'll only get yourself in trouble. Damn, I should have fixed the swing set earlier, but there was no real reason to. Tara is ten now, and more into listening to music with Karissa than playing on the swings. Seth, at twelve, wouldn't be caught dead near the swing set. And Sky ...well, Sky isn't here. There's been no rush, she thought. *Where are those kids anyway? Seth ought to be mowing the lawn. Oh yeah, I gave them permission to go swimming at Jen's*, she remembered.

"Hi, Billie," Jen's cheery voice rang out. "What are you up to?" she asked.

"Go ask the dictator in there," Billie said. "Mow the lawn, fix the swing set. Sheesh," Billie complained.

"Well, you really should fix the swing set. It *has* been broken for nearly two weeks," Jen observed.

"No one is using it, Jen. Why fix it?" Billie reasoned.

"Well, you never know when you'll need it again," Jen answered. Jen put an arm around her shoulder. "You look so sad. You miss her, don't you?"

"She's my baby, Jen. How can I not miss her?" Billie said, tearing up.

"Well, she's in a happy place right now, Billie. Keep that in mind," Jen said.

"I know, Jen. It's just hard. I miss her so much," Billie explained.

"We all do, Billie, we all do," Jen said. "Look, I'm going to go say hello to Cat, okay?" Jen said, leaving Billie to her own sulking.

Billie sat down hard on the stairs again. So much had happened in the last nine months. Her mother went home shortly after Sky came home from the bone marrow transplant, so she wasn't around for the worst of it.

At least the rift between us has been healed, she thought to herself.

They had all endured a lot of pain and anguish over the past several months...the bone marrow transplant, the weeks of repeated treatments and chemotherapy, weeks of vomiting, nausea, diarrhea and fatigue. Finally, when it looked like there was hope, Skylar developed Graft-Versus-Host Disease, a side effect of bone marrow transplant that attacks the skin, liver and intestines. Billie's heart broke at the thought of what her sweet angel had to endure. Then, finally, it was over. No more hospital, no more exams, no more treatments.

Damn how I miss her, Billie thought. "I hope you can hear me sweet angel. I love you, baby," she said.

"I love you too Mommy," came a small voice next to Billie's ear.

Billie turned her head sharply. "Sky! Sky-baby, you're home! Cat, Sky's home," Billie yelled toward the house.

She stood up and scooped the child into her arms. She swung her around in a circle then hugged her close, showering her face with kisses.

"Oh, Sky, I missed you so much. Why are you home early?" she asked.

"She's not home early, Billie," Cat said, stepping out onto the porch, with Jen right behind her. "The Camp Kwinisaki van just dropped her off, right on schedule. For some reason, you thought she'd be home next week instead of today. You've been so down since she's been gone, I thought it would be a nice surprise for you," Cat said

Billie set Skylar on her left hip then climbed the front porch steps and grabbed Cat around the waist, pulling her into a bear hug.

"Surprise isn't the word for it. Shock is more like it," she said, kissing Cat passionately and whispering the words, "I'll thank you *proper-like* later."

Billie released Cat and turned her attention back to the child. "So rugrat, how was camp?" she asked.

"It was a lot of fun. Mommy, there were other kids there with 'kemia, just like me."

"So, what did you do for fun, dumpling?"

"We played games, and there were horses, and clowns, and coloring, and swimming and, kickball, and...," the child droned on and on as Billie walked around the yard with her, intently listening to every word.

Never again would she take life for granted.

Note to Readers:

Leukemia is a cancer that starts in early blood-forming cells; most often of the white blood cells, however, any of the cells from the bone marrow can turn into leukemia cells. Leukemia cells often reproduce quickly and don't die out when they are supposed to, crowding out normal cells. These abnormal cells then spill into the bloodstream and travel to other parts of the body, such as lymph nodes, spleen, liver, central nervous system (the brain and spinal cord), testicles or other organs where they keep the other cells in the body from functioning properly.

Graft-versus-host disease (GVHD) can be a serious and life threatening complication of a bone marrow transplant. GVHD occurs when the donor's immune system reacts against the recipient's tissue. The new or transplanted immune system can attack the entire patient and all of their organs. This happens when the new cells do not recognize the tissue and organs of the recipient's body as itself. Over time and with the help of medicine to suppress the new immune system, it will be begin to accept its new body and stop attacking it. The most common sites for GVHD are GI tract, liver, skin and lungs.

To learn more about childhood leukemia, and how you can help fight this disease, visit the Leukemia & Lymphoma Society® official website at http://www.lls.org/, or The American Cancer Society at www.cancer.org/cancer/leukemia/.

Photo Credit: Brad Fowler, Song of Myself Photography

See her author page at www.karendbadger.com

About the Author

Karen D. Badger is the author of On A Wing And A Prayer, Yesterday Once More (a 2009 Golden Crown Literary Award winner for Speculative Fiction), In A Family Way, Unchained Memories, Happy Campers, Collective Identity Sweet Angel and Relative-ly Speaking (Books I, II, III, IV, V and VI of the Commitment Series), The Blue Feather, All My Tomorrows (sequel to the 2009 award winning Yesterday Once More) and her latest novel, 1140 Rue Royale...all released by Badger Bliss Books, which Karen co-owns with her wife Barbara Sawyer (aka, "Bliss').

Born and raised in Vermont, Karen is the second of five children raised by a fiercely independent mother, who remains one of her best friends to this day. Karen earned her B.A. in 1978 in Theater and in Elementary Education, and in 1994, earned a B.S. in mathematics. In addition to her novels, Karen is the author of many technical papers on photomask manufacturing, which she has presented at numerous semiconductor industry conferences, and is the holder if several technical patents. Karen is currently in her 38th year as a Principle Member of the Technical Staff with a prominent Semiconductor manufacturer in Vermont.

Karen and her wife, Barb (a retired Lt. Col., US Air Force) live in the beautiful state of Vermont—home of Ben and Jerry's. They spend their spare time with family as well as doing home improvement projects on both their homes in Vermont and New Mexico. They also enjoy camping, kayaking, motorcycling and singing Karaoke.

Please visit Karen's author website at www.karendbadger.com, or the Badger Bliss Books website at www.badgerblissbooks.com. Also like us on Facebook!

TITLES BY KAREN D. BADGER

www.badgerblissbooks.com

On A Wing and A Prayer
First edition published by Blue Feather Books, Sept, 2005
Second edition published by Badger Bliss Books – Sept, 2014
Third edition published by Badger Bliss Books – August, 2016
ISBN 13: 978-1-945761-01-0, ISBN 10: 1-945761-01-6

Yesterday Once More
First edition published by Blue Feather Books, July, 2008
Second edition published by Badger Bliss Books – Sept, 2014
Third edition published by Badger Bliss Books – August, 2016
ISBN 13: 978-1-945761-02-7, ISBN 10: 1-945761-02-4
2009 Golden Crown Literary Society Award - Speculative Fiction

In A Family Way – Book One of the Commitment Series
First edition published by Blue Feather Books, March, 2010
Second edition published by Badger Bliss Books – Sept, 2014
Third edition published by Badger Bliss Books – August, 2016
ISBN 13: 978-1-945761-05-8, ISBN 10: 1-945761-05-9

Unchained Memories – Book Two of the Commitment Series
First edition published by Blue Feather Books, Oct, 2011
Second edition published by Badger Bliss Books – Sept, 2014
Third edition published by Badger Bliss Books – August, 2016
ISBN 13: 978-1-945761-06-5, ISBN 10: 1-945761-06-7

Happy Campers - Book Three of the Commitment Series
First edition published by Blue Feather Books, Sept, 2013
Second edition published by Badger Bliss Books – Sept, 2014
Third edition published by Badger Bliss Books – August, 2016
ISBN 13: 978-1-945761-07-2, ISBN 10: 1-945761-07-5

The Blue Feather
First edition published by Blue Feather Books, July, 2014
Second edition published by Badger Bliss Books – Sept, 2014
Third edition published by Badger Bliss Books – August, 2016
ISBN 13: 978-1-945761-04-1, ISBN 10: 1-945761-04-0

Collective Identity – Book Four of the Commitment Series
First edition published by Badger Bliss Books – January, 2015
Second edition published by Badger Bliss Books – August, 2016
ISBN 13: 978-1-945761-08-9, ISBN 10: 1-945761-08-3

All My Tomorrows – Sequel to Yesterday Once More
First edition published by Badger Bliss Books – May, 2015 Second
edition published by Badger Bliss Books – August, 2016
ISBN 13: 978-1-945761-03-4, ISBN 10: 1-945761-03-2

Sweet Angel – Book Five of the Commitment Series
First edition published by Badger Bliss Books – June, 2015 Second
edition published by Badger Bliss Books – August, 2016
ISBN 13: 978-1-945761-09-6, ISBN 10: 1-945-761-09-1

Relative-ly Speaking – Book Six of the Commitment Series
First edition published by Badger Bliss Books – March, 2016
Second edition published by Badger Bliss Books – August, 2016
ISBN 13: 978-1-945761-10-2, ISBN 10: 1-945-761-10-5

1140 Rue Royale
First edition published by Badger Bliss Books – Sept, 2016
ISBN 13: 978-1-945761-00-3, ISBN 10: 1-945761-00-8

Relative-ly Speaking

Book VI of The Commitment Series

A BADGER BLISS BOOK

By

Karen D. Badger

CHAPTER 1

Sol rose over the rooftops, casting a bright orange glow over everything in his domain. Slivers of light entered every crevice, saturating, intruding, invading even the smallest slits, defeating the barriers intended to keep them out.

Soldiers of light attacked, conquering in parallel formation as they made their way through the Venetian blinds, landing on the occupants of the battleground. As the formation moved north, it became obvious that the enemy was defenseless, unable to escape the onslaught as the invading forces made their way across the hills and valleys created by the entwined bodies on the bed. Finally, victory was declared as the army of light reached its destination and planted its banner firmly in the face of the enemy.

"Billie," Cat said, nudging her sleeping wife.

"Hmmm," Billie murmured as she pulled Cat closer, wrapping her arms around her.

"Billie!" Cat said again.

"Whaaaat?" she said, annoyed at being awakened so early on a Saturday morning.

"Honey, please close the blinds, the sun is in my face. I can't sleep," Cat asked.

"Just roll over," Billie suggested not wanting to get out of the warm comfortable bed.

"Please, love?" Cat asked sweetly.

Billie opened one eye and saw Cat looking at her with puppy dog eyes. *Damn, I hate it when she does that!* Billie thought.

"Oh, all right." She got out of bed and closed the blinds, effectively casting out the slivers of light that had invaded their bed. She then climbed back into bed, and gathered Cat into her arms once more.

Cat kissed Billie on the cheek then snuggled into her neck. "Thank you, sweetheart," She said.

Soon, they were sleeping once more, bodies wrapped around each other like braided rope.

***

Brrrring...Brrrring...Brrrring.

Cat reached for the phone. "Hello?" she said groggily. "Mom? Mom, do you know what time it is?" Cat asked irritably.

"Yes dear, it's ten o'clock. You aren't still in bed are you?" Ida asked.

Cat shot up as if she had been goosed. "Ten? Oh my, God! Are you serious?" she asked, looking over at the digital clock to confirm what her mother had said. Sure enough, it read three minutes past ten.

Cat ran her hand through her hair and took a quick inventory of the bedroom. No Billie. *Damn it Billie, why did you let me sleep so long?* The last thing she remembered was nudging Billie awake to close the blinds.

"Caitlain, I just received a call from your sister," Ida said.

"Which one, Mom?" Cat asked, annoyed that her mother automatically thought she would know.

"Amy," Ida replied.

"And," Cat asked.

"Well, she suggested that it was time for a family reunion," Ida explained.

"Funny you should say that, Mom. Before Laurel went back home after Sky's illness, Billie and I mentioned organizing one so she could meet the rest of the family."

"You know, sweetheart, finding Laurel closed a lot of holes in our family trees. I mean, she's my sister, and Billie's mother and Grandma Alex's daughter. It *would* be nice to introduce her to the rest of the family."

Cat threw herself back down onto the pillows. "You're right, Mom. So, who is going to organize this thing?" she asked, dreading the answer.

"Well, dear, since Laurel is *your* mother-in-law, *and* Billie's mother, we thought that you and Billie should do it," Ida reasoned.

Cat reached over for Billie's pillow and covered her face with it, swearing up a storm into its softness while holding it tightly to her face so her mother wouldn't hear the cursing.

"Caitlain? Caitlain, are you there?" Ida asked after several moments of silence.

Cat was counting to ten in her mind. *Eight...nine...ten. Calm down, Cat, calm down. This is your mother you're talking to.*

"I'm here, Mom," she said after taking a deep breath to compose herself.

"Well, dear, what do you think?" Ida asked.

"I think, Mom, that I need to discuss this with Billie first," Cat said, hopefully buying herself some time.

"Okay, dear. Just give me a call when you've decided where and when we'll have it, all right?" Ida said.

"Mom," Cat began.

"I'll call Amy, Bridget and Drew and tell them to expect a call from you," Ida continued talking as if Cat had not spoken.

"Mom," Cat said again.

"This will be so much fun, dear. And you know Grams and Grandma Jo are getting on in years. It may be the last reunion they'll have with the family," Ida finished.

That did it for Cat.

Damn! she exclaimed to herself. "All right, Mom. I'll call you when I've worked out the details with Billie," she heard herself saying.

"Okay, honey. I'll talk to you later then. Kiss Billie and the babies for me. Bye, bye," Ida said, hanging up the phone.

"Bye, Mom," Cat said, dropping the phone onto her lap and reaching for Billie's pillow once more.

Exhausted after screaming into Billie's pillow for ten minutes…not to mention oxygen starved, Cat dropped the pillow into her lap and rested the back of her head against the headboard.

Why am I such an easy target when it comes to my mother? she asked herself. *My backbone just flies out the window where she's concerned!*

Cat inhaled deeply then closed her eyes and personally vowed not to exert such control over her own children. She opened her eyes and glanced at the picture of the kids on her bedside table. *Every day I'm amazed at the direction my life has gone,* she thought.

Almost nine years ago, it was just her and Tara…until that fateful day she walked into Billie's aerobics class and lost her heart forever. Over the course of the next few months, Billie and Cat fell in love. It wasn't until several months after they met that Cat learned Billie had a son…a son who was in the hospital in a coma after being hit by a car who passed his school bus.

So much had happened to them since they met. Cat's father, a neurosurgeon, was able to bring Seth back to them and they lived happily together as a family of four until that fateful day when Billie's ex-husband raped her while Billie was at work.

Their youngest child, Skylar was the product of that unholy act...an act that later became a blessing in disguise when Seth's paternal connection with her was her only salvation after she nearly died of leukemia two years earlier.

Cat looked back on that time and chided herself for the way she treated Billie during Skylar's illness. She was jealous of the special relationship Billie had with their younger daughter, and she essentially pulled rank on Billie as Skylar's only biological parent when the child preferred attention from her beloved Mommy over her. She was truly grateful her relationship with Billie survived that trauma although she would not have blamed Billie for leaving after the way she treated her.

Cat smiled. When it came down to it, their love endured every obstacle thrown in their path—including the bout with amnesia Billie suffered through after Cat's father, Doc removed scar tissue from Billie's brain...damage inflicted by a gunshot wound. Cat feared their lives would never be the same without a history to fall back on, but soon, Billie's memories returned and life became normal again...as normal as it could be while living unconventionally.

I thank God every day for our network of friends and family, Cat thought. *I don't know what we would have done without them over the years. Mom, Dad, Jen and Fred. We are truly blessed.*

Cat frowned. *I just wish I wasn't a mushball around my mother. Now we're in charge of organizing a fricken family reunion!*

"Ah!" Cat exclaimed as she threw the covers back and climbed out of bed. She threw on a T-shirt and boxer shorts before going in search of her wife.

"Billie!" she yelled as she charged through the house. "Billie, where are you?" she called as she entered the kitchen.

"Chill out, Cat," Billie said, coming in from the back yard. "What's got your undies in such a wad this morning?" she asked teasingly.

"Don't go there, Billie, I'm in no mood for it," Cat said irritably, her hands on her hips.

"PMS'ing, are we?" Billie quipped.

Cat picked up a dish towel and threw it at Billie.

Billie caught the towel and grinned. "You can do better than," she said as she lurched forward and grabbed Cat around the waist.

Cat tried to scramble out of Billie's grasp, but Billie held fast, nuzzling into Cat's neck and placing light kisses along her collarbone. Cat quickly settled down and pressed herself into Billie.

"Billie, why can't I stay mad when I'm around you?" she asked breathlessly.

"Because you can't resist my charm," Billie answered, nipping lightly on her neck.

"Hmmm, that feels good," Cat said as she arched closer to Billie. "I'd disagree, but I'm in no position to argue at the moment."

Billie stood to her full height and looked down Cat. "Wanna tell me what's got you so fired up this morning?" she asked.

"Why did you let me sleep so long?" Cat asked.

"Because, my love," Billie said. "You were tired. After last night's marathon lovemaking session, I'm surprised you're up as early as you are."

Cat smiled, remembering how sex crazed they had both been the night before. They just couldn't get enough of each other. They had made love so many times she actually lost count.

"Actually, I still *would* be sleeping if it wasn't for my mother," Cat said.

Billie frowned. "Your mother?"

"Yeah, she called a few minutes ago. By the way, where were you? I'm surprised you didn't answer the phone." Cat asked.

"In the back yard with the kids. I got them started putting a fresh coat of paint on the tree house," Billie answered. "So, what did Mom have to say?" she asked.

"Billie, she did it to me again!" Cat whined. "Damn it, why am I so weak around her?"

Billie raised her eyebrows, "What did she talk you into this time?" she asked.

"Us, love...us," Cat said.

"Us?" Billie asked.

"Oh yeah. You and I are officially in charge of organizing a family reunion," Cat moaned.

Billie's head snapped up. "Cool!" she said.

"Cool? Cool?" Cat said, astonished at Billie's casual attitude. "Billie, do you have *any* idea how difficult this will be?" Cat asked.

"Cat, we're talking about your family here, how hard can it be?" Billie asked.

"Billie, we're talking about *our* families. Are you forgetting that your mother is my mother's stepsister? We're talking about you and me, our kids, Mom and Dad, Amy and Joe and their kids, Bridget and Kevin and their kids, Drew, Grandma Alex, Grandma Jo, Laurel, Dylan *and* Jim...you know—your homophobic stepfather?" Cat reminded her wife.

"Shit!" Billie said, looking down into Cat's face.

"Shit, indeed, my love! Shit indeed!"

***

Cat and Billie sat at the kitchen table, fresh coffee and cheesecake in front of them. Cat scanned through her list as she tapped her pencil on the table.

"As far as I can tell, there will be about twenty-two people," Cat said. "Where are we going to sleep them all?"

"Well, we have a couple of choices, Cat. They can rent motel rooms for the week, or bring camping gear and set it up in the yard," Billie suggested.

"Camping gear? Billie, how can you even suggest camping after that horrible experience we had at Happy Trails?" Cat asked, seeing Billie visibly cringe at the mention of their disastrous camping trip with Fred and Jen.

"Maybe you're right. Sorry I mentioned it," Billie said, shuddering at the memory. "Well, there's always the motel," she added.

"That could get a little expensive," Cat observed.

"Well, I'm out of ideas, then," Billie crossed her arms on the table in front of her rested her chin on them.

Cat stood up and started pacing, tapping the end of her pencil on her chin as she walked. "What we need," she said, "is a house big enough for all of us."

Cat suddenly stopped and looked at Billie at the same exact moment Billie's head snapped up.

"SpireClyffe Acres!" they exclaimed together.

***

"Hi Grams, this is Cat."

"Caitlain, darlin', it's so nice to hear from you. How y'all doin'?" Alex asked excitedly. "How's the baby?" she added.

"We're all fine, Grams. Skylar is doing very well. She's on a very low maintenance dose of chemo, and seems to be tolerating it very well. Her hair has grown back in—curly this time! It really is very cute. So far, there's no sign of the leukemia returning. Dr. Berry is confident that we've beat it. So how are you and Grandma Jo?" Cat asked.

"Well, you know how it is. Josie is just as ornery as ever. I swear, Caitlain, that woman is gonna send me to an early grave. Just last week, she challenged the stable hands to a drinkin' contest, and they ended up tree climbin' of all things. It's a wonder she didn't fall and break that fool neck of hers," Alex exclaimed.

Cat chuckled at the thought of her rebellious grandmother climbing a tree.

"I do declare, sometimes I wonder why I stay with that woman!" Alex added.

"You stay with her because you love her, Grams," Cat stated mater-of-factly.

Alex smiled. "I'm pretty transparent, huh?" she said.

"Clear as glass, Grams, and you know what? Your granddaughter is just like you!" Cat added.

It was about a year ago now that they had discovered the blood connection between Billie and Alex. Billie had found Alex's daughter Laurel, and her grandson Dylan as well, in the process.

"Darlin', I can't tell you how happy I was to learn that Billie was my granddaughter. It is truly a blessing to have her in my life."

"Grams, I'm calling to ask a favor," Cat said.

"Of course, sugar. What is it that ya need?" Alex asked.

"Grams, Mom has put Billie and me in charge of organizing a family reunion, and we were wondering...," Cat began.

"A family reunion? What a good idea. Caitlain, I insist that we have it here at SpireClyffe Acres. We have plenty of room, a swimming pool, and tennis courts. Why, it's perfect. I won't take no for an answer," Alex exclaimed.

"Grams, you are a gem, you know that?" Cat asked.

"Why thank you, Caitlain, but you did say you needed a favor. What was it that you needed, darlin'?" Alex asked.

"Just to hear the sound of your voice, Grams. Thanks. I'll call you when we have a date for the reunion, okay? I love you Grams...and Grandma Jo too. Give her a kiss for me, will you?" Cat asked.

"I certainly will, sugar, if you kiss Billie and the kids for us. I'll talk to you later, Bye now," Alex said.

"Good bye, Grams," Cat said smiling.

You are a devil Alexandra Spirakis. You knew all along what the favor was. Don't ever change, Grams, I love you just the way you are, Cat thought.

www.ingramcontent.com/pod-product-compliance
Lightning Source LLC
Chambersburg PA
CBHW070857250626
47159CB00003B/1100